RUNNING OUT OF ROAD

RUNNING OUT OF ROAD

DANIEL FRIEDMAN

MINOTAUR
BOOKS
NEW YORK

First published in the United States by Minotaur Books, an imprint of St. Martin's Publishing Group

RUNNING OUT OF ROAD. Copyright © 2020 by Daniel Friedman. All rights reserved. Printed in the United States of America. For information, address St. Martin's Publishing Group, 120 Broadway, New York, NY 10271.

www.minotaurbooks.com

Library of Congress Cataloging-in-Publication Data

Names: Friedman, Daniel, 1981– author.
Title: Running out of road / Daniel Friedman.
Description: First Edition. | New York : Minotaur Books, 2020. | Series: Buck schatz series; 3
Identifiers: LCCN 2019041960 | ISBN 9781250058485 (hardcover) | ISBN 9781466862715 (ebook)
Subjects: LCSH: Death row inmates—Fiction. | Older men—Fiction. | Retirees—Fiction. | GSAFD: Suspense fiction.
Classification: LCC PS3606.R5566 R86 2020 | DDC 813/.6—dc23
LC record available at https://lccn.loc.gov/2019041960

Our books may be purchased in bulk for promotional, educational, or business use. Please contact your local bookseller or the Macmillan Corporate and Premium Sales Department at 1-800-221-7945, extension 5442, or by email at MacmillanSpecialMarkets@macmillan.com.

First Edition: March 2020

10 9 8 7 6 5 4 3 2 1

In loving memory of
Buddy and Margaret Friedman

PART 1

2011: SOMETHING I DON'T WANT TO REMEMBER

1

"Do you understand everything I've just told you?" asked the man in the white coat.

"Yeah," I said.

In fact, I had no idea what he'd been talking about. I remembered the droning of his voice, but not the words. I hadn't been listening, and my hearing hasn't been so good recently. Or maybe I had been listening, but somehow, what he said hadn't stuck. My mind had been wandering, but what had I been thinking about? I couldn't remember. Also, I couldn't remember who the man in the white coat was, where I was, or what I was doing there.

I looked up at the man, scrutinized his face. Clearly, he was a doctor; who else wears a white coat? He wasn't our regular doctor, though. Had our regular doctor died or retired? No. Probably not. I think I'd have remembered that. This doctor was maybe in his forties, and he had a dress shirt and a tie on underneath the coat, not those pajamas some of them wear, so this probably wasn't an emergency or a surgical kind of situation.

I was sitting in a leather chair. My wife, Rose, was sitting in an identical chair next to me. Between the chairs was a small wooden side table with a crystal vase of fresh-cut flowers sitting on it, where an ashtray should have been in any civilized place. I looked around for an ashtray. There were no ashtrays. I reached into the pocket of my Members Only jacket and found my cigarettes. I lit one. If the doctor told me to put it out, I could act indignant about it, and maybe nobody would realize I didn't know what the hell was going on.

We didn't seem to be in a hospital; the offices in those places usually seemed more institutional—cheap mass-produced furniture, tile floors, or occasionally thin wall-to-wall carpet. Flickering fluorescent tube lights embedded in low, drop-in ceilings.

This doctor was sitting behind a heavy wood desk, with a fancy-looking computer on it. Shelves lined the walls of the office, filled with books and little trophies and toys. I looked at the floor. Woven rug over hardwood parquet. The rug looked expensive. I was going to ash on that expensive rug unless this doctor offered me an ashtray.

He looked at my cigarette. I looked him in the eyes, daring him to tell me to put it out. He offered me his coffee mug, and I tapped my cigarette against the side of it.

So, this was definitely not the hospital. They'd never let me smoke in a hospital. And also, there was no piss smell. We must have been at one of the medical parks or a clinic of some kind. The doctor was one of the specialists.

I looked at Rose. She seemed upset. Embarrassed, maybe.

Had I said something that had embarrassed her? I almost certainly had. I grinned at her so she could see I wasn't sorry.

"If you have any questions, I am happy to answer them, or explain further," said the doctor. "I want to make sure you have all the information you need."

"Take it easy," I said. "I ain't stupid."

What could he possibly have been saying that was so important? What could he have to say that was new, or any different from what a procession of doctors had been telling me for the last fifteen years? That I was on a slow, steady decline, breaking down and wearing out, little by little? That every day, for the rest of my life, I would be a little weaker, a little slower, a little more shaky than I'd been the day before? That I was moving inexorably toward a single, predictable destination? No shit, Sherlock.

"You don't have any questions?" Rose said.

"I think I've got a handle on things," I said. "Are you ready to get out of here?" I gripped the armrests of the chair I was sitting in and lifted myself off of the seat, my arms shaking under my weight. My walker was parked by the door, and it was going to take me a while to totter over to it, so I figured I might as well get started.

But Rose put a hand on my arm. "Did you hear what this man has been saying? Do you remember what this man just told us?"

"Sure," I said. But it was clear I was caught. I couldn't really put one over on her. After nearly seventy years together, she had seen all my tricks.

"Who is he?" she said, gesturing at the doctor.

Okay, that was an easy one: "He's the doctor."

"Which doctor?"

I had two options. Either I could give in and tell her I had no idea who he was, or I could bluff. I hate admitting when I don't know something, so I decided to guess.

There were a number of possibilities. I had a cardiologist, a heart guy. He was older than this doctor, though, a bald man in his early sixties. I could even remember his name: Dr. Richard Pudlow. Funny name for a depressing cat. This man wasn't Dr. Richard Pudlow.

I had an ear, nose, and throat guy, and also an audiologist. I got a hearing aid last year, and going around with that thing jammed in my ear canal caused a lot of earwax buildup, so I had to go get that taken care of every few months. The audiologist would stick a little loop of wire down into my ear and dislodge a reddish-brown hunk of greasy foulness about the size of a pencil eraser. Going there was a real fun time. Lots of jokes about mining for treasure. But the audiologist was a lady doctor, and I was pretty sure this guy wasn't the ENT.

I had a gastroenterologist. I had an episode a while back where I started shitting blood. The gastro guy determined it was a sloughing of necrotic intestinal tissue and that it was normal, although they still put me on IV fluids and kept me for observation for three days on account of my advanced age and generally frail condition. When you get to be eighty-nine years old, occasionally your guts just die inside you. It's no big deal.

This doctor could have been the gastroenterologist; I couldn't remember what the man had looked like. But I remembered the smell; his office was in the hospital. So this wasn't the gastroenterologist.

That meant, by process of elimination, he had to be: "The neurologist. The dementia guy."

I looked at Rose to see if I had gotten the right answer, but she shook her head at me, and I could see tears in her eyes.

"This is Dr. Feingold. The oncologist," she said.

That rang a bell. A distant, quiet bell, but still a bell. I looked around again. This place wasn't as unfamiliar as I'd thought. I had been here before. Sat in this chair. Listened to the doctor talking at us. Lit a cigarette to be confrontational. Ashed in the coffee cup. I'd done it all before.

How could I forget? I used to be able to memorize a face, but lately the details that used to stand out in my mind seemed to blend together. Now I was sure I could recall having seen this man. It had just gotten so hard to keep a grasp on things.

"I've got the cancer?" I asked.

She shook her head again. "No, Buck," she said. "I do."

2

can explain it again, if you'd like," said Dr. Feingold.

"What's the point of that?" Rose asked. "It's not sinking in. Can't penetrate that thick skull of his."

I took another drag off my cigarette and tapped ash into the coffee cup. Before I started having the hearing issue and the memory problems, before I needed the walker to get around, nobody ever talked about me like I wasn't there when I was sitting in the room with them.

"Well, you don't need to make a decision immediately, but if we're going to engage in an aggressive course of treatment, sooner is always better," Feingold said.

"I never imagined I'd have to make a decision like this on my own," Rose said. "I try not to resent him. I know it's an illness, and he can't help it. And he was so strong for all of us for many years, and now I ought to be strong for him. But I need him, and he's just helpless. I feel like I am alone. Betrayed, is how I feel."

Feingold rested his elbows on his desk and leaned forward. His forehead crinkled, and his eyebrows knit together. He looked thoughtful and sympathetic. I wondered how many times he'd practiced doing this in front of a mirror. "Maybe now would be a good time to look for support somewhere else. Do you have children?"

"Brian is dead," I said, wanting to participate in the conversation. "We don't talk about it."

"We have a daughter-in-law and a grandson," Rose said. "I haven't told them about this yet. I don't want them to worry."

The doctor steepled his fingers under his chin. "If you trust them, now might be the time to lean on them. You need to think about authorizing someone to make medical decisions on your behalf in an emergency, if your husband isn't going to be able to understand those decisions or their implications. It's called granting a medical power of attorney, and it's a standard form. I can refer you to someone, if you'd like."

"Our grandson is a lawyer," Rose said.

"All right," said the doctor. "You can take some time to confer with whoever you need to and make a decision, but if we're going to move forward with proactive treatment, we should probably start within the next few weeks."

"Thank you," Rose said, and she stood up. I stood up as well, and I held Rose's arm to steady myself until I could get to the walker. We made our way, slowly and in silence, down a quiet, carpeted hallway, out a door, and into a waiting room. A very thin woman with a *schmate* covering her head was sitting in a chair reading a magazine. She looked up at us, her sunken yellow eyes staring out from the bottoms of deep purple-black hollows. I realized I was still holding a lit cigarette. I considered putting it out, but once you start making accommodations for even one cancer lady, you find yourself on a slippery slope. I decided, instead, to just get out of there as quickly as I could. With the walker, that wasn't very quick.

As Rose and I rode the elevator down to the ground floor, I felt I should say something, but I didn't know what. We walked in silence through the building lobby and out to the parking lot.

"Where did we park?" I asked. But Rose just pointed as our Buick pulled up to the curb. An aide from Valhalla Estates, the assisted-lifestyle community for older adults where Rose and I lived, was driving it. She was a heavyset black woman, and I knew I'd seen her a hundred times before, but I couldn't remember her name. She had some music playing on the radio, so loud I had to turn down my hearing aid. There were some trashy magazines with names like *Us Weekly* scattered on the front passenger-side seat; I guess she'd been out here waiting for us, and I didn't blame her at all for staying in the car instead of sitting in the waiting room and sharing space with the grim specter of death. Although, if she wanted to avoid sharing space with the grim specter of death, she certainly picked the wrong line of work when she applied for a position at Valhalla.

She shifted the Buick into park, climbed out, and opened the door for Rose. Then she held my arm as I climbed into the backseat. This was a laborious process. First I grasped the doorframe with my left hand as I clung to the walker with my right. Then I had to lift my quivering left leg an agonizing fourteen inches to step into the car. Leaning on the aide's thick, soft arm for support, I slowly lowered my body onto the seat, and then I used my arms to help lift my right leg over the lip of the Buick's chassis. When I was finished, my forehead was damp and my breathing was ragged. Of all the indignities I faced on a regular basis—people talking about me like I wasn't there, the walker, people yelling at me so I could hear what they were saying—having to ride in the back of my own car was the worst.

"You need help with your seat belt, Mr. Buck?" she asked. I waved her off, so she closed the door behind me, folded up my walker, and put it in the trunk.

Rose seemed like she was about to say something, but then her handbag started chirping. She found the cellular telephone and flipped it open.

"Hello?" she said, and then she paused while the person on the other end spoke.

"This is Mrs. Schatz, his wife," she said. Then the person on the other end said something else, before Rose responded, "I don't think he'd be up for that. He's almost ninety years old, and he has dementia."

"Who is it?" I asked. Rose shook her hand in my face to shut me up.

"No, thank you," she said to the person on the line.

"I want to talk to him," I said. Actually, I yelled it. Rose hesitated, but there was no way the person on the other end of the call hadn't heard me. She gave me a dirty look, as well as the phone.

"This is Buck Schatz," I said into the receiver. "What do you want?"

"Mr. Schatz, my name is Carlos Watkins." The voice was thin and reedy, but cultured. Carlos Watkins sounded like the talking heads on TV, but not the right-thinking, plainspoken ones I liked. He sounded like the liberals on MSNBC. Come to think of it, he sounded a little like my grandson.

I made a noise into the phone, a deep, phlegmy rattle that let Carlos Watkins know I was unimpressed by his diction. "Sounds like an ethnic name," I said.

That caught him by surprise, I think. He stopped talking to process that. Then: "Uh, yeah, I guess it is. My mother is Dominican. I'm black. Is that a problem for you?"

I laughed. "Son, if that was a problem for me, I'd have to be a damn fool to have spent the last ninety years living in Memphis. Is it a problem for you?"

"I think it's at the root of almost every problem in this country," Watkins said.

I rattled again. "We're just going to have to agree to disagree on that," I said.

On the other end, I heard the sound of Watkins shuffling some papers, and then he said, "Detective Schatz, I'm the producer of *American Justice*, a serialized journalistic project made in collaboration with National Public Radio and broadcast over the air and on streaming Internet audio."

"Well, I ain't giving you any money," I said. "I've got all the coffee mugs and tote bags I will ever need."

The aide—I wished I could remember her name—had

climbed into the front seat and was pulling the car out of the clinic's parking lot and onto Humphreys Boulevard.

"I'm not calling to solicit donations," said Watkins. "I was wondering if you would be willing to sit for an interview with me."

"Right now?" I asked. "I've got a lot of stuff going on, at the moment."

"No, not right now. Cell phone audio is less than ideal for recording, and I'd like to meet you face-to-face. I'll be in Memphis later this week, and I am happy to come visit you at your place of residence."

"What do you want to talk to me about?" I asked.

"*American Justice* is a show about criminal justice in the United States, the people who operate it, and the people it operates on, with a focus on the intersections of race, class, sexuality, and gender, and how those factors interact with the systems that disseminate state-sanctioned violence against individuals and groups whose lives and activities are deemed to be illegal by those who hold power."

"That sounds like fun," I said. "I once took a road trip to the Grand Canyon and stood at the intersection of Colorado, Utah, New Mexico, and Arizona. Four states at once. It was really something."

"So, almost the same thing," Watkins said.

"I've been retired for forty years. I don't operate any systems anymore. What do you want with me?"

"I'd like to talk to you about Chester March," said Watkins.

So, this reporter was looking for a whole lot of trouble. "I haven't heard that name in a long time. Is he still alive?"

"Yes, for the moment. But the state of Tennessee is planning to put him to death within the next few weeks, if his lawyers aren't able to get a court to stay the execution."

"Good," I said. "The sooner, the better."

"He'll be the oldest person executed in the United States since the death penalty was reinstated in 1976."

"He must be very proud."

"He is a frightened, feeble old man who is about to be killed with a lethal injection."

"I'd be pleased to hear he's frightened, but I don't think he's capable of feeling fear or any other emotion. Chester is a reptile."

"Our program will include our extensive interviews with him, so our listeners will be able to judge that for themselves, but you are a big part of his story, so we'd like to hear from you and get your side of things."

"You've talked to him already?"

"I have, and I intend to talk to him some more as my work progresses. Do you have a problem with that, Detective Schatz?"

"You can talk to whoever you want. Just be careful. That fellow is a damned snake, and he lies as easy as he draws breath. It ain't easy to get a true word out of a man like Chester."

"How would you accomplish such a feat?"

"Come again?"

This time his voice came through loud and slow as he carefully enunciated each word: "How would you extract the truth from a man like Chester?"

Then I heard a rattling noise that wasn't coming from my throat, and I realized it was the sound of the phone shaking in my hand.

I lit a cigarette. "I ain't stupid, you know," I said to Watkins.

The aide in the front seat shook her fleshy arm at me. "Quit it with the cigarettes. We talked about this, Mr. Buck. I know you ain't forgot. My little boy got asthma. He don't need to be smelling your smoke on me."

"It's my goddamn car, isn't it?" I said to her. "Crack the window."

In my ear Watkins said, "What does that mean?"

"I know you're trying to set up some sort of smear on me with your little program. Why should I help you do that?"

"I am going to tell this story whether you participate or not. If you'd like to tell me your side of it, I'm willing to listen. But your input is not required."

"I'll think about it," I said, and I flipped the phone closed. This was the start of a real mess, and maybe I wouldn't be able to handle this reporter on my own. "We're going to have to call William," I said to Rose.

"Yes," she said. "I guess it's time we told him about the cancer."

"Who has cancer?" I asked.

TRANSCRIPT: AMERICAN JUSTICE

CARLOS WATKINS (NARRATION): In the state of Tennessee, they send the worst of the worst down to the Riverbend Maximum Security Institution, in Nashville. About 750 men live in this complex of twenty low-slung buildings, and two-thirds of them are "high-risk inmates," convicted of serious violent crimes and considered to pose a continuing danger to society. Sixty of those high-risk inmates have been sentenced to die by lethal injection. Riverbend is where Tennessee's death row inmates live, and Riverbend is where they will be executed, unless they're spared by Providence, a court order, or death by natural causes.

Of those sixty condemned, half are black, even though black folk comprise only 17 percent of the state's population. And half of the state's death row inmates hail from "West Tennessee," and that mostly means Memphis.

Philip Workman was put to death here at Riverbend in 2007 for the 1982 killing of a police officer in the parking lot of a Memphis Wendy's restaurant. Ballistics experts had some doubts about the evidence that convicted him, four of the trial jurors later repudiated their verdict, and two Tennessee State Supreme Court justices asked the governor to grant clemency, but none of that was enough to stop Workman's execution. He tried to donate his last meal, a vegetarian pizza, to the homeless. The state denied his request.

Riverbend is also the home of serial killer Bruce Mendenhall, a long-haul trucker who traveled America's highways murdering sex workers. Mendenhall isn't on death row; he was sentenced to life for the 2007 murder of Sara Hulbert. But he's facing more charges here in Tennessee, as well as in Alabama and Indiana, and he's under investigation in five other states, so he may yet get his date with the needle.

It was from an inmate who dwells in these bleak environs that I recently received a letter. It's not terribly uncommon for journalists to get letters from prisoners. Prisoners send a lot of letters. Writing letters passes time, and passing time is the chief occupation of those who are trapped in the teeth of the American criminal justice apparatus.

But this letter stood out immediately as unusual. I've asked the man who sent it to read it aloud for you, and then I'll tell you more about him and the circumstances in which he finds himself. I apologize for the poor audio quality.

CHESTER MARCH: Dear Mr. Watkins,

I listened to your recent feature on the plight of three prisoners who have spent decades in solitary confinement at the Angola penitentiary in Louisiana, and I thought it might be worthwhile to reach out to you, and to share my experience.

My name is Chester March, and I have been on death row in Tennessee for about thirty-five years. Death row isn't quite as restrictive as a segregated unit; I am allowed to have books and a small radio. These things go a long way toward keeping me sane. However, condemned inmates here are confined in an eight-by-ten space for twenty-two hours each day, I take my meals alone in my cell, and my visitation privileges are extremely limited.

I am one of the oldest men awaiting execution in the United States. Tennessee doesn't relish keeping a man around who holds that distinction, and it seems my appeals are soon to run their course. I wonder if you and your listeners might be interested in hearing my story before the state kills me by lethal injection. I just learned that I have an execution date scheduled in two months.

I am in this place because I was hunted and persecuted by a famously brutal police detective, and convicted on the basis of a confession extracted during a torturous interrogation, in violation of my constitutional rights. I have spent decades fighting for a new trial, but the criminal justice system refuses to acknowledge the insufficiency and illegality of the evidence supporting my conviction.

My appellate lawyers, who work on my behalf at no cost to me, seem competent and dedicated, which is something I cannot say of my trial counsel or about some of the lawyers who worked on my previous appeals. However, I no longer believe my salvation can come through the system in which they operate. The only way I will be spared is if there is a public outcry against the injustice perpetrated against me. You are my last hope, Mr. Watkins.

Yours in Christ,

Chester A. March

WATKINS (NARRATION): Compared to most prison correspondence, this is grammatically polished and well structured. Erudite, I'd even call it. It aroused my curiosity, and if I'm being honest, it also tickled my ego a little bit. It was like getting the message from *Star Wars*. "Help me, Obi-Wan Kenobi, you're my only hope!" I had to learn more. How could the man who wrote this letter be sitting in a Tennessee prison, awaiting execution? And when I began to look into the circumstances of Chester A. March, I found he is quite different from most prisoners.

The American carceral state inflicts its cruelties primarily upon the underclass. Black men are locked up in proportions that more than triple their representation in society at large. And among the whites who find themselves behind bars, they too emerge primarily from disadvantaged communities.

But not Chester March. Chester March is the wealthy son of one of Mississippi's agricultural oligarchs, a descendant of slaveholding planters, a graduate of Ole Miss, and a brother in Sigma Alpha Epsilon. He is, it goes without saying, a white man. And yet even a man like this, born with the privileges of whiteness and of aristocracy, could not protect himself from the violence of the state, which has locked him away for decades, and which plans to kill him. The machine is designed to process the marginalized, but it will crush anyone unlucky enough to be fed into it.

You might have noticed that this story has a ticking clock; Chester March is scheduled to be executed. After I got this letter and pitched the story to NPR, I spent about two weeks doing background research and making contact with some of the people involved. Each episode of *American Justice* airs about a week and a half after I finish editing the audio, so by the time you hear this, we'll be about a month away from the date Chester March will either be put to death or given a stay of execution. So this is an interesting, experimental project: long-form, serialized coverage of a developing story. This season of *American Justice* will be six hour-long episodes, released once a week, and we'll learn what happens to Chester in the fifth. As I record this, I don't know how the story will end.

But along the way, you'll find out how Chester came to be in his current situation, you'll meet the heroic lawyer who is trying to save Chester's life, and we'll try to talk to the man who waged a twenty-year campaign to bring the full weight of the criminal justice system down on Chester: a notorious Memphis police detective named Baruch Schatz.

3

William Tecumseh Schatz Esq. arrived on a Delta flight from New York with a stopover in Atlanta. He used to be able to get here direct; Memphis was a hub for Northwest Airlines. But Delta bought up Northwest in '08, and since then, there have been far fewer direct flights from LaGuardia. Memphis is still the international hub for Federal Express, but that won't get you here nonstop unless you want to ride in a crate.

The Memphis terminal opened in June of 1963, one of the first two-level airports in the country and a masterpiece of cutting-edge modern architecture by the acclaimed Memphis designer Roy P. Harrover, who built it with huge tapering columns that made the terminal look like a tray of martini glasses.

With its sparkling new facility complete, the Memphis municipal airport was rechristened the Memphis International Airport. It was a time of great optimism, and Memphis felt like a city on the rise. I shot a bank robber in the face that summer and got to shake hands with the mayor at a ceremony honoring my bravery. My son was about to turn ten.

A few months later, though, the president was killed in Dallas, and after that, we had several years of racial unpleasantness, culminating in a certain unfortunate incident at the Lorraine Motel, and then the Vietnam War. Once we got through all of that *mishegas*, the jet age was at an end, the river port was being automated, and I was nearing retirement. The celebration promised by that giant tray of martinis never quite seemed to happen.

William T. Schatz—who used to be called Tequila by his brothers in Alpha Epsilon Pi, by the way—never knew what it was like to hope or to believe that an international airport would make this an international city. As he trudged through Harrover's masterpiece, dragging his carry-on suitcase behind him on its squeaky plastic wheels, he probably just thought the place was small and dated, a decrepit monument to a failed dream in a crumbling region that never quite got over its humiliation in the War Between the States. A place you couldn't get to from the civilized world without first making a stopover in Atlanta.

His mother—my daughter-in-law, Fran—was waiting for him outside the terminal, and she took him to lunch at a chain Mexican restaurant where he ate two full baskets of chips with salsa, and drank five Diet Cokes. In New York, you see, the Mexican joints don't give you free chips, and none of the restaurants do free refills on the fountain drinks, so he gorges on that trash when he comes home.

Rose always tells me to leave him alone about it, because he says he doesn't eat like that when he's off on his own and he doesn't come here often, so I shouldn't start fights over trivialities when he's in town. And I know he is a grown man and I should mind my own business. But something he is eating up there is making him go soft around his midsection, and also, it's unseemly. I've sat there and watched him do it, and I was disgusted. And I wasn't happy to have to go to a *verkakte* Mexican joint in the first place, because I don't like ethnic food and those places always smell funny.

Anyway, sitting at that table, as he picked at the last of the chips, not minding that the paper lining of the basket was soaked with so much grease that it had become transparent, Tequila's mother told him what Rose didn't want to have to be the one to tell him, and what I couldn't seem to remember for more than a few hours.

Rose had got the lymphoma. It isn't the worst kind of cancer, but even the best kind of cancer is still cancer. The doctors caught it pretty early, and in a younger patient, the prognosis would be very favorable. The usual treatment was a course of oral chemotherapy and targeted radiation. But chemo drugs and radiation wreak havoc on even a fit human body, and Rose was eighty-six years old.

The doctor had walked us through the side effects of chemotherapy: anemia and fatigue. Nausea. Vomiting and diarrhea, which meant we'd have to be really careful about dehydration. Hair loss. Her fingernails and toenails would fall off. And the big ones: thinning skin and easy bleeding and heightened vulnerability to infection.

If she took a fall while she was undergoing these treatments—and she had fallen before—she was likely to rip open like an overstuffed garbage bag.

As for the infection, well, lymphoma is a cancer that starts in the lymphocytes, which are white blood cells—the immune system. Chemo attacks the cancer by attacking the lymphocytes, and when you kill off the lymphocytes, you strip the body of its defenses against things like influenza, strep throat, and the common cold, any of which can be extremely dangerous for someone who is elderly and immunosuppressed. It's very easy for something like that to progress into pneumonia, and when you are old and weakened from cancer treatments, pneumonia will kill you.

The alternative was not to take the chemo and not to do the radiation and just die of cancer. I hit the goddamn ceiling when Rose told me that this was even under consideration—actually, I hit the ceiling each of the half dozen or so times she had told me about it. But the case for refusing the treatment and letting the cancer run its course made a certain kind of morbid sense. It would likely take eighteen months to two years before the cancer spread everywhere, and then she could go into hospice and drift off on a morphine cloud. She'd make it almost to ninety.

That's a good run. Maybe a good enough run. If she underwent cancer treatment, she might die anyway, and she might die sooner because of it, weak, bald, emaciated, and drowning from the inside with her lungs full of fluid. Even if she fought the disease into remission, how much longer could she expect to live, and what kind of quality of life would she have? Was it worth the suffering she was certain to endure if she took poison drugs and assaulted her body with radiation? Would it leave her wheelchair-bound? Bedridden?

After Tequila's mother told him the news, she brought him over to Valhalla, so we could all have a fun conversation about it, together.

"What do you think I should do?" Rose asked, after the hugs, condolences, and various formalities had been exchanged.

"I don't know," said our grandson.

"Well, a fat lot of use you are, then," I said.

Since we only had two chairs, Tequila and Fran were sitting on the bed. Our space at Valhalla was tiny, even smaller than Tequila's studio apartment in New York. Besides the chairs and the bed, we had a shallow closet, a chest of drawers with the TV sitting on top of it, and a pair of large speakers Tequila had ordered from the Internet so I could turn the TV volume up loud enough for me to hear what people were saying and for the neighbors' walls to shake. We also had a small refrigerator, a microwave oven, and a tiny square of counter space with a couple of cabinets mounted on the wall above it. The kitchenette was situated opposite the bathroom, which was fine, since we had no room for a table and ate on TV trays next to the bed on days when we didn't feel like getting dressed to go down to the common dining room. The whole space was maybe 350 square feet, which was plenty for me. When things were close together, I didn't have to move around as much.

"I'll figure it out," Tequila said. "It's just that you blindsided me with this. I'm still trying to absorb it."

"Why did you think your mother told you to come home, when you're taking the bar exam in six weeks?" I asked. "You had to know it wasn't for good news."

"Actually, I just thought she wanted me here so she could make sure I was watching my Barbri course videos," he said.

That got a bitter laugh out of Fran. "Are you?" she asked.

"I'm a little behind," he said. "But it will be fine. Everyone from NYU passes."

"Great," I said. "That will make you feel extra special when you don't."

He bit his lower lip and sort of puffed himself up. "There are some things you should take care of right away, whether you decide to undergo treatment or not," he said. "You need a document giving medical power of attorney to Mom. That will allow doctors to talk to her about your condition and show her your medical records, and it will allow her to make decisions on your behalf if you're in a situation where you can't make them for yourself. You also need a living will, which absolves her of having to make some of the most serious of those decisions. It's a document that directs your medical treatment, so that you are the one who gets to determine how you will be treated in an emergency. Basically, it stipulates that you don't want radical measures taken to keep you alive when you're comatose or brain-dead. If you reach a point where you are end-stage metastatic, you don't need to have your ribs cracked by doctors performing CPR if you stop breathing, and you don't want to be kept alive on a ventilator or a feeding tube."

"Can you draft those for us?" Rose asked.

"I shouldn't," Tequila said. "I haven't even taken the bar exam yet, and I am not going to be taking one in Tennessee. These are pretty standard documents, though. A local lawyer should be able to draft them, witness them, and notarize them for maybe a few hundred dollars. I can find somebody who will take care of it for you."

"What do you think I should do?" Rose asked him.

"You should definitely put a do-not-resuscitate instruction in a living will," he said. "If you get to that point, they're not going to be curing or saving you. The best they can do is prolong your suffering. And not for very long."

"Yes, but how do I decide whether to undergo the chemotherapy and the radiation?"

He lay back on our bed, with his feet dangling over the edge, like a sullen teenager. "Oh, God. I have no idea. I can do some research online. If you'd like, I can talk to your doctor."

"So, what you're telling us is that you have nothing to contribute, and your presence here is in no way useful," I said.

He sat up and clenched his fists. "Get off my nuts, Grandpa," he said. "I didn't know I was walking into this shit."

I pointed a finger at him. "Let's take this out into the hallway."

"What?"

"You've bothered your grandmother enough. Let's go outside."

He ran a hand through his hair. "Are you asking me to fight you?"

"What? No. I'm not going to kick your ass and put you in the hospital a month before your bar exam, as much as you probably deserve it. Let's just talk outside, so you can stop upsetting your grandmother."

I lifted myself off of the chair, grabbed onto the walker, and started pushing it toward the door.

"I don't understand," said Fran. "Where are you going?"

"Just out for some air," I said.

"I know what he wants to talk to William about," Rose said. "Some fight he got into with a man from the radio. He thinks if he goes out into the hallway, I won't know what he's up to."

"He got in a fight with a man from the radio?"

They were talking about me like I wasn't in the room again. I was hearing all of it, because I had only made it about a third of the way to the door. Our room was maybe thirty feet from end to end, but I needed ninety seconds to cross it. Maybe a little less, if I was in a rush to get to the toilet.

"Yes. A journalist, I think. It's something to do with one of his old cases. He keeps finding these doorways back into his past, like a Pevensie child finding portals into Narnia. And meanwhile, I'm dealing with cancer. I've had to remind him three times in the last two days that I am sick, and every time I tell him, it's like I'm telling him for the first time. But he hasn't needed any help remembering a stupid phone call from a reporter."

"Do you want me to stop him?" Fran asked. "I feel like we have some important things we need to discuss."

"Let him go. William will keep an eye on him. There's no reasoning with him when he gets like this, anyway. If we call downstairs, I think we can get somebody to send up some coffee."

"How is the coffee here?" Fran asked.

"Disappointing," said Rose. "Just like everything else."

Then Tequila opened the door, and I shuffled through it.

TRANSCRIPT: AMERICAN JUSTICE

CHESTER MARCH: Hey, how you been?

CARLOS WATKINS: I'm all right. How are you?

MARCH: You know me. Every day is a new adventure.

WATKINS (NARRATION): Death row inmates aren't allowed any visitors other than their lawyer, and, as their execution nears, a religious adviser. They don't get to see their families. They can make occasional phone calls, if they have enough money to pay the extortionate per-minute rates the phone company charges prisoners, and they can send a limited amount of mail that is screened and heavily redacted by prison censors. They get an hour in the yard each day. Otherwise, they're in their cells. It's the most maddening existence I can imagine, and Chester March has been living it since 1976.

By the way, that's why the audio quality for my conversations with Chester is a bit worse than it would be otherwise—all our conversations have been over the phone, and I have to record both sides. I've never been able to meet Chester face-to-face. I'm in Nashville right now, but the closest I can get to Chester is Riverbend's gate.

MARCH: Regular prisoners get to have jobs—they can cook or work in the laundry. Some of them get trained to do maintenance on the facility. Plumbing or electrical work. There are group counseling sessions, and GED classes, and even some college courses the men can take. I don't get to have a job. I never thought I'd be jealous of something like that, the right to mop some floors or change out light-bulbs. But the state figures there's no point in me learning or doing anything. No point in me bettering myself, or keeping myself busy, or even staying sane in this dump. I'm a dead man. I've been dead since Gerald Ford was president.

WATKINS: What do you do to pass the time?

MARCH: A lot of fellas on death row, they just get real fat. They say, when the ghost leaves you, you lose seven ounces, but while you're waiting for your big day, most folks here seem to put on about two hundred pounds. If you can die before the state can kill you, that's the only way you beat the house. Since they don't give us any sharp objects, or even shoelaces to hang ourselves with, diabetes is the way most of the guys here try to punch their own tickets. I know a man who ate so many Oreos, he lost a foot.

WATKINS: How many Oreos does that take?

MARCH: Who can count that high? I'll tell you something, though: You eat fifty or so of those cookies every day for a week, and your shit will turn black.

WATKINS: Black?

MARCH: Yeah, and dry. Chalky or—I don't know—powdery? Never seen anything like it. Eating all those cookies dries your guts out so much that, when you fart, it's like your ass is coughing.

WATKINS: Does it smell like chocolate?

MARCH: You'd think that, but no. It smells evil. Like rotten eggs, but a hundred times worse. The stink carries into the other cells. And the air circulation in here isn't so great, so that really lingers, especially in the summertime.

WATKINS: This has happened more than once?

MARCH: More than once? It happens constantly! That guy has been eating as many Oreos as he can get his hands on for fifteen years. He came in here in '96, and he was just a scrawny kid. Looked like maybe he was what they call a tweaker, but you don't ask a man about his past. Not in this place.

He didn't stay skinny for long, though. When they took him to the hospital for his surgery, they had to haul him out on a reinforced gurney. They cut his leg off just below the knee, got him on insulin, and then they brought him back here to keep waiting for them to kill him. He's probably 450 pounds, and that's without the leg. These days, he goes around in a wide-load wheelchair.

(LAUGHTER)

WATKINS (NARRATION): Every funny story about death row is really a sad story, though. These aren't just stories about poop and bad smells, but stories about mental and physical illness, about the toll it takes on the mind and body to live for decades in a desolate place without hope or joy or, indeed, much human contact of any kind.

Is it okay to laugh at stories about the harm the state is doing to people like Chester March and the skinny tweaker kid, ostensibly on behalf of all of us? I guess it has to be, because if you don't laugh, you'll have to cry.

4

The hallway on our floor had two sitting areas carved out of the spaces between the rooms, where there were sofas and little side tables with artificial flowers. Maybe the person who designed the place had envisioned them as gathering spaces, where active older adults would congregate to gossip and reminisce and share in their enjoyment of the residential amenities offered by the Valhalla Estates Assisted Lifestyle Community. I'd never seen them used for that purpose, though. Mostly, it was just a place to stop and rest on the way to the elevator, and it was much appreciated by those among us who couldn't make it all the way down the hallway without a break.

Even though it was only midafternoon, the common areas on my floor were empty, and the hall was as quiet as a mausoleum. There might have been a few televisions on in some of the rooms, but they were too low for me to hear, and the carpet muffled the sound. And most of my neighbors were probably napping. I usually dozed in the afternoon myself; I'd gotten by on five hours per night until around my eightieth birthday, but the amount of time I spent asleep had tripled in the previous five years. Training for the marathon, I suppose.

I pushed the walker toward a rarely used couch, and Tequila followed me.

"You know the real reason why I asked you to come into town, right?" I asked.

"Grandma has cancer."

"Yeah, but what are you going to do about that? You can't even draft the drop-dead instruction."

He flopped down next to me. "It's a do-not-resuscitate, and everyone should really have one."

"Thanks for your advice, Dr. Kevorkian. What I need from you is help dealing with a pesky journalist. This man from the radio is digging into an old case I worked, looking to cause trouble."

"I'm still kind of stuck on the cancer thing, if I'm being honest," he said. "Why are you worried about what someone might say on the radio? Nobody even listens to the radio anymore."

"I'm worried about your grandmother as well," I said. And I was, to the extent I could remember what was happening. For some reason, trying to hang on to the news about Rose's illness was like holding a live, wriggling fish. "But I can't have somebody tearing down my past. It's all that's left of me."

"Okay. Tell me what's going on, and I'll figure out what we can do about it."

"There's a man I put on death row up in Nashville named

Chester March. He's looking for a technicality that will save his skin, and he thinks he can get off by claiming I beat his confession out of him. He's got this NPR producer, Watkins, listening to his nonsense."

Tequila held a hand up. "Wait a second. You retired before I was born. How has this guy been on death row that long?"

"I don't know why they haven't killed him yet," I said. I pulled out a Lucky Strike, and stuck it between my lips. "Ask your liberal president."

"Barack Obama was fifteen years old when you retired."

"That's not the point." I dug my lighter out of the pocket of my Dockers and started flicking it.

Tequila draped his arm over the back of the sofa and crossed his legs. If nothing else, three years of law school had taught him to take up space. Eating all that Mexican food probably helped as well. "Grandma has cancer, and I am taking the bar exam in a few weeks. In the scheme of things, this just doesn't seem very important."

"It's important to me, Sambuca. Is there anything we can do to get rid of this reporter?" The lighter spouted flame, and I lit the cigarette. I wasn't supposed to smoke in the building's common areas, but there was nobody around, and if someone had a problem with me, what were they going to do? Send me to the principal's office?

Tequila shrugged. "If he says something false and damaging to your reputation, we can sue for defamation, I guess. But you can only do that after you've already been defamed. There's no way to, like, get an injunction to force NPR to kill the story.

Protections for the press are First Amendment freedoms, and courts can't impose prior restraints that prevent people from speaking."

"So what can I do?" I asked.

"Not much," he said. "But maybe we can call your representative at the police union. They might have some suggestions."

"I don't even know if I have his card," I said. "It's probably not the same guy anymore, anyway."

"Not a problem," he said, and he started tapping the screen of his Internet phone. I sat there and watched him do that for maybe thirty seconds, and then he dialed a number and set the phone on speaker.

"That seemed a little too easy," I said as the phone rang.

"Most things are easy," he replied. That had not been my experience in nine decades on this planet, but I never had a *Star Trek* communicator that told me everything I needed to know about everything.

A woman's voice on the line: "Memphis Police Association."

"Hi," Tequila said. "I am here with my grandfather, who is a retired Memphis police detective. He's hoping he can speak with his union representative."

"Okay, let me transfer you."

The phone played classic rock while we held. I flicked ash on the carpet. Tequila grinned at me. "See? Easy."

The music stopped, and somebody picked up. "You got Rick Lynch."

"Hi, Rick," Tequila said. "I'm here with my grandfather, who is a retired Memphis police detective. We're trying to get in touch with his union rep. Is that you?"

"Can your grandfather speak?" Lynch asked.

"Yeah," Tequila said.

"Then how about you shut the fuck up and let him. Ain't my job to talk to people's grandkids." I liked this guy.

"Are you my union rep?" I asked.

"Maybe. Who are you?"

"I'm retired detective Baruch Schatz."

"Aw, shit!" Lynch said. "I've heard of you. I didn't know you were still alive."

"I get up three times a night, just to check," I said.

"Well, what can I help you with today, Baruch Schatz?"

"A man I arrested, Chester March, is about to be executed. He's trying to get his sentence overturned by claiming I coerced his confession, and he's got a reporter from NPR who is listening to him."

"When did you put this guy away?" Lynch asked.

"Seventy-six," I said.

"Okay, did you murder anybody?"

"What? No!"

"Is this reporter going to try to say you murdered anybody?"

"I can't imagine why he would. I expect he's gonna say I whupped this suspect in the interrogation room."

"Mmm-hmm," Lynch said. "Well, there's no statute of limitations on murder, but anything else you might have done, it's too late for anyone to charge you on. So you're in the clear. I've never heard of the department opening an internal investigation this long after the fact, especially not into the conduct of retired personnel. I don't think you've got anything to worry about."

"But this reporter is still going to go on the radio and tell this story about me," I said, and I flicked my ash again.

"Detective Schatz, I don't know how things used to be done, but in the Year of Our Lord 2011, the Memphis Police Association ain't in the business of silencing journalists," Lynch said. I stopped liking him.

"We were hoping you could help us with public relations or crisis communications," Tequila said.

"Son, this is a police union. You must have us confused with an advertising agency."

"Is there anything you can do to help me with this?" I asked.

"If you are charged with a crime or subjected to a departmental investigation, we can get you a lawyer and back you up. If this reporter calls me, I'll be happy to tell him you were a great detective and that our position is that this guy March deserves to be executed. But there's not much else I can do."

I rested my elbows on my knees. "That's just terrific."

"Eat a dick," Tequila said, and he hung up the phone before Lynch could respond.

"So, what's next?" I asked my grandson.

"I think you should ignore this reporter and this whole situation, and just focus on supporting Grandma," Tequila said.

"But if I don't talk to him, he'll tell the story without my side of it."

"So what? Journalists write and broadcast stories about death penalty cases all the time. Nobody pays much attention, and the reporters almost never prevent people from getting executed. If you don't talk to this reporter, you can't make an inculpatory admission."

"A what?" I asked. This damn kid and his law-school Latin.

"A damaging statement. The reporter has got nothing but old

records and the killer's self-serving narrative. He needs a climax for his story, and he wants it to happen when he confronts you and makes you admit to wrongdoing. He's trying to get you, and all you have to do to avoid being gotten is stop taking his phone calls."

"Okay, maybe that makes sense," I said. "But I just can't let March broadcast his lies on NPR and not respond. I can't let that animal have the last word."

Tequila smacked a hand against his forehead. "Okay, well, why don't you tell me what really happened."

"Not much has happened yet. The reporter called me on the phone and said he's been talking to March and he wants to talk to me," I said.

"For fuck's sake," Tequila said. "Tell me what happened between you and March. What did you do to him? What is he telling this reporter?"

"Oh," I said. I stubbed out my cigarette on the armrest of the sofa, and hid the spent butt underneath a cushion. Then I lit another one. "Well, that's a whole thing."

PART 2

1955: JEW DETECTIVE

5

The woman sat in the chair on the other side of the desk from me and sobbed. I had gotten used to looking at people in this state, but I never managed to get comfortable with it. I lit a cigarette.

"If you need a minute to compose yourself, you're free to step into the powder room," I said, gesturing toward the toilets.

Her eyes widened, and her mouth fell open. "No!" she shouted. I must have looked alarmed, because she said, "I mean, I am afraid that if I leave, you won't be here when I get back. I've come to this police station four times, and this is the first time anyone has let me speak to an officer."

"Detective."

"What?"

"I'm a detective."

"That's even better," she said.

The shield was new, and very important to me. I'd earned it in the face of some pretty harsh circumstances. It had been tough for me to even become a cop at all; I'd caught a bullet overseas and messed up my shoulder pretty good. It took three surgeries and a couple of years of rehabilitation before I was able to get a medical clearance to sign up for the academy. I'd gone to Memphis State on the GI bill in the meantime and got me some liberal arts. I joined the department in 1949.

An officer with a college education could sit for the detective's exam after two years on patrol; men without college had to wait three. I took the first test I was eligible for and earned top marks. They told me they didn't have an opening for me, but they somehow had openings for guys with worse scores. It wasn't a mystery why: I had the wrong kind of name, prayed in the wrong kind of place, and I didn't belong to the right social kkklubs.

It was another three years before I got called up. It only happened after a spectacular display of heroics that got my picture in the paper, and I wasn't well liked in the detectives' bureau. Which was probably why this lady that nobody wanted to deal with was sitting in front of me.

I tapped my cigarette against an ashtray. "So what is it I can do for you, Miss . . . ?"

"Ogilvy. Hortense Ogilvy."

I nodded. "Of course you are."

"A friend of mine has gone missing."

I read once that, for at least a short time, in the flower of their youth, all girls are beautiful. But whoever wrote that never met Hortense Ogilvy. Miss Ogilvy had very large gums or very small teeth, or probably both. There was visible inflammation around the gumline, angry red with a few pockets of yellow-green pus. Her lips didn't quite stretch far enough to cover that whole disaster, so the gums were constantly exposed: florid, spit-slick, and glistening. I'd seen a mouth like that once before: on a bloated cadaver we'd fished out of the river. I caught a whiff of something foul, and I wasn't sure if I was actually smelling Miss Ogilvy's mouth or having a vivid sense memory of the stink of that particular corpse. I wondered if she would take offense if I tried to smoke two or three cigarettes at once.

"A friend of yours?" I asked.

"Yes. My friend Margery Whitney." Miss Ogilvy made a face like she'd bitten into a lemon. Her swollen gums blushed purple with disgust. "Well, she's Margery March now. That's her husband's name. Chester March."

"Margery March?"

"Yes, sir."

I exhaled a plume of smoke out of my nostrils and then tried to breathe it back in. "She should have turned down his proposal just to avoid that name."

Hortense clenched her fists. "If you ask me, she should have turned down his proposal for a lot of reasons."

"Too bad nobody asked you," I said.

"What is that supposed to mean, Detective?"

"I'm not sure yet. Why don't you tell me why you think Margery March is missing."

"We're quite close, and we talk every day or so. We had a standing lunch date every Wednesday that we'd kept almost religiously until she disappeared. I haven't seen or heard from her in nearly three weeks."

"Anything happen between you that might explain why she is making herself scarce?" I really couldn't blame Margery for taking a break from Hortense. I was ready for one myself, and I'd only known her for about five minutes.

"Nothing whatsoever," Miss Ogilvy said. "We were thick as thieves, and then she was just gone. Her sister hasn't heard from her, either. And the neighbors haven't seen her around, which is unusual."

"What does the husband say?" I asked.

"That she's out. Whenever I visit."

I dropped my cigarette butt in the ashtray and lit another one. "Usually, a family member initiates a missing-person report."

"Her family is up in Nashville. All she has here is Chester."

"And you think Chester might have done something to her?"

"Oh, I hope not."

This conversation was becoming circular and annoying. In a nonchalant way I figured might seem unintentional, I blew some smoke in her face. "Well, what do you think happened?"

She coughed and waved a hand in front of her mouth. "That's why I came to you. So you would find out."

"Terrific," I said. "Sounds like fun."

6

I took a drive to Chester March's stately manse on Overton Park Avenue to get a look at the guy and see if I could figure out how much of a piece of shit he was.

The houses in the Evergreen neighborhood of Midtown Memphis were built around the turn of the century, but in the antebellum style—the mansions were fronted by ostentatious colonnades, the columns held up the heavy second-story balconies, and the balconies shaded the wraparound porches.

The nostalgic elegance of the neighborhood was giving way to shabbiness, though. By the mid-'50s, the rich had already begun fleeing Midtown and moving out to the suburbs and unincorporated areas of Shelby County. The construction of the new highway loop, as well as the recent proliferation of fully enclosed automobiles with heating and air-conditioning, meant it was no longer necessary to live in close proximity to the downtown business district, and a recent decision by Chief Justice Earl Warren was set to render the Memphis City Schools unacceptable to most of the better-heeled whites.

I parked on the street; there was a car parked in Chester's driveway, a red Buick Roadmaster Skylark. It was a nice enough ride that even if you were rich enough not to have to care about things, you probably still wouldn't want to leave it out in the elements. The house had an attached garage, but the door was closed. I wondered what he was keeping in there instead of his car.

I found March sitting on his porch in a rocking chair, drinking something with a lot of ice in it out of a highball glass. Next to him, a large fan noisily agitated the soupy July air. The fan was powered by an extension cord that ran through the open front door of the house. I peered into the foyer, but there was nothing in plain view that appeared incriminating, so I didn't have any justification or probable cause that would allow me to toss the house or frisk the occupant. Why couldn't things ever be easy?

I sized Chester up. He wore his hair in a short, clean cut, and he used just enough pomade to keep it in place. His jacket was white summer linen, and his shirt collar was white and crisp, despite the intense heat and the oppressive humidity. Whoever did his laundry must have been some kind of wizard, or else he was in the habit of wearing his linens just once and then throwing them out, because they showed no indication of ever having been sullied by proximity to human skin.

He had a fine aquiline nose and a well-defined, arrogant jaw. Some folks might have thought him a handsome man, and maybe he even came across that way in pictures, but there was something off about him, a coldness to his manner and a flatness to his affect that made his fine features seem too sharp and jagged.

I was wearing summer-weight wool by Sears, Roebuck that afternoon, but wool doesn't come in a weight that is appropriate for July in Memphis, so I was doing a pretty good job of *schvitz*ing through my suit. All my shirts had yellowish stains around their cuffs and collars that Rose could never quite get out. I suppose I'd have to admit that Chester looked better than me, though I would not have required much provocation to ugly him up some.

"Are you the man of the house?" I asked him.

He took a long sip from the glass and then dabbed at his lips with a linen handkerchief. "None other," he said. I think he was trying to seem bored by my presence, but the slightest crease appeared in the middle of his forehead, revealing his annoyance. He was a man accustomed to deference, and a man accustomed to everyone knowing exactly who he was. He did not seem to be a man who was accustomed to fielding pointed questions from pushy Jews in damp, rumpled suits.

I climbed the porch steps and positioned myself so the big fan would blow my cigarette smoke in March's direction. "That's a mighty nice automobile," I said, pointing at the Skylark. "Is it yours?"

"Yes, it is," Chester said. I waited a few seconds in case he wanted to talk about his car. Most people with cars like that liked to talk about them. I liked talking about cars, and I liked people who liked talking about cars. But Chester didn't say anything. I did not like Chester.

I asked, "Is your wife here?"

His lips turned up, flashing a set of straight, white teeth at me.

"Usually, when a stranger comes around looking to liaise with a lady, said stranger will exercise a bit more discretion with regard to her husband."

I showed him my shield. "People are worried about Mrs. March. I just want to make sure she's all right. So, is she around?"

The crease in Chester's forehead became more pronounced. "People should mind their own business," he said.

"I asked you a question."

He took a sip from his drink and smacked his lips. "Ooh, that's nice. You know, the custom around these parts is to drink whiskey cocktails in warm weather, but this is much more refreshing. It's white Cuban rum with lime juice, cane sugar, and a sprig of mint. I'd have my girl fix one for you, but I'm sure an upstanding officer such as yourself wouldn't take a drink while you're on duty, and I'm not sure I'd like you to stay around long enough to properly enjoy it."

"Where's your wife, Mr. March?"

He smiled his mirthless smile again. "She's out, I guess."

"When will she be back?"

"You know, I didn't think to ask."

I pointed toward the open front door. "Can I take a look around inside?"

"I would prefer you didn't," he said. I considered pushing that issue, but decided against it. A guy like that would have a swarm of needle-toothed lawyers on retainer. If I wanted to get Chester, I'd need to be very careful not to give them any opportunity to challenge my evidence.

"What if I hang around until Mrs. March gets back?"

He shrugged and took another sip from his drink. "Well, I've no inclination to entertain you while you wait. Of course, you may do whatever you'd like once you're beyond the edge of my property. I'd appreciate it if you'd stay out of my eyeline, though. I don't enjoy looking at you."

I went back to my car, parked on the curb, and sat in it for half an hour, watching March as he sat in his rocker, drinking his icy drink and letting his fan ruffle his hair. Then I left. My unmarked vehicle had no air conditioner, and my shirt was sticking to my chest. And Margery wasn't going to be coming back; I was pretty sure.

TRANSCRIPT: AMERICAN JUSTICE

CHESTER MARCH: So, the first time I met Buck Schatz was when he came to my house to tell me my wife was missing.

WATKINS: He came to tell you? You didn't already know?

MARCH: She was always what you might call a strong-willed woman. She went off on her own sometimes—trips with her friends or visits to her parents. So when she didn't come home at night, I never really worried much. Women were becoming independent in those days, and as a cosmopolitan gentleman, I had no objection to that. I never expected Margery to be waiting around with dinner on the table when I got home, and, in any case, we had a girl who came in and kept the house up and did the cooking so Margery was free to follow her whims. I was all right on my own and never minded a little peace and quiet, and Margery always came back. Until she didn't.

WATKINS: You were eventually convicted of murdering her.

MARCH: On the flimsiest of evidence, in a kangaroo courtroom, twenty years later. But you know that, or you wouldn't even be talking to me.

WATKINS: They found her body.

MARCH: They claim they found skeletal remains, decades after the alleged murder. Completely unidentifiable. I don't know where they got that skeleton. Nobody knows where they got that skeleton except Detective Schatz, and the only thing you can trust about a cop is the fact that a cop is going to lie.

You know, my lawyers keep asking for DNA tests to be performed on those remains, and the state just fights tooth and nail against it. If they're gonna put me to death, they should at least be willing to perform scientific tests on the alleged evidence.

WATKINS: That seems reasonable. What's their basis for objecting to the test?

MARCH: I think they don't want to do the tests because they've got something to hide. But what they say is that it would be disrespectful to re-exhume the body. They say it would cause distress to the family. Hell! If they really believe that's even her, she's been dead fifty-five years. Margery ain't got any family still alive that remembers her.

WATKINS: Except you.

MARCH: Well, Carlos, I expect that what is going to cause me more distress is the lethal injection. Oh! The other thing they say is that the remains are so old that DNA results will come back inconclusive. If a DNA test is inconclusive, I should get a new trial!

WATKINS: What about the statement you gave to Detective Schatz?

MARCH: You ever heard the phrase "fruit of the poison tree," Carlos? It's got a nice ring to it, don't it? Like something out of the Bible. The fruit of the poison tree. It means that any evidence collected in violation of a suspect's rights by police misconduct is untrustworthy. Inadmissible. That coerced statement is the fruit of the poison tree. It never should have been presented to a jury. Evidence gathered based on the things they say I told them should have been excluded. What that man did to me should never happen in America.

WATKINS: We're definitely going talk about that, but we're getting a little ahead of ourselves. Let's get back to the first time the two of you met.

MARCH: You ever see a guy, and the look of him just scares you? That was Schatz. He wasn't a tall man, but he had some mass to him, and he carried himself in a way that let you know he was dangerous. You can look at Buck and tell he's the kind of guy who would know the right way to hit you in the throat with his elbow and make it so you couldn't swallow solid food for ten days. Living where I've been living the last thirty-five years, you meet a lot of fellas who will posture and boast and threaten, but it's pretty easy to figure out which of them will step up and which of them will back down.

WATKINS: And Buck Schatz was the kind to step up?

MARCH: Buck Schatz was the kind who seemed like he was just looking for an excuse to hurt somebody. He had these dark, deep-set eyes and heavy brows. And that big Jewish nose, like a hawk's beak. That's what he looked like. A huge predatory bird. But that might give you the wrong impression of him, make him sound like he was light on his feet or something. He actually had this clumpy way of walking, like maybe something was a little bit wrong with him.

WATKINS: He got shot, fighting in Europe.

MARCH: Oh yeah? How'd that happen?

WATKINS: He was in a prison camp, and one German guard shot him in the back to stop him from beating another guard to death with his bare hands.

MARCH: That sounds like something that would happen to Buck Schatz. Did he tell you about that?

WATKINS: No. I got it from military records and research in

newspaper archives. I haven't managed to pin Schatz down for an interview yet. I've called him on the telephone a couple of times to set a meeting, but he's being cagey.

MARCH: Keep at him. He'll talk to you.

WATKINS: Because he's the kind of guy who steps up rather than backs down?

MARCH: Because that son of a bitch can't resist conflict. Do you know about Schatz and his cigarettes? The guy chain-smokes, constantly. It's unbelievable that he's lived this long, the way he pollutes his body. He is always surrounded by a cloud, like the Pigpen kid from the Snoopy comic strip. And he's real aggressive with it. It's a power thing for him. He'll blow smoke on you, or he'll throw his butts and ashes on the floor, and he'll look you right in the eye while he's doing it, like he's daring you to confront him about his refusal to follow even the most basic norms of polite society. He thinks it's funny. This is a very childish man.

WATKINS: We were talking about the day you met him, when he came to tell you your wife was missing.

MARCH: Some busybody friend of Margery's had reported her missing, so he came around to check out what was happening. I guess he didn't like the look of me, because he had it in for me almost from the start. He was really pushy, and he wanted to look inside the house. Of course I was not going to give a police officer permission to come into my domicile. Anyone who has ever even met a lawyer knows better. When I turned him away, he went and sat in his car, just staring at me. He waited like that for maybe half an hour. Just a scary guy, sitting there, breathing smoke, and figuring out how to ruin me.

WATKINS: And then what did he do?

MARCH: He ruined me.

7

———

The smart thing to do is not to do anything," I said as I hacked at a tuna croquette with a fork. The croquettes were pretty simple to make—just canned tuna, bread crumbs from a box, and chopped onions, fried in vegetable shortening—but they were one of my favorite meals.

"Why is that smart?" my mother asked. She roughly wiped ketchup off of Brian's face. The baby was three. Bird was sixty-three. "This woman is dead, the husband killed her. Go get him."

"I think she's dead, but I don't know she's dead." I dunked a piece of tuna in ketchup and popped it into my mouth.

"What's the difference?"

"Have you ever heard of Schrödinger's cat?" I asked.

"What are you talking about?"

"Imagine you've got a cat, and the cat is in a box. And there is also a vial of poison in the box, which might or might not shatter and kill the cat. Until you open the box, you can't know if the vial has been shattered, so you don't know if the cat is alive or dead. So, the argument is that the cat exists in a state of being both alive and dead."

Mother frowned. "I don't understand. What kind of evil person puts a cat in a box with poison?"

"It's not a literal cat," I said. "It's a thought exercise."

"But you have to be a real degenerate to want to think about torturing animals."

"The point is that, since the cat is sealed in the box, you don't know whether the vial of poison has shattered. The point is how you treat that uncertainty."

She shrugged. "Why wouldn't you just open the box and look?"

"It's used as an analogy for thinking about particles that are difficult to observe. But also, there's value in not knowing. That's how it is with investigating missing people." I said. Rose came into the room carrying a bowl of canned peas that she'd heated up on the stove. I helped myself to a big spoonful. "Once you know something, an unpleasant chain of events can follow from that knowledge."

Rose offered my mother the peas. Bird sniffed at them, wrinkled her nose, and waved them off. "So you pretend to be ignorant, and this killer gets away with everything? Where's the value in that?"

"We've got a list of all the year's murders downtown," I said. "It's got the names of the victims, the names of the detectives investigating, and whether we solved them. I don't want to be the man who finishes the year with his name on that list next to a bunch of murders that aren't solved. Chester March is rich and clever. The wife has been missing for weeks. He's had plenty of time to destroy the evidence. I can call this a murder. I can start this process. But I don't know if I can finish it."

"What happens if you don't? What happens if you walk away?" Rose asked.

I shrugged and bit into a chunk of tuna. "Then she's the cat in the box. Nobody knows if she's alive or dead, so there's no name on the list downtown. We look for people who go missing, but there's no accounting for the ones we don't find. There's nobody counting how many we solved, like there are with murders. There are lots of reasons people go missing. Sometimes they get on a bus and just skip town. Maybe Margery March met a man and ran off with him."

"But you know Margery March didn't get on a bus," my mother said.

I lit a Lucky Strike. "Suppose I start down this road but I can't find the body. It takes a bulletproof circumstantial case to convict somebody of murder if you don't have a corpse. Every one of those reasons I could have used to walk away from the case without calling it a murder becomes a defense lawyer's argument at trial. If we haven't found a body, how do we even know she's dead? And if we don't know she's dead, how can we convict her husband of murdering her?"

Mother reached across the table, plucked the cigarette from my lips, and ground it into the ashtray. "I didn't raise you to be a coward. Your father, *alev ha-shalom*, would be ashamed," she said. "He died fighting for what he believed in."

I tapped my pack of Luckys against my palm so that one

popped out. "And you always said he was a fool. That he died because he thought his principles would protect him. You said he believed in a world governed by justice and fairness. A world that doesn't exist." I struck a match.

Mother lunged across the table and smacked the unlit cigarette out of my mouth. "Principles don't protect you. That doesn't mean you live without principles," she said. "It just means you have to protect yourself." For emphasis, she produced a six-inch serrated hunting knife from someplace under her skirt and dropped it on the dinner table.

"How does he protect himself if he keeps tilting at windmills?" Rose asked. "You know how hard he had to work to make detective. You know all the bigots in that department don't believe a Jew can do that job. They're looking for an excuse to call him a failure. He's got a family to feed. He has a son. And I know he pays some of your bills as well, Bird. Why does this woman's disappearance have to be his problem? He has enough problems already."

"Either he's a man or he's not," Mother said. She dropped her fork onto her plate and pushed the plate toward the center of the table. "By the way, Rose, you can't cook for shit." She wiped her mouth with her napkin and tossed it onto the plate.

"Watch your language in front of the kid, Mother," I said.

"You can't cook for shit, Mommy!" Brian said. "Cook shit!"

"You don't have to eat here," Rose said, and she scooped up the baby, grabbed Mother's plate, and stormed off to the kitchen, pausing just long enough to give me a dirty look. Maybe I should have stuck up for her; God knows, if any man alive had said something like that about my wife, I'd have put him face-first through the nearest wall without hesitation. But this was my mother. What did Rose expect?

I took another bite of my croquette, and Mother sat there, glowering. The dining room was silent except for the sound of my knife cutting through the fish and breading. Mother was right, of course, about Chester March. She was right about the food, too. The croquettes were too oily, and a little bit burned.

I grabbed the ketchup bottle and shook it until a big, gelatinous gob fell onto my plate.

Mother took care of me on her own after Dad was killed. It wasn't easy for a woman to make a living and raise a child by herself in those days, but I never wanted for much. She was tough and smart, and she was right about most things. You could fight Hitler. You could fight the Klan. You could fight crime. But if you tried to fight with Bird Schatz, you were probably going to get your ass kicked.

"Of course I'm going after March, Mother," I said. "I don't let people get away with the kinds of things he has done."

"Good," she said.

I tapped my pack of Lucky Strikes against the table again, but she shook her head at me, and I put it back into my pocket.

8

Once I decided to treat Hortense Ogilvy's report about her missing friend as a criminal investigation, it meant I was going to have to do some actual work. You wouldn't know from watching police shows on television that detectives have to do real work sometimes. But we do, and it's a pain in the ass.

The first thing I needed to do was verify that Margery March was, in fact, missing, and to make sure my witness wasn't just a crank. I checked to see if Hortense had a criminal record and didn't find anything. I pulled her traffic record from the local DMV. She'd gotten a parking ticket once, but a judge had fixed it for her.

Using the date of birth from her driver's license, I figured that she'd graduated high school in 1948. The Memphis Public Library kept archives of *The Commercial Appeal* on microfilm, so I took a drive down there and looked through April, May, and June of that year, to see if they'd written anything about her. I found a photo of her attending a cotillion in the grand lobby of the Peabody Hotel. Her dress was lovely, but she was not. She appeared to be grimacing, but based on the context, I decided that was just how her face looked when she smiled. The boy escorting her looked like he would rather be anywhere else. The accompanying article said Hortense was going to attend Southwestern Presbyterian College.

The library also kept yearbooks from the local colleges, and I was able to use those to verify that Hortense Ogilvy had been at Southwestern from 1949 to 1953 and had graduated. Margery Whitney attended from '49 to '51, so that was probably how they knew each other.

I went back to the microfiche and flipped through the wedding announcements from the spring of 1951, until I found an article about Margery Whitney's marriage to Chester March. Chester had graduated from University of Mississippi, and he was employed with his father's cotton concern outside of Tupelo. The article mentioned that Chester's best man, a guy named Murray Bottom, had delighted the attendees with a story about how Chester used to shoot stray dogs. I decided I wanted to talk to that guy.

The operator found me a listing for a Murray Bottom in Oxford and patched me through to him.

"Howdy," I said. I had the story about Hortense's cotillion in front of me. I checked the byline. It was written by a guy named Al Waters. "I'm Al Waters from *The Commercial Appeal* in Memphis, and I am writing a story about Chester March. I was hoping you could tell me some things about him, sort of as background."

"What kind of story are you writing about Chester?" he asked.

"I write for the society page," I told him. I tried to guess what a rich guy might do that would get written up in the newspaper. "I'm doing a piece on Chester's charity work."

"Oh," said Bottom, sounding relieved. "I thought he might be in trouble."

I laughed. "Now, why would you say a thing like that?"

"No reason, no reason. I'm sure he's doing a lot of good, with his charity. I just always thought there was something a little strange about that guy."

"You were the best man at his wedding," I said.

"Yeah. That was one of the things that was strange. Why would he ask me? I knew him when we were kids. My father services and repairs farm machinery, and old Mr. March was an important account for him. Pop always wanted me to let Chester hang around with my crew, so I was friendly to him, but I never thought we were close. And I hadn't even heard from him in several years before he called to ask me to be in his wedding. I didn't want to do it, but, you know, his family is a big chunk of our business. You're not gonna print any of this, are you?"

"Naw," I said. "Just background."

"Maybe a lot of guys were off in Korea when they had the wedding. Maybe he didn't have anybody else who could attend."

"Why wasn't Chester in Korea?" I asked.

"I think he got a deferment because his job on his daddy's farm was vital agricultural work."

"What does he do for his father?"

He was silent on the line, maybe starting to see through me. "Can't you ask Chester these questions if you're writing a story about him?"

"An important guy like Chester March just expects you to know these things when you go in to talk to him. I always find it's best to find out as much as I can before I sit down with my subject, so I waste as little of his valuable time as possible."

He took his time chewing on that, and then he said, "I guess that makes sense, but I don't really know what Chester does for his father. I've been down to their land to service some of the equipment, and I've never seen Chester around. He lives in Memphis, and Mr. March doesn't have much business up there. To tell the truth, I got the impression Chester just had a make-work kind of job to get the deferment and stay out of the war."

"How'd you stay out of it?" I asked, even though I had no real reason to want to know.

"I didn't," Bottom said. "I got a chunk of my leg shot off in '50, and then I came home. I walk okay now, but I had a rough time of it for a while."

That made me like him a little better. "I caught one myself, in France. Made a real mess of my shoulder."

"And now you write for the society page." He sounded skeptical. I wasn't sure how much more bullshit I could feed this guy.

"I've got our article about Chester's wedding here, and it says you gave a real ripper of a toast at the reception," I said. "You had everyone in stitches, apparently. Can you tell me that story?"

"That was a few years back. Refresh my memory?"

"Something about shooting dogs."

"Oh, I don't really remember how I told it to make it sound funny. It's not a funny story. Chester had a .22 rifle, and he used to like to shoot dogs with it. He said they were mangy, flea-bitten strays, but people just let their dogs run in the country back then, so I don't know how he'd know if they were strays or not. A .22 is a small-caliber rifle. You use it to hunt squirrels. If you shoot a dog with a .22, it won't die right away, unless you get it through the head or the heart. Chester used to like to shoot them through the guts and watch them bleed. I didn't like that. I like dogs. I didn't want to hang around with him, but it was real important to stay on his family's good side. Old Mr. March was an important account for my dad. Anyway, I'm sure Chester grew up all right. He's a married man now, and he does charity work."

"Yeah, I think he's a good sort," I said. "Thanks for your time."

I liked dogs, too. And I was really starting to wish ill on Chester.

Having established that Miss Ogilvy was not self-evidently a nutcase and that something was off about Chester, I felt comfortable contacting Margery's family in Nashville. I had the operator patch me through, and I got her mother on the line. I told her I was Al Waters from *The Commercial Appeal*, and was trying to get in touch with Margery for a story.

She told me Margery hadn't called in a few weeks. I asked if that was unusual, which probably stretched the credible limits of what Al Waters might ask, but Mrs. Whitney didn't catch on. She told me her daughter usually called more often, but long-distance wasn't cheap. She didn't seem worried. I didn't want to worry her until I knew for sure what had happened.

I went back to the DMV files and found Margery's records. She drove a light blue 1953 Packard. I checked to see if a car matching that description had been found abandoned anywhere and came up empty.

I took a drive out to Overton Park Avenue, found a space on the street down the block from Chester's house, and waited for him to leave. Once I saw him drive off in the Skylark, which he was still parking in the driveway, I went over to the house, lifted the garage door about six inches, and took a look inside. The Packard was there. If Margery had run off someplace, she'd done it without her car. I was tempted to see what else he might be hiding, but I didn't want to risk searching the garage without a warrant. Nothing could be worse than finding a murder weapon or some human remains during an illegal search and getting all my evidence thrown out of court.

So, I shut the garage, walked over to the door, and banged on it for about ten minutes, in case somebody other than Chester was in there. Nobody answered.

9

This was looking pretty straightforward to me. Margery was dead, and Chester had probably killed her. But my hunch wasn't going to be enough to convict him, especially since I had no idea where the body might be.

Contrary to what you might have read in detective novels, it is possible to commit a perfect murder. You bury a body under concrete, dissolve it in acid, or dump it properly in deep water, and nobody will ever find it. But most people don't manage that trick the first time they try. They bury bodies in shallow graves, so animals uncover them; or they use the wrong kind of acid, and it doesn't dissolve the corpse; or they dump the body in a lake, but they don't weigh it down enough, and it bobs to the surface when it begins to decompose and bloats with gas.

If Chester knew how to make Margery disappear, I figured that this might not be the first time he had done something like this. He might have had some practice. I pulled all the files for unsolved murders and unaccounted-for disappearances of women between fifteen and forty years of age from the previous five years and took them to my desk. There were a couple dozen of them, which was more than I expected. Less than a quarter of total murder victims were women, and in most cases, when a woman was murdered, detectives didn't need to look beyond her husband or her lover to find a culprit.

But certain women—prostitutes, dopeheads, and the kinds of women that hung around truck stops—had a tendency to fall prey to random assaults and sadistic drifters. It was real tough to pin down a suspect who was a stranger to his victim and often had no connection at all to the community. In a solid 90 percent of murders, there's somebody out there who knows who did it, and all a detective has to do is find that witness and get them to talk. But these women were falling prey to men nobody knew, and they weren't the kind of women whose murders the department was prone to making a great effort to solve. Out of twenty-seven women whose murders had gone unsolved, twenty-three were colored. I set aside all the files where the victim had last been seen getting into a semitruck, and all the files where the victim had last been seen in the company of a colored suspect. That left me with only one.

A witness named Bernadette Ward had seen victim Cecilia Tompkins speaking to a well-dressed white man on the evening of May 11, 1953.

Ward described seeing Tompkins and the well-dressed white man getting into a new-looking red car with a description that matched Chester's Buick Skylark. She didn't get the plate number, but she described the fabric top of the convertible, the whitewall tires, and the way the headlights and the front grille looked like a scowling face. Late-model luxury cars were uncommon in Bernadette Ward's South Memphis neighborhood, and so, for that matter, were well-dressed white men.

Nobody saw Tompkins again until her corpse washed up on the banks of the Mississippi fifty miles south of town on May 18.

She died from blunt-force trauma, and her body was covered in chemical burns that the coroner believed had occurred postmortem. The killer had attempted to dissolve the corpse using acid or some other abrasive, and he dumped the remains in the river when that didn't work. Both Ward and Tompkins were colored prostitutes, so nobody looked very hard for the man Ward had seen.

The detective investigating Tompkins's murder decided she'd been killed out of state and closed the file, with the blessing of Inspector Byrne, who oversaw the homicide division.

I found Bernadette Ward working on the same corner she'd been on two years earlier when Cecilia Tompkins disappeared. When I climbed out of my unmarked car and she saw I was white, she looked nervous. I showed her my shield, which didn't make her any more comfortable. But she didn't try to run away, which I appreciated. I always resented the ones who made me chase them.

"I ain't seen nothing, I ain't done nothing, and I don't know nothing," she said. Her voice was rusty and jagged, the kind of voice a woman only gets from being strangled by somebody who means it, and probably more than once.

According to the DOB that was printed under her mug shot, she was five years younger than me, but she looked five years older.

I'd been starved, beaten, and shot. Recovering from my war wounds had taken a lot out of me. I'd spent time in a foxhole and in a prison camp, and I had not chosen a low-stress occupation. But I suspected Bernadette Ward could tell me a few things about rough living that I didn't yet know.

"Whatever you're getting up to out here, I don't care about it," I told her.

She leaned against a streetlamp and crossed her arms. "Well, you're gonna have to excuse me if I don't believe you."

"I'm here to ask you some questions about Cecilia Tompkins and the white man who took her," I said.

She laughed—bitter and off-key. "Now I know you're lying. Nobody gives a damn about Cecilia Tompkins. The police made that real clear to me."

I thought about telling her that I cared about Cecilia Tompkins. But she wouldn't have believed it, and I didn't even really believe it. If I had cared, I would have been here sooner. The disappearance of Cecilia Tompkins hadn't been my case; I hadn't even known about it. But the file had been sitting there, waiting for me or anyone else who wanted to make trouble for himself, and I had never been interested in that kind of trouble. The only reason I was in South Memphis talking to this woman was to get something on Chester.

If I had been responsible for investigating the Cecilia Tompkins killing, would I have struck it from the list of Memphis murders using the same justification the investigating detective had used? Would my mother have said the same things to me she'd said about Margery March if I'd told her about the killing of a colored hooker?

I could lie to myself, but my lies probably wouldn't work on Bernadette Ward. "I think the man you saw on the night Cecilia disappeared has killed a white woman," I said.

"Oh, so now you gonna look for him."

I reached into my pocket and fished out my pack of Luckys. "I don't think I need to tell you how the world works."

"Why should I help you?" she asked.

"You don't have to. But if you do, I might catch the man who killed your friend." I offered her the pack of cigarettes. She took one, so I lit it for her, but I didn't let her hold my lighter.

"What do you need me to do?"

"I have some photographs. I need you to look at them and tell me if you see the man who killed Cecilia."

"Do I have to go with you to a police station?"

"Not right now. I've got the pictures with me." The best photo of Chester I had was a mimeographed copy of his wedding announcement in *The Commercial Appeal*, so I had trimmed Margery out of the picture and pasted Chester onto a sheet of heavy paper. I had done the same with similar newspaper pictures of fifteen other men. I handed the stack of pages to Bernadette. She leafed through them and stopped on Chester's picture, which was in the middle of the stack. She glanced at the rest of the photos, but went back to Chester.

"This is him," she said. "I've never seen these others."

"Are you sure?" I asked. I tried as best I could not to convey to her whether or not I was pleased with her identification.

"Two kinds of white men come around here. One is the kind that's got a taste for a little something dark, a little something— you know—voodoo."

"Taboo?"

"Call it what you want, policeman. Point is, that white man is gonna pay you, and he's gonna be pretty clean, and it's gonna be easy money. But sometimes, a white man comes around here because he's looking to do something nasty to somebody that white cops won't care about. That white man will beat you so you can't work. Maybe he'll cut up your face so nobody will want you anymore. Maybe he'll dump you in the river like that man in the picture did to poor Cecilia. When you see that white man, you had better recognize him, and you had better know to stay away. I ain't never gonna forget that man."

"When I arrest him, I may need you to identify him in a lineup, and I may need you to testify at trial."

"Well, maybe I'll be here," she said.

TRANSCRIPT: AMERICAN JUSTICE

CARLOS WATKINS (NARRATION): Edward Heffernan is a law professor at Vanderbilt University. He's also leading the team of appellate lawyers that is racing the clock to get a stay of execution that will save Chester March's life. I checked in with him to see what's going on with the case and what Chester's chances are.

Before you hear from him, I want to give you a sense of this guy: First of all, if you're imagining Gregory Peck as Atticus Finch, stop doing that. Ed Heffernan and Gregory Peck are both white guys, but that's where the similarities end. Heffernan is around fifty, skinny and bald, with glasses so thick they distort the shape of his eyes. He's an average-size guy, maybe five feet ten, and a hundred and seventy pounds or so, but he carries himself in a way that somehow diminishes his stature. After I met him the first time, I described him in my notes as being five-six, and when I went back to see him again, I was shocked to realize he's actually taller than I am. But his head's always down and he holds his arms close to his body. He's easy to underestimate.

The students in his capital appeals clinic joke about his fondness for Kirkland Signature clothing; that's the store brand at Costco. Ed wears their sweaters and chinos most days, unless he's in court, and then he dresses in his Men's Wearhouse best. You would never know from looking at him that Edward Heffernan is a former clerk to Justice William Brennan, that he's one of the most respected appellate lawyers in the country, that his law review articles have been cited dozens of times in important federal judicial opinions, or that he's an instrumental figure in the fight to abolish the death penalty.

EDWARD HEFFERNAN: We have two interrelated arguments before the Tennessee Supreme Court for staying Mr. March's execution. The first is that it is unconstitutional under the Eighth Amendment, which bars the use of cruel and unusual punishments, to carry out a lethal injection on a person of Mr. March's advanced age. The dosages recommended by the state's lethal injection protocol are measured for a healthy middle-aged man. Injecting that into an elderly person could have unpredictable results. The second prong of our argument is that the state's lethal injection protocol is unconstitutional as applied to anyone. It has been a few years since Tennessee has executed someone, and there's some new research that raises questions about the physiology of what happens to a person when these chemicals are administered. Several states have issued moratoria on the death penalty, halting all executions while they reevaluate their protocols, and we think that's appropriate in Tennessee as well.

WATKINS: What about Detective Schatz's conduct during Chester's interrogation, and the admissibility of the statement Chester gave to police?

HEFFERNAN: Those questions have been raised by previous appeals. Personally, I believe the confession and the evidence the police discovered because of it should have been excluded from Mr. March's trial, and I find the circumstances of that interrogation appalling. But judges, especially here in the South, will give the police the benefit of every doubt they reasonably can to avoid throwing out evidence they view as credible. From a legal perspective, those issues are exhausted, and we're trying to make the best arguments we've still got to save our client's life. As you're well aware, Chester is scheduled for execution in a few weeks. Time is of the essence, and we are focusing on our strongest arguments to stop or at least delay the execution. Of course, if somebody like you managed to uncover some new information, or raised significant public outcry over the circumstances of this conviction, that might change something, especially since Mr. March has a clemency petition in front of the governor. So everyone on the defense team really appreciates what you're doing.

WATKINS: Tell me why you think the lethal injection is unconstitutional.

HEFFERNAN: Now, there's a subject I love to talk about! Throughout the twentieth century, states cycled through a number of execution methods. The goal has always been to find a method of killing human beings that doesn't appear to be violent. And it has always been impossible, because violence is inherent in the act of executing someone.

We used to hang people. It did the job quick, but folks didn't like the optics. Or the noise it made when someone's neck snapped. For a while people thought that electrocution would allow us to shut somebody down like flicking off a light switch. It didn't quite work out that way. Electrocution causes horrible burns, and sometimes hemorrhages. And there's a smell. A person's veins are full of blood, and their digestive tracts are full of food at various stages of being turned into waste. Electrocuting somebody is like sticking all that into a high-powered microwave oven.

WATKINS: I don't even want to imagine what death by electrocution smells like.

HEFFERNAN: I know firsthand. It is unpleasant.

WATKINS (NARRATION): Y'all, I have spent hours interviewing this man, and I cannot tell if this is just the way he talks, or if he has, like, a very dry sense of humor. Sometimes I think he's messing with me a little.

HEFFERNAN: As an alternative to electrocution, some states tried execution by gas chamber, but people thrash around when they're choking to death on poison gas. Corrections officials tried restraining the subjects to prevent that, even strapping their heads down, but, once again, a lot of people found it unpleasant to bind a human being to a gurney in order to force them to breathe poison gas. And witnesses can still see the victim struggling against the restraints. There's no way to gas somebody to death that isn't awful to watch. So currently most states have settled on lethal injection. Throughout these iterations on death penalty methods, the states prioritized the appearance of a peaceful death over methods known to actually minimize the pain and suffering of the condemned.

WATKINS: What's the difference in a humane death and a death that only appears to be humane?

HEFFERNAN: We know the fastest and most painless way of killing a large mammal. Massive, instant trauma to the brain. We do it literally a million times a day in various industrial slaughterhouses. We even have a tool for it: a pneumatic gun that fires a bolt through the skull of a pig or a cow. We know it causes no pain when we do this to animals, because pain causes the release of a hormone into muscle tissue that fouls the taste of meat.

The firing squad, the guillotine, and the gallows all perform the task of quickly destroying the brain, to varying levels of effectiveness. A hollow-point bullet in the head, of course, is the swiftest death we know how to inflict. A man executed by firing squad will be dead before he ever hears the shot. That's how they execute people in China. A human head may survive a few seconds after decapitation, or after the neck snaps by hanging, which is functionally the same thing—the noose and the guillotine both sever the brain from its source of oxygen. These methods are pretty fast, but possibly slow enough for the victim to be briefly aware of what has happened.

But there's no way to inflict massive brain trauma or decapitation without making a mess. And we've developed a great distaste for messiness. You know, we don't go out and kill a chicken for dinner anymore; we get it plucked, cleaned, drained, and shrink-wrapped at the supermarket, and we don't want to know about the process that got it there. Nobody wants to see the blood or handle the guts or look into the eyes of the thing that is dying at their whim. Are you familiar with the utilitarian arguments for ethical veganism?

WATKINS: I think I know what you're talking about, but we're kind of getting off the topic of Chester March and the death penalty.

HEFFERNAN: If you are ever reporting a story about animal rights or the hidden horrors of food production under late capitalism, please feel free to contact me. Someday in the future, contemporary treatment of animals will be regarded as an atrocity as great as colonialism or genocide. And factory farming and modern networks of retail distribution have dramatically increased the ease with which we can consume the flesh of sentient beings, and therefore the amount of flesh we consume.

WATKINS (NARRATION): If I ever report that story, I will contact Ed Heffernan. It turns out that in addition to being a leading figure in the fight against the death penalty, he's also considered to be one of the legal academy's foremost moral philosophers and has written extensively about how legal rules ought to be informed by and based in ethical principles. I've got to break up the recording here, by the way, because Ed talked to me about the atrocities of the food production system in America for quite some time, despite my repeated attempts to get him back onto Chester and the death penalty. And while it's an interesting topic, it's not what we're doing here.

I've got to admit, at first I was a little perplexed by Ed's tendency to segue from the death penalty into animal rights, like the plight of the folks trapped in the criminal justice system is equivalent to the plight of some chickens. It seemed like a waste to be preoccupied with that when Chester has so little time left. Personally, I am of the opinion that this country needs to reckon with the way it treats black people and the underclass before it worries about the way it treats livestock. But, to Ed, both of these fights are the same fight, his fight to force society to organize itself in an ethical way. I can see how he connects the systems that funnel hundreds of thousands of black and brown men into the criminal justice system with the mechanism by which millions of animals disappear into industrial slaughterhouses. And I can see how we all become complicit in these systems that operate invisibly and conveniently.

But still, that stuff is a little bit esoteric, and *American Justice* only gets an hour per week. So, although Ed spent a solid twenty minutes explaining to me why we will never have a just society without massive reforms to agriculture, I am going to cut the audio around those digressions and try to streamline the conversation for you.

HEFFERNAN: . . . And we don't like messiness in the criminal justice system any more than we like it at the dinner table. We want this process to appear clinical, professional, and infallible. So, to avoid messes, states have historically preferred methods of execution that avoid the appearance of violence and leave a corpse that superficially appears to be intact. But these methods are less reliable, slower, and likely to cause more pain.

Over the course of the twentieth century, about 3 percent of executions were botched—and when I say they were botched, I mean the execution protocol failed to cause death. When you try to kill somebody and fail, you generally inflict horrific suffering. Botched executions are torture. It is morally untenable and illegal under the Eighth Amendment to employ an unreliable method of execution.

The firing squad is 100 percent effective, and hanging is about 99 percent. It's when you start electrocuting people that we see mistakes; about 3 percent of the time, when you try to electrocute somebody, they survive. Bad press over torturous failed electrocutions in the 1980s spurred the adoption of lethal injection as the preferred method of execution in the United States. But lethal injection is the least effective method of killing a person we've ever devised. It has a failure rate of about 7 percent.

WATKINS: Why is it so ineffective?

HEFFERNAN: Part of it is the complexity. The lethal injection protocol involves the sequential administration of three different drugs: First, a sedative, to render the condemned unconscious. Then, a muscle relaxer or a paralytic agent; that's for the benefit of the witnesses.

It prevents twitching or convulsions when the third drug, a poison called potassium chloride, is administered to stop the heart.

An executioner can foul things up at any stage. If the sedative is improperly administered or the dose is too small, the condemned will be conscious through the process. If the paralytic agent is improperly administered, the inmate will thrash around on the gurney. And if there is some mistake with the potassium chloride, then the condemned won't die. Or at least, he won't die quickly.

This is a medical procedure, but very few medical professionals will participate in executions or advise corrections officials on how to kill people, because doing so would violate the Hippocratic oath to do no harm. So the person in charge of the sedation will not be a trained anesthetist. The person inserting the intravenous line will not be a nurse.

WATKINS: It actually seems surprising they carry it off successfully as often as they do.

HEFFERNAN: The definition of a successful execution by lethal injection is flexible. Unlike the firing squad or the guillotine, potassium chloride doesn't kill instantly even when it's administered properly, so several minutes can elapse after the injection before the subject enters cardiac arrest. If the condemned is paralyzed by the second drug, then those minutes will appear peaceful, but that doesn't mean he isn't suffering. Poison kills much slower than a bullet to the head, and death by poison isn't painless. These are chemicals that dissolve your insides.

WATKINS: How can a barbaric practice like this continue in an advanced society?

HEFFERNAN: We're doing all we can to put a stop to it.

10

With the witness identification of Chester as the likely killer of Cecilia Tompkins, along with the information I collected about the disappearance of Margery March, I now had enough evidence to get a warrant to search the house on Overton Park Avenue. Usually, I would run a request for a warrant past Inspector Byrne, but he wasn't at his desk, and I wasn't in the mood to wait around for him, so I went ahead and swore out my affidavit detailing the evidence I'd collected and had a messenger take the paperwork over to the courthouse for a magistrate to sign.

Once I had the document, I grabbed a couple of uniformed bulls—Cadwalader and Branch, I think their names were—and went to execute the search. I drove my unmarked, and the officers followed in a patrol car.

In most cases, the best time to go search a house was around four in the morning. It was just safer that way. Suspects were at their most compliant and cooperative in the early hours when they were hungover and lethargic instead of drunk or high and potentially irrational. But I felt like there was a slim chance Margery March was alive in that house and in need of rescue, and a somewhat greater chance that Chester was actively in the process of destroying evidence.

Later in my career, I think I probably would have waited a few hours and gone after Chester at night, which would have given me time to loop Byrne in on what I was up to. The actual facts didn't justify going over there in the middle of the day. Margery had been missing for a couple of weeks before Hortense Ogilvy came to speak to me, so my victim was probably dead long before I even knew she existed, and Chester had plenty of time to clean up his mess before I got onto his trail. My sense of urgency wasn't really justified by the circumstances. The truth was, I was just hot to get the son of a bitch.

So it was maybe 6 P.M. when I knocked on Chester's door. He didn't respond, but I knew he was home because the Skylark with the scowling face was parked in the driveway. I knocked some more. This was a courtesy; my paperwork said I had a right to bust the door in.

Eventually, Chester answered, dressed in a linen suit with his hair slicked immaculately. He eyed the two uniformed officers with casual disdain.

"Is there something I can do for you gentlemen?" he asked. Real sarcastic inflection on the word "gentlemen."

"People are concerned as to the whereabouts of your wife," I said.

"People's concerns are no concern of mine," Chester said.

"Well, they're my concern, and I've got a warrant to search these premises for Mrs. March or evidence of what might have happened to her," I said, jabbing a lit cigarette close to his face. "Step aside and let us in."

Chester squared his shoulders and planted his feet. "Suppose I don't allow you to enter my house?"

I laughed at him. "That would pretty much make my day. I hope you try that. But I wouldn't advise it."

"What if I want to call my lawyer?"

"Call whoever you want. But we got an order to search this dump, and it's signed by a judge, so we ain't waiting around," I said. With the hand that wasn't holding the cigarette, I gave Chester a rough shove. He took a step back from the doorway, and I strode past him.

We entered into the house's grand foyer, which was about what you'd expect to find in your standard-issue turn-of-the-century, antebellum-style Memphis mansion. To the left was the formal dining room. To the right was a sitting room, and in front of us was the grand staircase to the second story. I noticed that the floors and all the surfaces were clear of dust, and I wondered who had been keeping the house up if Margery had been gone for weeks, but then I remembered Chester had mentioned having hired help.

I drew my .357 from its holster, and Cadwalader and Bench followed suit. Before we began searching for evidence, we'd need to do a quick check of every room in the house, to make sure the place was clear of any accomplices who might be lying in wait to try to ambush us. I gestured toward a closet underneath the staircase, and Brunch opened it and looked inside. He turned toward me and nodded, and we did a quick sweep through the kitchen, the den, and a small office, where Chester picked up a telephone and started dialing.

"The police are here," he said into the receiver, while I checked another closet. "No, I told them they couldn't come in, but they came in anyway."

I gestured to Brundle to keep an eye on the suspect, and Cadwalader and I climbed the staircase to clear the upstairs.

"He showed me a piece of paper. He said a judge signed it," Chester was saying. "Are they going to arrest me? They can't arrest me, can they? There's no body!"

We methodically checked the three upstairs bedrooms and a billiards room; I opened each closet, and I made a note to scrutinize all the grout and the drains in the two full bathrooms on the second floor.

Satisfied that there was no one in the house who was going to jump us, I turned to Cadwalader and said, "Let's go have a look at the garage, and then we'll start tearing this place apart."

"Aye-aye," said Officer Bumble, who wasn't supposed to be standing there.

"What are you doing up here?" I asked him. "Why aren't you keeping an eye on the suspect?"

"You didn't tell me to do that," he said.

"I pointed at him, and then I pointed at you," I said. "The implication was clear."

He scratched his chin. "I didn't get that at all."

I dropped my cigarette, ground it into the rug with the heel of my shoe, and lit another one. "Where is Chester now?"

Officer Bungle shrugged. "Last I saw him, he was talking on the phone with his lawyer."

And that's when I heard the luxurious purr of a Buick nailhead engine starting up. I took off at a dead run, shoving Officer Butthole aside, clearing the staircase in three bounding strides, and barreling through the front door just in time to see the Buick turn out of the driveway and float down the block.

There are a lot of reasons why it's real dumb to try to run from me, and on that particular day, one of those reasons was the car I was driving: 1955 happened to be the year that Ford replaced the aging Crestline chassis with its new Fairlane model. This development came on the heels of Ford's 1954 move to phase out its flathead engine in favor of the cutting-edge Y-block design, an absolute monster whose eight cylinders displaced 292 cubic inches.

If you put a Y-block V8 in a Fairlane, you get what Ford called the Thunderbird, one of the greatest police vehicles ever to come off of a Detroit assembly line. Chester's Buick Roadmaster Skylark was a fine luxury automobile, to be sure, if you wanted a silky-smooth ride, the best air conditioner then available in an enclosed vehicle, and a burled walnut dash. But the Skylark couldn't outpace the Thunderbird, which could go from zero to sixty in 9.4 seconds and reached a top speed of about 120 miles per hour. Even if the Skylark could have outrun the Thunderbird, Chester wasn't a good enough driver to shake me. His head start wasn't shit.

I turned the key in the ignition, and 193 horses roared to life. I was gone before Cadwalader and Boner even got out the front door. I was already doing forty when I reached the corner, and instead of braking, I eased off the gas and released the clutch, then popped the handbrake to lock the wheels as I gunned the engine into the spin. When the car straightened out, I had closed twenty yards of distance.

"They call that a bootlegger's turn, you dirty son of a bitch," I said.

Chester must have panicked, because he ran a stop sign, swerved onto North Parkway, and started accelerating, weaving in and out of afternoon traffic. I knew he couldn't make a turn at speed, and the Skylark couldn't outrun the Thunderbird on a straightaway. It may have looked to him like he had plenty of road in front of him, but he was caught.

Chester got about half a mile before I closed the distance between us. He ran through a red light, which gave me enough clear space to nudge the corner of the Skylark's bumper doing seventy-five without pinballing him into any bystanders. The impact threw the Skylark into a spin, and it bounced over the curb and slammed into a tree. The Thunderbird spun in the opposite direction, but I cut the wheel and popped the handbrake and brought it to a clean stop in the street.

Chester stumbled out of the wreck of his five-thousand-dollar car. He had a ragged cut on his forehead where his face had hit the steering wheel. In his hand was a long chef's knife he must have grabbed from his kitchen.

I climbed out of the Thunderbird and tossed what was left of my cigarette on the ground. "What do you think you are gonna do with that, Chester?" I asked.

"You can't do this to me. You can't come into my house. You

can't chase me," he said, slashing at the air for emphasis. "You have no right. No right!" He staggered toward me.

If I'd met Chester five years later, I'd probably have drawn my sidearm and decorated the pavement with the part of him that thought it was a good idea to menace me with a blade, but I was a gentle idealist in those early days of my career, and therefore I was more amenable to engaging in knife fights with psychopaths. So, instead of my gun, I grabbed my blackjack truncheon—a ball of lead the size of a baby's fist wrapped in soft leather and mounted on a coil of stiff spring. I called the blackjack Discretion, because it was mine to exercise as I saw fit.

I approached Chester, holding the club out like a fencer's sword to defend myself in case he lunged at me, but he seemed dazed from the crash. I smacked his fingers, and the knife clattered to the ground. He looked, with confusion, at his empty hand and then at the weapon lying on the asphalt. He seemed to be considering trying to pick it up. I decided to put an end to that idea. I spun my arm in a full circle, like a pitcher winding up a fastball, and then I thumped him in the nuts with the blackjack. He collapsed to his knees and started vomiting. I kicked the knife out of his reach and brought the truncheon down between his shoulder blades.

I've walloped people with a variety of blunt objects in my time: side-handled nightsticks, telescoping batons, saps, and, on occasion, a heavy steel flashlight. But the blackjack was always my favorite tool for busting skulls because the lead weight was so soft. That meant that, when it hit something, it yielded instead of bouncing or vibrating, so almost none of the energy of the swing was wasted. Hitting somebody with it was like dropping a sandbag off a third-floor balcony onto the roof of a car.

A good whack from the blackjack sent Chester sprawling into his puddle of sick. I put a knee on his neck to keep him from lifting his face out of the mess, and I set to work getting handcuffs onto him, as he feebly resisted.

"You're under arrest, Chester March, for killing your wife and for killing Cecilia Tompkins. And whatever else you've done, we'll find out about that, too." I clicked the cuffs into place, checked that they were secure, and then I grabbed a handful of his hair and pulled him back up to his knees. "They've got a special chair up in Nashville, and it has your name on it. They're gonna strap you into it, and they're gonna run twenty-four hundred volts of God's holy justice through you. Your blood will boil in your veins. Your flesh will cook like sausage, and your eyeballs will fry in their sockets like sunny-side-up eggs. All the fat in your body will render and melt. And I will be there to see it. I will watch you die."

"You have no idea who you're talking to," Chester said. "You have no idea who I am."

"You're a scumbag," I told him as I shoved him into the passenger seat of the Thunderbird. "And you're gonna be a country-fried scumbag pretty soon."

TRANSCRIPT: AMERICAN JUSTICE

CHESTER MARCH: So I opened my front door, and this smoke-belching monster was standing there, leering at me. He was flanked by a couple of the most thuggish-looking uniformed cops I ever saw.

CARLOS WATKINS: What did you feel, in that moment?

MARCH: Terror. Abject terror. I'd asked around about this guy.

Learned his reputation. Buck Schatz had already gunned down three men he claimed were criminals at that point—he'd go on to kill a dozen more. And for some reason known only to him, he had his sights set on me.

WATKINS: What did you do when he showed up at your house?

MARCH: He said he had a paper signed by a judge, and he was coming inside to search the premises. I didn't want to let him in until my lawyer arrived, but he told me he'd kill me if I tried to stop him. I couldn't keep him out, but I immediately called my attorney.

WATKINS: What did the lawyer say?

MARCH: He told me I was probably about to be arrested and started asking me whether I expected Schatz to find evidence in the house. He wanted to know if a murder weapon was in there, or if the body was hidden there someplace. There was nothing like that, and Schatz didn't find anything, but my own lawyer was assuming I'd killed Margery. I was frightened, and probably not thinking straight. That's when I tried to run.

I had a beautiful car back then. A deluxe Buick Skylark. It was a fast car, but a smooth ride. I loved that car; it was really something to see. I took off in it, but Schatz had this huge black Ford muscle car, and he ran me down and rammed me off the road. Absolutely totaled the Skylark. Twisted the chassis and buckled the axles and crushed the engine, though some of that might be from the tree I hit after he bumped me. His car was barely even dinged.

I had the Skylark's clutch open and the pedal on the floor, and I remember watching the Ford growing larger and larger in the rearview. That was Buck Schatz—a huge, relentless shadow bearing down on me. There was nothing I could do and no way to escape. I remember stumbling out of the wreckage, and then he grabbed me and beat me with a club. I took a hit below the belt. The pain was unbelievable. I don't want to get too graphic, but something ruptured.

WATKINS: According to his report, you came after him with a knife.

MARCH: I don't remember any knife.

WATKINS: Chester, why did you run?

MARCH: I don't know. Lots of innocent people run from the police. This powerful figure has come for you and means you harm, and there's just this drive, like an instinct, to put distance between yourself and the predator that is out to destroy you. It's not a rational decision. I can't justify it. When you feel the devil's hot breath on the back of your neck, when you feel his fingers closing on your throat, all you can do is give in to the fear. Nothing has ever scared me as much as Buck Schatz scared me.

I remember what he told me after he beat me into submission and locked me into handcuffs. He said, "I will watch you die." And very soon, barring a miracle, he's going to make good on that promise.

11

made Officer Branch stand guard over Chester in the car while Cadwalader and I searched the house. Despite the suspect's freak-out, there wasn't much incriminating physical evidence.

We found a half-empty three-gallon jug of sulfuric acid in the garage, which could have caused the burns on the body of Cecilia Tompkins. I noticed a strong bleach smell in one of the upstairs bathrooms, so I combed over every surface and found two small brown stains, which I photographed and took samples from to test for blood.

In the master bedroom, I checked Margery's closet. It was full of her clothes. A jewelry box on the dresser contained several expensive-looking rings and necklaces, the kinds of things no lady would flee her home without. And I found a matched set of luggage in the attic, monogrammed "M.W." It appeared to be complete. If she was alive somewhere, she'd run off without her car, her clothes, her valuables, or her suitcases. Seemed unlikely.

I took Chester for a ride downtown, had him photographed and fingerprinted, and then left him in a windowless interrogation room to mull over his situation for a bit.

Chester's lawyer, a respected pillar of the community named Jefferson Pritchard III, had arrived before we even got our suspect processed, but we could make a lawyer wait until his client asked for him. I figured Chester would want to see Pritchard almost immediately. The smart ones always did. But I'd learned that people were generally stupider than I expected them to be, so I figured I might as well take a shot at getting a statement out of my murder suspect.

I'd made a few conciliatory gestures to try to get him into a talkative mood; after he was done getting his picture taken, I shackled his hands in front of him rather than behind him. I'd moved him directly to an interrogation room without making him sit in a holding cell, and I had given him a cup of coffee and some ice to put on his injured ballsack.

I had a little speech I liked to give men in Chester's situation. I told them that the evidence against them looked bad. I told them that witnesses had identified them and fingered them as the perpetrators of monstrous deeds. I told them I wanted the whole story, that I wanted to get it right, and I wanted to give them a chance to tell their side of it. If they opted not to talk, I'd tell them, we'd have to proceed to trial with an incomplete record.

I didn't think Chester would bite; he was going to want his lawyer. But it was worth taking a run at him after he'd had an opportunity to think about his predicament and consider what the rest of his life was going to be like. So I was sitting at my desk killing some time when Inspector Byrne found me.

"In my office," he told me. Considering I'd just made a murder bust, he should have looked happier.

I followed him down the hallway. Byrne opened his door and revealed Henry McCloskey, an assistant district attorney, waiting for me.

"Schatz, why the fuck have you arrested Chester March?" McCloskey asked. He was sitting when I entered, but he rose and got right in my face as he spoke. I'm not going to say Henry McCloskey had poor oral hygiene, because I have no knowledge of his daily practices, but if he was assiduous about those things, I had to assume from the smell of his breath that he brushed with shit-scented toothpaste, flossed with shit floss, and then gargled hot diarrhea mouthwash. He made me long for the company of Hortense Ogilvy.

Obviously, I lit a cigarette. "Chester March killed his wife," I said.

"That will be news to the medical examiner's office. They have not performed an autopsy reaching that conclusion. They have not even received a body." He was a big man, and he loomed over me. I got a good close-up view of the inflammation around his nostrils. There was an ingrown hair on his upper lip, a thick, greasy stub surrounded by an overfilled yellow inner tube of pus. He was, by any assessment, very handsome.

"Mrs. March had been missing for a couple of weeks before we began our investigation," I said. "Chester had time to dispose of the remains. But a murderer who hides a body is still a murderer, and we've got a strong circumstantial case."

"A circumstantial case? Schatz, do you know who this boy's daddy is?"

"I don't give a goddamn who his daddy is."

"Maybe you ought to, because the district attorney got a call tonight from a United States senator, and the senator gives a goddamn. And I intend to do as the senator asks, and drop these charges. You are going to turn that boy loose and apologize."

I tapped my ash into the ashtray on Inspector Byrne's desk. "The hell I will. Chester March killed at least two women, and I intend to see him executed."

McCloskey erupted with a deep belly laugh that filled the small office with the smell of what he was full of. "Let's say I were willing to prosecute this loser of a case. What evidence have you collected for me that will persuade a jury?"

"Margery March has been missing for several weeks. Her friend Hortense Ogilvy hasn't been able to find her. The neighbors haven't seen her. Her family hasn't heard from her. Her blue Packard is parked in Chester's garage. Her clothes are in the closet at the house. Her luggage is in the attic."

"So what?" McCloskey said. "Maybe she eloped with a man who bought her a new wardrobe."

"You know she didn't."

"Where's the body?"

"I haven't found it yet."

"Then why have you brought that boy in?"

I sat down heavily in one of the chairs. McCloskey was still standing. "For God's sake, he had a vat of sulfuric acid in his garage," I said.

"So what? Maybe he used it to clean engines."

Now I laughed. "Clean engines? With sulfuric acid? I don't think you've ever worked on an engine, Henry, and I doubt Chester March has either."

"They got heavy machinery on those cotton farms. People clean machines with acid. People use acid to open up drains. You can buy acid at a hardware store. No jury is going to convict Chester March of murder because he had sulfuric acid in his garage."

"My witness, Bernadette Ward, described his car as the last one Cecilia Tompkins got into. Ward identified Chester in a photo lineup. And Tompkins's body was scored by chemical burns that could have been caused by Chester attempting to dissolve her remains with acid."

"Who the fuck is Cecilia Tompkins?"

"She's the victim of an unsolved murder—"

"A whore. A negro whore. You think a jury is going to ruin that nice young man's life over a dead negro whore? You think they'll believe a word from the mouth of the other negro whore you want to put on the witness stand?"

McCloskey had a real big head. Long forehead like the monster from the Frankenstein movies and a big caveman jaw. And his neck spread out beneath it rather than narrowing. I bet he needed to buy the king-size pillowcases to make his Klan hoods. He had little-bitty ears, though. And beady, close-set rat eyes. If you went to a cross burning, you could probably pick out which one was him really easily, because he'd be the goon in the giant hood with tiny eyeholes, and also, you'd be able to smell his shit-breath.

"Chester attempted to flee when I executed a search warrant on his house, and he tried to attack me with a knife after I ran him down," I said.

"And who is going to testify to that? You?"

"I'd imagine so."

"So you want the district attorney to risk the ire of a U.S. senator to take a murder case to trial against the finest legal defense team a very rich man's money can buy, and all you've got for evidence is the contents of a jug of battery acid and the dubious testimony of a negro whore and a Jew detective?"

"Officers Cadwalader and Branch went with me to execute the search warrant and can confirm that March attempted to flee."

McCloskey leaned against the wall and crossed his arms. "Had you placed him under arrest?"

"I've never seen a man take off like that while officers were searching his property."

"But did you place him under arrest?"

I didn't see a way out of that one. "No. Not until after."

"Then he was free to leave, wasn't he?"

"He killed those women, Henry."

His lip turned up. There was a thick coat of caked-on yellow gunk between his teeth, so maybe he didn't floss with shit after all. "You're a damn fool, Schatz."

"At least I ain't ugly," I said.

"Well, you ain't pretty enough for me to put up with your bullshit," McCloskey said. He turned to Byrne. "Get Chester March out of here. And keep your Jew on a shorter leash from now on. I don't enjoy having to come down here at night to deal with this nonsense." He elbowed past me and slammed the door.

Byrne produced a pipe from his jacket pocket, so I lit another cigarette.

"I didn't want you as a detective," he said.

"I know that," I said. "I figured it out while I was waiting three years to get called up after I aced my exam."

He nodded and lit his pipe, and he puffed on it while he ruminated over the next thing he was going to say. I let him. He had a normal-size head, and probably could have used a normal-size pillowcase to make his hood, but he would have needed at least a queen-size sheet for his robe because he was such a tub of guts. It would have been tougher to pick out which one was him at the cross burning. There were a lot of fatties in the Klan.

"You should have spoken to me before you went to the judge to get that warrant."

I made a guttural noise that conveyed to him that I acknowledged the point without necessarily agreeing with it.

"I know why you didn't, though."

It was because I thought he was a halfwit, and because I had no respect for him whatsoever.

"It's the nature of a Jew to be shifty. It's what everyone expects from you," he said.

I should have been wondering if he was gearing up to fire me, but I was busy trying to figure out if I could shoot Byrne, run down the hall to catch McCloskey, shoot him as well, and then plausibly claim I had killed them both in self-defense. Probably not.

"That being said, you did some good police work on this. It was real crafty of you to see if you could tie your suspect to those unsolved cases when you couldn't find the wife's body. Most detectives wouldn't think to do that. Your people's traits may be a little better suited to this line of work than I realized."

This surprised me. I realized my hand had slid inside my jacket and my fingers were on the grip of my sidearm. I withdrew them. I still wasn't going to thank this fat Irish prick, though.

Byrne continued: "I don't like you much, and I expect you don't like me much. But that doesn't mean I like what Chester March is. I know why you took up this line of work. I know about what happened to your daddy. Lot of men on this force could tell you similar stories. I could tell you a similar story. No, I don't much like what Chester March is, the kind of man who could do that to a woman. Makes me sick." He took a deep pull from the pipe, slowly exhaled the smoke out through his nose, and then spat a wad of brown phlegm into the ashtray.

"What can we do if the district attorney won't prosecute?" I asked.

He adjusted himself on his chair so he could get to a pouch of pipe tobacco in his jacket pocket. "If a U.S. senator had called the district attorney's office to get March released, I'd expect to see the district attorney down here himself, unless he had some reason to stay away. Maybe there's no senator, and McCloskey is acting on his own. Maybe March really has those kinds of connections, but the matter is so dirty that the district attorney didn't want to handle it personally."

"Doesn't matter either way if McCloskey ain't willing to prosecute that boy."

Byrne nodded. "Yep. I've seen things like this before. Shit don't stick to people like Chester March the way it does to regular folks. We're gonna have to turn him loose in the next couple of hours, and whatever happens to him between now and then is all the justice those women he killed will get."

This was surprising. "What, exactly, are you saying?"

Byrne leaned back, and the swivel chair groaned with effort. "He was in a car wreck tonight, wasn't he? Maybe he got a little more hurt in that accident than we had previously realized."

"Seems like there'd be consequences for doing what you are suggesting, especially for a Jew nobody wanted in this bureau in the first place," I said.

Byrne laughed. "I guess you've got no reason to trust me. But, out of the two of us, I ain't the one descended from a duplicitous race. And I've got no inclination to get in the way of a Jew or anybody else giving a woman-killing piece of shit a well-deserved beating. Just don't kill him."

"I'll take your suggestion under advisement," I said. I rose from the chair, left the office, and closed the door behind me.

I was alone in a department full of men who hated me for what I was. They believed my racial defects rendered me incapable of doing my job and would have loved to have proof of it. I had worked for years to ascend to my current fragile position, and I had a wife and a young son who were dependent on my income.

I didn't know Margery March, but I had done everything a conscientious detective could reasonably do to get justice for her. I could look my mother in the eye and tell her I'd stood by my principles. But principles don't protect you; you have got to protect yourself. And now it was time to be sensible. I'd done as much as I could do. As much as I should do. As much as the law allowed me to do.

I opened the door to Chester's interrogation room. His suit was dirty and wrinkled from when I'd thrown him on the ground and rolled him in his vomit. His head was wrapped in gauze, covering the cut on his forehead. He was holding a bag of ice over his bruised nethers. But he still thought he owned the place, the son of a bitch.

"I don't know why you've kept me waiting here this long when I know my lawyer is already here," he said. "You can't treat me this way. You know who my father is? You had better take these manacles off of me. And you had better apologize."

I thought about those women he killed. I thought of my father, dead in a ditch. I thought about my mother, constantly looking over her shoulder and hiding razor blades in the hems of her skirts. I thought of Bernadette Ward and all the people like her who lived their lives in fear of men like this. Why were they afraid, while he felt he had nothing to fear, even when he was caught dead to rights? He should be afraid. Him and everyone like him. Someone needed to give them something to be afraid of.

"I don't hear you saying you're sorry," said Chester March.

He didn't, and he wouldn't. Instead, I let him hear the sound of his teeth breaking.

TRANSCRIPT: AMERICAN JUSTICE

CHESTER MARCH: After I met Buck Schatz in 1955, I never saw my-self again when I looked in the mirror. I needed five reconstructive surgeries, and that's not counting the dental procedures. They had to rebuild my nose using grafts of skin and cartilage from other parts of my body. I needed artificial cheek implants to hide the deformities caused by the fractures to my jaw, my cheekbones, and my left eye socket. I look, more or less, like a normal man now, but I don't look like me anymore.

CARLOS WATKINS: And the dental work?

MARCH: That was extensive. He hit me five or six times with a metal club. Knocked a bunch of my teeth clean out of my head and shattered most of the rest. The ones in front had to be pulled out, because there wasn't enough left of them to put crowns on. I wore dentures through the '60s; that was really the only option at that time. I got implants around '72, which turned out to be sort of a blessing. It's hard to take care of your teeth in prison, and ceramics don't rot.

WATKINS: And he faced no repercussions for doing this to you? There was no criminal or disciplinary investigation into his conduct?

MARCH: As far as the police were concerned, I had been injured in a car wreck, and my father wasn't interested in anyone hearing anything different. If I had pursued justice against Schatz, then everyone in my family's orbit, all of society in Memphis, Oxford, and Nashville, would have known my wife's disappearance was suspicious and that the police had been after me about it. It would have been embarrassing and harmful to my father's business. And even though the prosecutor had dropped the charges Schatz wanted to bring, my lawyers advised me that those charges might come back if I made trouble for the police department. The lie that was convenient for the police was also convenient for me. I am ashamed to say it, but I let Buck Schatz get away with his crimes. He was free to go on brutalizing others for decades because I didn't stand up to him.

WATKINS: I don't think you should blame yourself for that.

MARCH: Even though I was not convicted or even tried, there were still repercussions for me—even beyond the injuries. Schatz kept coming around, returning to the scene, so to speak. Before he tried to arrest me, he'd always driven this ridiculous unmarked muscle car. But after his charges didn't stick, he started driving by my house all the time in a black-and-white police cruiser. He'd flash his lights and wail his sirens, and all the neighbors would come to their windows. He'd already been questioning them, and they were wondering where my wife had gone, and then this police car was always staking out the house. Eventually, one of my father's business associates heard about it, and at that time, my presence became detrimental to the company. So my father encouraged me to leave town.

WATKINS: That must have been difficult for you.

MARCH: Baruch Schatz ruined my life. The company was called March and Sons, Inc. We had been prominent landowners in Mississippi before the Civil War, and lost everything to the Yankees. The plantation holdings were broken up. But my great-grandfather was a resourceful man, and he knew the business. So, he started his company to bale and package and ship the cotton the new owners were growing on the land he'd lost. And within ten years, he'd got it all back and then some. And that land and that business stayed in the family for almost a hundred years, and it was set to go to me, and then Schatz ran me off from my birthright. I moved to San Francisco for a while, and while I was out there, my father died. He hadn't handed me the reins. He hadn't introduced me to the folks I needed to know to move our product. I wasn't situated to run that business, so I had to sell it off. There is no March and Sons, Inc., anymore. And no more March sons either, probably on account of Schatz smashing my gonads.

PART 3

2011: KIND OF RACIST

12

So you fucked up the investigation, the DA dropped the charges, and then you bashed the guy's face in with a stick?" Tequila asked. He leaned forward, and the sofa squeaked. All the furniture in Valhalla's common areas was upholstered with a slippery plastic that the staff could hose down easily if someone shit themselves on it. "That is not a story you should tell on the radio."

"The man said his program is about race and class and the criminal justice system," I said. "If my witness hadn't been a colored prostitute and I hadn't been a Jew, Chester would have been convicted of murder in 1955, and he'd have gone to the electric chair decades ago. I did everything right, and it didn't matter."

William sniffed. "I wouldn't really say you did everything right."

"What did I do wrong?"

"Did you talk to the maid?"

"The maid?"

"The woman who cleaned Chester's house. She had been in there between the time Margery disappeared and when you started investigating. Did you speak to her?"

"I never ran into her. I spoke to the neighbors. I got a witness identification of the man and the car from Bernadette Ward. What could the maid have told me?"

"I don't know, because you never asked her. She was inside the house, cleaning up his messes. God knows what she might have seen. You should have tracked her down. But that's not even the point. This reporter is going to be on Chester's side. You're the racist, classist system with your boot on everyone's neck in this story. I mean, you literally put your boot on Chester's neck."

"That makes no sense. Chester was a rich white man. And it was my knee on his neck, not my boot."

"You don't get it."

I lit a cigarette. "Then explain it to me."

"Okay. He starts from the premise that the system is racist, classist, sexist, and broken. Then he looks for abuses. He finds you. You spent thirty years on the Memphis police force basically just being a bull in a fucking china shop and an inveterate corner cutter. He uses your misconduct as evidence supporting the thesis that the criminal justice system is corrupt, and then he tags the rest of that stuff onto it."

"That makes no sense. I'm not a racist."

"You kind of are."

"You've obviously never met a real racist."

"Grandpa, that's exactly what a racist would say."

I stubbed out my cigarette on the glass top of the coffee table, and I tossed the spent butt on the carpet. Then, I gripped the rails of the walker and slowly started to lift myself to my feet. "How would you know?"

He reached out a hand to help me up. I waved it off. "This reporter wants to give you a rope to see if you will hang yourself. He is not a person you should be talking to."

"I can deal with him."

"I don't think that's true," Tequila said. "Not with your mental situation."

"My mental situation is fine," I said.

He walked ahead of me, put his hands on the rails of the walker, and got up in my face, like Henry McCloskey had. "If your mental situation is fine, why are we even talking about this, and not about Grandma's illness? I'm having a hard time making some radio show nobody listens to a priority when I just found out my grandmother has cancer."

"I just found out, too."

"No, you didn't. You've known the whole time."

"What this journalist is saying may not matter to you, but this was my work, and I am proud of it," I told him. I lit another cigarette. "Chester March is a serial killer. He committed those murders, I caught him, and he got the death sentence he deserves, and anyone who says otherwise is a goddamn liar."

Tequila paused long enough to do some simple math, and then said, "Wait, so the district attorney's office released Chester without charges in 1955, and you didn't convict him for another twenty years?"

"Yeah."

"So there's another story—a story about what you did in 1976? And that's the story this Watkins guy thinks should get the conviction thrown out?"

"There's two sides to that as well," I said.

"Grandpa, you cannot talk to this journalist."

"You don't understand what it's like."

Tequila let go of the walker. "You're threatened by somebody telling you that the history you've idealized wasn't as great or as honorable as you remember it being. I can't fix this for you, because what you're trying to protect isn't real, and Grandma is sick. She might die. You can't be living in the past right now. You've got to be here—in this awful moment—with the rest of us."

I threw the cigarette on the carpet without bothering to stub it out. Tequila stepped on it, leaving a black smudge. "Your grandmother and I have been together fifty years longer than you've been alive. She knows who I am, and she knows how I feel, and she knows why this is important."

"When that journalist calls, just don't pick up your phone," he said.

"How will I know it's him if I don't pick up?" I asked.

"The number of an incoming call comes up on the screen."

I fished the flip phone out of my pocket and squinted at it. "Who can even see the tiny numbers on this thing?"

"Just don't answer the cell phone at all. I'll talk to him. I'll deal with this. You focus on Grandma."

"You don't understand," I said.

"Yes, I do," he told me. "I understand basically everything, because I am very smart. I'm much smarter than you ever were, even before your brain started calcifying or liquefying or whatever it's doing in that thick skull of yours. Go get some rest. To-morrow is another day, and it's going to be a shitty one."

TRANSCRIPT: AMERICAN JUSTICE

CARLOS WATKINS (NARRATION): Chester March agreed to give me ac-cess to all the files pertaining to his case, and Edward Heffernan—who you may remember is the Vanderbilt law professor who is leading Chester's defense—was kind enough to allow me to dig into six bank-er's boxes stuffed with documents that he had in his office.

I took the first box down to Vanderbilt's Alyne Queener Massey Law Library to start sifting through the materials. It's a beautiful space: two stories of books with high ceilings, warm organic light, heavy cherry-wood furniture with ergonomic chairs, and carpets the color of money.

Vanderbilt is the third-best law school in the southeastern United States, according to the influential *US News and World Report* ranking. Only the University of Virginia and Duke have it beat. Upon graduation, the students who were sitting around me would be near the front of the line for elite jobs paying six-figure starting salaries at the best law firms in Nashville, Atlanta, St. Louis, New Orleans, or anywhere in Florida.

The library wasn't terribly crowded at that time; it was midmorning on a Wednesday, and most of the law students were probably in class. But I couldn't help noticing that I was the only black person in there. Everyone at the law school had been very polite toward me, but I still felt uneasy in this bastion of privilege. Vanderbilt's law school is only about 7 or 8 percent black. The city of Nashville is about a quarter black, and the Riverbend prison is nearly half. The only institution in the state of Tennessee more racially inclusive than Riverbend is the 90 percent black Memphis City School system.

I opened the boxes. Inside, I found Chester's confession. It is an eight-page report based on four hours of interrogation conducted by Baruch Schatz. Seven pages, actually, and really closer to six: The first page is a signed waiver that states Chester was informed of his rights and waived them, and the last page is mostly blank, except for Chester's signature, certifying that the report accurately represents his statements to police. This small stack of paper got Chester March condemned to death.

Schatz wrote the report. Chester signed and dated those first and last pages. He initialed each of the other pages, to indicate that he'd seen them and that they were consistent with his statements. There are no audio or video recordings of the interrogation, but interrogations weren't typically recorded in 1976.

Schatz's report says Chester confessed to the 1953 killing of a sex worker named Cecilia Tompkins. According to the report, Chester said he had been thinking about killing a woman since adolescence, and he'd decided to try it. He attempted to dissolve the body using sulfuric acid, and when that failed, he dumped her in the Mississippi River. Chester further admitted that, two years later, he killed his wife Margery. He beat and strangled her in the kitchen of their Memphis house and buried her body on a wooded tract of land his father owned in Mississippi. He also confessed to the 1976 killing of a woman named Evelyn Duhrer, who had rented a room to him in her home.

Appended to the confession was a report from Schatz, documenting the excavation of the area where Chester said he buried his wife. A forensic team discovered skeletal remains under a layer of calcium oxide—quicklime—and three feet of dirt. A report by the coroner notes that a full autopsy was impossible, due to the advanced state of decomposition, but that the body was that of a Caucasian woman, about five foot three, which was Margery March's height, and while some of the teeth were missing, those that were present matched Margery March's dental records. The coroner concluded that the condition of the remains was consistent with death by beating and strangulation as described by Chester in the report.

While I was reading, I got a collect call from Chester at the prison.

CHESTER MARCH: Did you catch up to Ed Heffernan?

CARLOS WATKINS: Yes, we spoke. He gave me your records. They make for interesting reading. I'm looking at your confession right now.

MARCH: It looks bad, doesn't it? Schatz certainly knew his business.

WATKINS: And you admitted to these things?

MARCH: I have no idea what I said to him. I don't remember talking to him at all. Take a look at the exhibits from my appeal in 1986.

WATKINS (NARRATION): I found the file in the box. It contained X-ray photographs of Chester's head. They're dated one day after Schatz's interrogation report.

MARCH: You find the pictures?

WATKINS: Yes.

MARCH: You're looking at what they call a concussive brain injury, and a cranial fracture. Whatever I said in that room, I was not in my right mind when I said it. And listen: When you talk to Buck and you hear him make references to busting heads or stoving people's skulls in, he's not embellishing or being colloquial. That is what he went around doing to people in a very literal sense. He busted my head. Imagine tapping a soft-boiled egg with a spoon. What that does to an eggshell is what he did to me. I'm lucky to be alive. Or maybe not. Maybe I'd be better off if he'd just killed me.

WATKINS (NARRATION): In the 1986 appeal, Chester's lawyers argued that the statement should not have been admitted at trial, due to Chester's head injury. The Tennessee State Supreme Court ruled that Chester couldn't get his conviction reversed for that reason because Chester's lawyer hadn't objected to the admission of the statement on that basis at trial.

In 1992, a different team of appellate attorneys hired a handwriting analysis expert to examine Chester's signatures on the statement. The expert said that the handwriting on the documents, when compared to existing samples of Chester's handwriting, was clumsy and tremulous. This showed that Chester had signed his confession while in a diminished cognitive state, due to his traumatic brain injury.

Since handwriting analysis was not typically used for this purpose in 1976, Chester's lawyers argued this analysis was evidence produced through newly available forensic techniques that had not been available at trial. This kind of argument was often used in the early '90s to get new trials in cases where DNA testing created doubts about the factual determinations of old cases. But a panel of appellate judges did not see Chester's handwriting analysis as equivalent to new DNA evidence, and they denied the appeal.

In 1996, Chester's lawyers tried to get a court to order the alleged remains of Margery March exhumed. They argued that the forensics used at the time to identify the remains were no longer accepted science, that it could no longer be said that the remains had been identified as Margery beyond a reasonable doubt, and that it was unconstitutional to perform a contemporary execution on the basis of such outdated evidence. The Tennessee Supreme Court upheld the conviction and refused to dig up Margery's alleged body.

In 2002, a different appellate team came back to the head injury.

They tried to get around the fact that the courts had already ruled on the issue by arguing that advances in neurology and our progressing understanding of the effects of traumatic brain injuries raised new constitutional questions about the admissibility of Chester's 1976 statement. The state supreme court wasn't having any of that and upheld the conviction again.

If you are recognizing a pattern, you're not alone. Every one of these appeals is an objection to carrying out a modern execution that is justified by abandoned and repudiated police practices and outdated, outmoded methods of evidence gathering. Chester March has been on death row for thirty-five years, and the men who are going to kill him are following orders given by a judge and jury two generations removed.

Here's something to think about: William Faulkner, who is still revered in these parts, said that "the past is never dead. It's not even past." And here in Faulkner's South, the past is still killing people.

Here's something else to think about: William Faulkner was only twenty-five years old when Buck Schatz was born. Some people would like to believe we've moved past the pernicious aspects of our history, but that history is still with us, and here in Tennessee, a man is going to be put to death on the say-so of that history. In the procedural history of Chester March's appeals, we see the decrepit, liver-spotted hand that operates the levers of the death machine that is American Justice.

13

awoke at six thirty. Rose was still sleeping. My habit was to go downstairs on my own in the mornings, get some coffee, and flip through *The Commercial Appeal*. Usually I'd get up—by myself, if I was feeling strong, and with assistance from an aide the rest of the time. There was a cord on the wall above the bed that I could pull to call for help. If I pulled it, somebody would come into the room—the doors here didn't lock—and haul me out of bed. Rose would sleep through it. Or at least she'd pretend to, as I slowly dressed myself.

I had reached the point where putting on pants had become a difficult process. The staff was willing to help out with that as well, but I wasn't quite ready to hand over that much of my dignity. So I would sit in a chair with the walker in front of me, and I would pull the pants over my feet and get them up around my knees, before lifting myself up and leaning on the walker to pull them up the rest of the way. Most days, I could stand on my own long enough to zip the fly and fasten my belt, but I usually needed to thread the belt through the loops on the pants before I put them on, because I had a lot of difficulty reaching behind myself. I was lucky that my fingers were still dexterous enough to fasten buttons and operate zippers, but my wardrobe choices had, nonetheless, shifted toward sweaters and pullovers in the last couple of years, after favoring oxford shirts for decades. It was easier to find the sleeves in a pullover, and there was nobody to look sharp for anyway.

I didn't pull the cord for assistance, though. I didn't clamber for the walker. I didn't undertake the burdensome ritual of struggling into my clothes in the dark while Rose slept. I looked at the ceiling and listened to her breathing.

She got up a little after eight.

"Surprised to see you still in bed," she said, after she checked the clock on the nightstand.

"I guess I was pretty tired," I replied.

We both dressed quietly, her with a bit less difficulty than me, on account of the fact that she was slightly younger, and she had never been shot.

Then we padded down the carpeted hallway and took the elevator to the ground floor to find some breakfast. Before I came here, I hadn't been a huge fan of breakfast food, but I'd learned to like it at Valhalla, because the dining room was less crowded during breakfast than it was during other meals. I grabbed a plastic tray with some chlorine-smelling dishes and tarnished flatware. The forks and knives were stainless steel, and I didn't know that even could get tarnished, but everything at Valhalla found a way to become decrepit. I scooped some overcooked scrambled eggs out of a buffet tray warmed by a Sterno can, and I grabbed a bagel—the kind that comes frozen in a package. Rose picked some honeydew melon out of the bowl of fruit salad to go with her eggs. I don't think Rose ever bought a honeydew melon at the grocery store in all the years I was married to her. I'm not sure anyone does. I only ever saw it on buffets and in fruit salads. I think it lasts longer than other cut fruit; cantaloupe turns to mush after a couple of hours at room temperature, and honeydew stays firm. But stability is a questionable virtue in a fruit nobody enjoys. And if stability was the goal of the salad, why was there so much banana in it? Cut pieces of banana turn brown and slimy real fast. Nobody wants to eat a fruit salad full of bland honeydew and slimy banana.

That's what it means to consign yourself to a place like Valhalla. Filler fruit for the rest of your life.

The honeydew on the breakfast bar looked underripe, and its flesh was mostly white. Even if it had been juicy and green, we'd have barely been able to taste it, and it still would have been an inferior fruit. Considering how much they charged us each month, you'd think this dump could at least serve strawberries. Everybody likes strawberries.

We sat at our usual table, at the far back corner of the dining room. I had to walk farther to get there than I'd need to if I'd been less picky about where to sit, and it wasn't easy to move the walker across the rug with a tray perched on top of it. But I preferred to eat in a spot where nobody could sneak up on me from behind.

At Valhalla, the smallest tables in the dining room are set for four people. Since it's less crowded in the morning, it's less likely somebody will try to sit with us, so breakfast is the one meal of the day I am not usually forced to eat while having a conversation about things I don't care about with people whose names I can't remember.

But, while Rose and I picked at our eggs in eloquent silence, some guy came over and sat at our table.

"Hello, Schatzes!" said this putz, whose high spirits were entirely inappropriate under the circumstances.

"Hello, Gus Turnip," Rose said. She enunciated the name loudly and slowly because she knew I had no idea who he was.

"What kind of a name is Turnip?" I asked.

"Scots-Irish," said Turnip. "We've had this conversation before. My people were Scots-Irish, and yours were Jews from Eastern Europe. You told me about your great-grandfather, who was born in a Lithuanian shtetl and burned Atlanta with Sherman."

How had I told this guy those things, when I was pretty sure I had never met him before?

"Buck's just giving you a hard time, Gus," Rose said.

"She's right," I agreed. "I'll do that."

Turnip smiled at her. His teeth were the color of an old sidewalk. "I just wanted to see if y'all were going to be joining us for Lunch Bunch this week."

"Nope," I said. "Got other plans."

I didn't remember who Gus Parsnip was, but I remembered Lunch Bunch. Eight or ten of the inmates met up every week in the lobby, and one of the aides loaded them into a van and took them to TGI Friday's or Applebee's to enjoy a lousy meal with lousy company.

"Maybe we could go, Buck," Rose said.

"I'm pretty sure we have that other thing we need to do, and also, I don't want to," I reminded her.

She set her fork down on her napkin. "You always talk about how much you hate the food here. Why don't you want to go for a meal out?"

"Our grandson is in town," I said.

"He's busy studying for the bar exam. We have the time."

"Why are you being so persistent about this?"

"Why are you being so obstinate?"

Gus Pumpkin was looking uncomfortable. "I didn't mean to start a controversy. Why don't y'all check your schedule, and if you feel like joining us, just show up, and we'd be delighted to have you."

"Thank you, Gus," Rose said. "It was so nice to see you."

"Well, I have my breakfast here," Gus said, gesturing at the plate he had set in front of him. "I thought I might join y'all."

"It was good talking to you, Potato," I said. "I guess we'll be seeing you around." Then I lit a cigarette, even though smoking was banned in the common areas of the building.

"Oh, all right, then," Gus said, and he gathered up his breakfast and carried it to a table on the other side of the dining room.

When Gus was safely out of earshot, Rose started laughing. "Did you see the look on his face when you called him a potato?"

"What did you say his name was?" I asked.

"Turnip."

"So, pretty much the same thing," I said.

"Mr. Schatz!" called one of the aides from across the room, waving a finger at me.

I stubbed out the cigarette, and Rose started laughing again.

"I know they're annoying, but I worry about you, Buck," she said. "If I'm not here, are you going to eat all your meals alone?"

"If you're not here, I doubt I will find solace in the Lunch Bunch," I said.

Still laughing, she put her head in her hands.

"Can you picture me at Friday's splitting an order of loaded potato skins with Gus, who is, himself, a loaded potato skin?" I asked. "Do you think they sing songs together in the van when they're riding to the restaurant?"

"I just worry about you," she said. "I worry about a lot of things."

"When did I tell him about my great-grandfather? And why?"

"I don't know," Rose said. "But we've got an appointment with your neurologist today, to talk about your memory problems."

"Wonderful. That guy's always a real ray of sunshine," I said.

TRANSCRIPT: AMERICAN JUSTICE

CARLOS WATKINS (NARRATION): It's about a four-hour drive from Nashville to Memphis. I thought I might get to see the Smoky Mountains, but it turns out that I was heading in the wrong direction. West Tennessee is mostly flat—mostly farmland. I drove past thousands of acres of what I think were soybeans. Memphis is a transportation hub, and I was sharing the highway with a lot of tractor-trailers heading in and out of it; I got good gas mileage riding in their draft, and I was pleased that I was lowering my carbon footprint, until I thought about how much diesel all those trucks were burning. These are the systems of convenience that Ed Heffernan is always talking about, running invisibly in the backgrounds of our lives, making things effortless for us, and causing mounting and irreparable harm.

With so much freight traveling along the highway, there are a lot of stops along this stretch of I-40. Gas stops. Truck stops. Rest stops. IHOP, Denny's, Shoney's, the Cracker Barrel, and, every so often, a Waffle House. Lots of little towns with names like Fairview and Dickson and Bucksnort. Places that might seem inviting, if you're white. But I wanted no fellowship at the Cracker Barrel, and I did not take the exit to visit the world-famous Bucksnort Trout Ranch. I gassed up before I left Nashville and stayed on the highway until I saw the Mississippi River, and I listened to Memphis music the whole way down.

If you look at the travel brochures in the lobby of any Motel 6 or Holiday Inn Express in these parts, you'll always see the pasty, swollen face of Elvis Presley on the front of them, but Memphis is one of the cultural capitals of black America. It is as important, in its way, as Motown or Harlem. Memphis had Sun Studio, where B. B. King, Rufus Thomas, and Junior Parker laid down the blues, as well as Stax Records, the birthplace of Southern soul, and home to Booker T. & the M.G.s, Isaac Hayes, and Otis Redding.

Memphis is where Dr. Martin Luther King gave his Mountaintop speech, and where a white supremacist murdered him for being a leader in the struggle for civil rights. The Lorraine Motel, where Dr. King died, is now the National Civil Rights Museum.

Memphis is also home of one of the predominant regional styles of barbecue, and Memphis pork ribs and shoulder are among the greatest of the many contributions black folks have made to American cuisine. The Memphis tradition is to rub the meat with garlic, pepper, paprika, and sometimes brown sugar, and then slow-cook it over hickory wood for upwards of eighteen hours. You can get Memphis barbecue wet or dry—either cooked with sauce, or just with the spice rub—but either way, the meat is so tender you can cut it with a plastic fork. The folks at Jim Neely's Interstate Bar-B-Que are among the finest practitioners of this art on the planet.

And I know you're listening, Ed, and I'm sorry, and I acknowledge the grievous wrongs perpetrated on livestock animals—which are sentient beings—by the American food industry. But some of us just ain't strong enough to practice ethical veganism. Not in Memphis, anyway. Those ribs. My God, those ribs. They serve them on plastic cafeteria plates with white bread, baked beans, and macaroni and cheese, and they are worth the drive down from Nashville all by themselves.

But if all that isn't enough for you, you can go to Graceland and check out Elvis's Jungle Room, which is a monument to the aesthetics of 1970s design. Green shag carpeting, wood-paneled walls, and earth-tone window dressings. Dude had a couch upholstered in fur. And there are a bunch of statues of monkeys in there for some reason. And all his weird, kitschy junk is maintained in pristine condition, like his fur couch is a holy relic.

I've been to the Smithsonian and seen the first ladies' inaugural gowns, and the lace is all faded. There's a touch of discoloration. If you look close enough, you might suspect that dust has touched those garments. Not so, however, with the relics in the Jungle Room; they are immaculate. In the Jungle Room, it will always be 1973. Time has not been permitted to soil or tarnish the King's sacred trinkets. I would be remiss not to point out, of course, that nobody bothered to preserve the home furnishings of Otis Redding and Rufus Thomas with such care. But the white people in the group I toured the house with were awestruck by the experience of being in the place where Elvis lived and died. A lot of visitors find it worthwhile to add this to their itinerary; Graceland gets about five times as many annual visitors as the Civil Rights Museum.

If this sounds a little bit like a travelogue, there's a reason for that; I persuaded NPR that *American Justice* could do with some local color, a sense of place. Just because Chester March has spent the last thirty-five years in an utterly featureless eight-by-ten cell doesn't mean that this program needs to feel like being shut up on death row. And just because we're documenting the process by which a state slowly and inexorably prepares to kill an old man for no good reason doesn't mean that listening to this broadcast needs to be a totally soul-crushing experience. Beyond the high walls of Riverbend, there's good music, and there's delicious pork shoulder, slow-cooked over smoldering hickory and pulled by hand. And, if you're into that kind of thing, there's Graceland.

If you ask me, I deserved to listen to some music and eat some barbecue after my hours of interviews with Chester and with Ed Heffernan and my days of sifting through the boxes in Ed's office. It is demoralizing to pore over the X-ray images of Chester's smashed skull and the transcripts from his sham of a trial, or to read the perfunctory opinions in which indifferent judges dismissed his appellate lawyers' futile bleats of protestation against the state's plan to murder their client. But we shouldn't have to forget about life's joys when we think about the people who are locked away from them. Indeed, it is necessary to remember the pleasures of living free in order to comprehend the magnitude of the injustice that is perpetrated upon the victims of the prison-industrial complex.

And it was in that spirit that I convinced NPR to put me up in the lovely Peabody Hotel while I was down here. Lest you fear that your generous donations to public radio are being ill-used, I should point out that the Peabody, for all its grandeur, was surprisingly cheap. A standard room only cost $250 per night. Memphis is an affordable town, though. A platter of pork with two sides at Neely's costs only ten dollars; in New York, you can only eat at Wendy's for that much if you forgo the upsize on your combo meal.

My initial research indicated that Robert E. Lee and Nathan Bedford Forrest had stayed at the Peabody, but when I asked the desk clerk about that, he testily informed me that the original Peabody Hotel, built in 1869, had been demolished in 1925 in preparation for the hotel's move to its current location, a block away. Those towering figures of American racism may have, admittedly, found shelter at this hotel's predecessor, but he assured me that the current facility had entertained no Confederate visitors.

While I was quizzing the clerk about the hotel's checkered history, a gaggle of white people gathered around a large fountain in the middle of the elegant lobby. There was a noticeable excitement among the crowd, as if these folks were anticipating a visit from Jimmy Buffett or the start of a slave auction. Then a gentleman in a full livery with tassels on his epaulets and little gold buttons on his jacket unrolled a red carpet leading from the elevator to the fountain.

My curiosity was piqued. Who was about to appear? Was it Martha Stewart? Or the ghost of Elvis himself? What could justify such pomp?

When the elevator door opened, a procession of mallard ducks emerged, waddled in single file down the carpet, climbed a little staircase into the fountain, and began splashing around in the water. All the white people applauded, and I could see why; it was whimsical, delightful, and a little surreal. I watched the ducks until they climbed out of the fountain and returned to the elevator. After the door closed behind them, the man in the livery rolled up the red carpet.

The state of Tennessee will put Chester March to death in less than three weeks.

14

The neurologist held a deck of vocabulary flash cards, made for teaching little kids to read. He laid four of them out in a row on his desk in front of me. The first had a picture of a car on it, with the word "C-A-R" written beneath it, in big block letters. The second had a picture of a fluffy white cartoon cat, with "C-A-T" written under it. The third was a picture of a cartoon bus, anthropomorphized so that its headlights were eyes and its front bumper was a mouth. It leered out of the image with a hideous rictus grin, and I couldn't help but think of Bernadette Ward's description of Chester's Buick Skylark. "B-U-S." The fourth was a picture of a house with red shutters on the windows and a bright blue door and flowers in front of it. "H-O-U-S-E." House.

"Car, cat, bus, house," the neurologist said. He picked up the cards and put them back into his deck. "Do you think you're going to be able to remember those?"

"Sure," I said. "The car I can't drive anymore, Schrödinger's cat, the bus I have to ride because I can't drive my car, and the house I had to leave to go move into the retirement home."

"You don't take the bus," Rose said, looking up from the magazine she was flipping through.

"How come you Indian guys are all named Patel?" I asked the doctor.

"My name isn't Patel," he said.

"Well, I can't remember what your name is, so I am going to call you Patel," I told him.

"You can do whatever you need to do to feel comfortable, Mr. Schatz," he said.

As you get older, you have fewer friends left with each passing year, but you get more doctors. The less time you have left to you on this planet, the more of it you have to spend in sterile rooms waiting for bad news. Needing a dementia specialist wasn't a good-news situation, but at least this doctor didn't make me take my pants off, most of the time.

"So how come you Indian guys are all named Patel?" I asked him.

"Why don't you tell me what was on the cards we just looked at?" Patel asked.

I could do that. My mind wasn't completely gone. "The car I can't drive anymore, Schrödinger's cat, the bus I have to ride like a schmuck because they won't let me drive, and the house I wanted to die in but I had to sell."

"For God's sake, Buck, nobody makes you ride a bus," Rose said.

"It's the principle of the thing," I told her.

"That doesn't even make any sense."

Patel took the cards and put them carefully in the drawer of his desk.

"Mr. Schatz, can you tell me what day of the week it is today?" he asked.

"I mean, the days all blend together where I live," I said. "Maybe one night is hamburger night and one night is Salisbury steak night, but it's the same meat either way, and there's nowhere to go and nothing worth a damn on the television."

"So you don't know what day it is?"

I shrugged. "Tuesday or Wednesday, I think," I said.

"Who is the president of the United States?" he asked.

I snorted. "Nobody I voted for."

"Jesus Christ," Rose said.

"Jesus Christ holds no sway here," I said. "We're Jews, and Dr. Patel is a Hindu."

"I'm actually Muslim," said Patel. "That's why my name is Dr. Ahmed Mohammed."

Had I known that already? I couldn't imagine I had. But how could I not have? "I'm going to keep calling you Dr. Patel," I said.

"Behave yourself, Buck," Rose said.

"Do you know who the president is?" asked Patel.

"Barack *Hussein* Obama."

"Very good," said Patel. "You got his middle name and every-thing. Do you remember what was on the cards we looked at a minute ago?"

I nodded. "The car I can't drive anymore, Schrödinger's cat, the house I wanted to die in, and the garbage truck they'll haul me away in when I finally kick the bucket."

"Okay," Patel said. "If this were an ordinary checkup, I would say Mr. Schatz suffers from mild to moderate dementia, but I am not seeing much of a change from where we were at our last visit six months ago. But you say his condition has worsened significantly, Mrs. Schatz?"

"He's having severe lapses in his memory," Rose said. They were doing the thing again, where they talked about me like I wasn't there.

"Do you find he is lucid some days and incoherent on others? Or is he lucid at certain times of the day, like in the mornings, with his mental state deteriorating in the evenings?"

"It's not that he's incoherent, exactly. He just forgets important things," Rose said. "He can remember all the details of a police investigation he worked on fifty years ago, but he can't seem to remember what happened during a doctor's appointment yesterday."

"Does he forget lots of different things, or does he forget the same things over and over?" Patel asked.

"Mostly certain things, over and over. Things about our son. Medical things. But he remembers every ridiculous thing he hears on talk radio. He can't shut up about that."

"It's not my fault the liberals are out to destroy this country," I said. I reached into my pocket and found the pack of Lucky Strikes.

"Quit it," said Rose, putting a hand on my wrist. I put the cigarettes away.

"I'm going to refer you to a specialist, and see if we can find out what's going on in that head of his," Patel said.

"Is there any point to that?" Rose asked. "You can do the

CAT scan or whatever, but regardless of what they find, nobody's going to be doing brain surgery on somebody as old as Buck."

"That's true," Patel said. He crossed his legs at the knees and leaned back in his heavy leather executive office chair. "But I'm not referring him to a radiologist. I'd like for him to visit with a psychologist."

I pulled my Luckys out again, and this time, Rose didn't stop me. I lit one. "See? Just like I said. Liberals destroying this country."

"And how is that supposed to help us, Doctor?" Rose asked.

"I think it's worth exploring the possibility that Mr. Schatz's memory lapses have causes other than the progression of Alzheimer's-type dementia."

"What else could be causing it?"

"Well, that's what I think Dr. Pincus might be able to help figure out. I've had some suspicions about the causes of Buck's difficulty for a while, and I talked to my colleague after you called and scheduled this appointment. He agrees he might be able to help, and he's holding an appointment open for you this afternoon. I can't promise his intervention will provide relief. As I'm sure I've told you before, dementia is a progressive condition that we try to manage but cannot cure. But what my colleague proposes is an entirely noninvasive procedure."

"Depends on your definition of the term," I said.

Rose turned toward me. "At least he's Jewish."

"And he's clearly very busy," I said.

"I think you'll like him," said Patel.

"Do I have a choice?" I asked.

"No," said Rose.

TRANSCRIPT: AMERICAN JUSTICE

CARLOS WATKINS (NARRATION): So, several episodes of *American Justice* have aired now, and y'all are getting to know Chester March and his plight as I'm continuing to report on this developing story. You have been sending lots of e-mails and tweets, and I love that. I love when people engage with these vital stories, and I love hearing what listeners have to say. I can't respond to everyone, but we're reading everything you send us, and we're seeing some questions recurring. So I want to take a moment to talk about some things folks keep asking in the e-mails, and on Twitter, and in the comments sections on the articles we post on the NPR website.

Everybody wants to know if Chester March is innocent. And, look, I'm down here in Tennessee doing the reporting. I've got drafts of the scripts I am working on for the next couple of episodes here. I've got all the information I've presented, and a lot of what I am going to tell you. I've read the court transcripts and the appellate briefs and the newspaper articles and all the primary sources. And I am sorry for those of you who consider this a spoiler, but I just don't know.

I am not in possession of any new evidence that will exonerate Chester. If I had anything like that, I wouldn't keep it under wraps while the state is already beginning its preparations for the execution. I'd turn that evidence over to Ed Heffernan, and he would get it in front of a court right away. If I learn anything new that materially changes my understanding of these crimes, you'll probably hear about it first when you see me in *The New York Times* or on CNN. This is a story with a real person's life at stake, and I'm not messing around or holding anything back.

There's not going to be a twist ending—at least, not one that I have planned. There's no reversal. There's no big surprise in the works. My sleeves are empty, folks. This is a story about a man who was convicted of murder thirty-five years ago and whose time has finally run out. It's a story about his lawyers filing his last-ditch appeals. If Ed Heffernan can't get a court to stay this execution, or if he can't convince the governor to put a moratorium on the death penalty in the state of Tennessee, then this story is going to end with Chester March getting a lethal injection.

And if you've become emotionally invested in Chester and his story, you need to be prepared for the idea that this is how it's going to end. I have already got my press credential to attend the execution. Don't think that I won't let it happen. Don't think that NPR won't let it happen. There is nothing we can do to stop it. I'm trying to change the world by shining a light on horrible things. But I can only witness these things and relay what I have witnessed to you, the listener.

Is Chester March a murderer? Maybe. And as far as I know, there's no evidence that will change that assessment. But can we be so sure he did it that it is unreasonable to doubt his guilt? I don't think so. And that is the question we're asking here: Can we say that this process and this evidence are sufficient for us to feel comfortable killing this man?

What we're trying to do here is a little different from a typical true-crime program. We're not exploring or analyzing the crimes Chester allegedly perpetrated but, rather, the crimes he is a victim of. We're looking at systems: the police investigation, the interrogation that yielded his confession and the trial that ended with him being sentenced to death, and the appeals that affirmed that sentence.

American Justice is, to borrow a cliché, a story about putting the system on trial. Because if this system puts Chester March to death unjustifiably, the system will be guilty of murder.

Of course, if you know anything, if you have any new information about Chester or his alleged victims, get in touch with us. Right now.

15

The ride back to Valhalla was tense and quiet. I didn't like being pushed into doing things, I didn't like people trying to get inside my head, and I didn't like talking to strangers. And with my memory steadily degrading, almost everybody was a stranger. I was so upset about having to go talk to Patel's head-shrinker that I didn't even bother to antagonize the aide who was driving the car. This seemed to worry her a great deal. She insisted on holding my arm as I lifted myself out of the back-seat, and after she parked the Buick, she followed us through the lobby, into the elevator and down the hallway to our room, hovering behind me all the way, as if she was scared I might collapse. Which, in all fairness to her, was a real possibility.

I shut the door in her face, pushed the walker over to the bed, sat down, and kicked off my shoes. I used to care a lot about my shoes. You can tell a lot about a man's character by looking at his shoes; they tell you about the kinds of choices he makes, whether he is fastidious or sloppy, and about how he sees himself and what he aspires to.

For most of my career, I wore cordovan oxfords that I shined myself, twice a week. They were the shoes of a striver, a man on the make. They showed that I was careful and deliberate. They represented the version of myself I wanted to show a world that aimed to pigeonhole me on the basis of my race.

These days, tying a shoelace takes too much out of me, so I wear slip-on canvas sneakers. They look like nurse's shoes, and they say a lot about me as well. They tell you a story of resignation, a story of decline. They tell you about the stream of compromises that have steadily eroded my foundation and turned me into the rickety ruin I have become. But I can step in and out of them without bending over. My doctor—one of my doctors—told me that his goal in treating patients like me is to get us through the day with as little pain as possible. So, slip-on shoes. There's nothing left for me to aspire to anymore, anyway.

Just as I was lying down on the bed, the cell phone rang.

"Don't pick it up," Rose said.

I picked it up. "I'm not supposed to talk to you," I said to Watkins, who was the only person who would be calling me on that line.

"Says who?" Watkins asked.

"My grandson," I told him.

"Your grandson gets to tell you what to do?"

"Nobody tells me what to do."

"That's for sure," said Rose.

"So why does it matter what your grandson says if nobody gets to tell you what to do?" Watkins asked.

"He thinks you have it in for me," I said. "He thinks there's nothing good that can come from you and me talking. He thinks I shouldn't dignify your little program with any response except silence."

"Mmm-hmm." Watkins was unimpressed. "And what do you think?"

"I think he might have a point."

"He said, as he did exactly what he had been advised not to do," said Rose.

"He's not recording this," I told her.

"Yes, I am," Watkins said. "Anytime we talk, I'm running the recorder. I'm probably not going to use this, though. It's not much good to me. I'd like to sit down with you in person and have a real conversation."

"I think I am going to take my grandson's advice," I said.

"There's a first time for everything," said Rose.

"Mr. Schatz, I'm just trying to tell this story—the whole story—the best way that I can. We're serious about journalism at NPR, and I'm after the facts. If you're willing to share your side of this story, we'll put it in front of our listeners. If not, the story I broadcast is going to be missing that piece of the puzzle, and that would be a real shame."

I laughed. "You're not going to fool me with that. I invented that," I told him.

"What do you mean? What did you invent?"

I cleared my throat. "Listen, son, if you want a lawyer, you've got a right to a lawyer. You give me the say-so, and I'll walk out that door and find you one. But if that happens, we're done talking. I'm going to have to file the paperwork charging you with murder one and pass this case along to the district attorney, and that's who you're dealing with from now on. The district attorney is a good man, I guess. But he's a politician. All he cares about is getting convictions and showing his constituents that he's tough. Whatever you've got to say, he's not interested in hearing. Now, me—on the other hand—all I want is to get to the truth. And that includes your side of the story. So if you want a lawyer, you can have one, and I'll go fill out my paperwork. Or I can find us some coffee, and you can say your piece, and I am willing to listen. It's up to you."

"I never thought of you as the good cop," Watkins said.

"I was the best cop," I told him.

"Well, if you want to square that with what you did to Chester March, I'll open up my air to you."

"I've got nothing to say about Chester March."

"Suit yourself."

TRANSCRIPT: AMERICAN JUSTICE

CARLOS WATKINS (NARRATION): I have contacted the Memphis Police Department several times about Buck Schatz. They won't provide anyone to sit with me for a recorded interview. Clarence Mathis, the media relations officer for the Memphis Police, sent me this written statement, which I will read in its entirety:

Baruch Schatz is one of the most decorated detectives in the history of the Memphis Police Department. He retired in 1976. No officer currently employed by the Memphis Police worked with Detective Schatz or has any firsthand knowledge of his methods or professional behavior. No officer currently employed by the Memphis Police Department investigated Chester March, or any of the murders he has been convicted of. No Memphis Police officers have provided testimony in any court proceedings regarding these cases in the last two decades. We have responded to your requests to provide copies of Detective Schatz's records, and we have complied to the extent required by law. We have no further information to provide to you regarding this matter. You may find it more productive to contact a local historian; there are several who are well versed in the history of the Memphis Police.

When I received that, I was angry. I felt they were stonewalling me a little bit. But on further reflection, maybe this is fair. They don't know Buck Schatz. They don't employ Buck Schatz. There's no institutional memory to tap into here; nobody currently working there knows anything about this case. All they can do is look at the same documents that I have already looked at and tell me things I already know. Nonetheless, I was hoping that an official with the Memphis Police would try to defend Schatz's conduct or else repudiate his actions. They weren't willing to do either.

So I called up the Memphis Police Association, which is the union that represents Memphis police, including retired police. One of the first things a journalist learns when covering crime is that you always call the police union when the police department won't talk to you. These guys are less constrained by bureaucracy, and they tend to be larger-than-life characters who give great sound bites. They also represent Schatz, so they have to speak to me.

RICK LYNCH: Hi there, I'm Rick Lynch. I'm a former police detective, out of St. Louis, and now I work for the Memphis Police Association, negotiating with the city and dealing with media on behalf of Memphis police officers.

WATKINS: How well do you know Buck Schatz?

LYNCH: I spoke to him recently—him and his grandson. They wanted to let me know you might be getting in touch. I'm not exactly a young man, but I ain't old enough to have been around during Buck's heyday. So what I know about him is what is in the records. I went through them after I got your e-mail. It's a thick folder, and it's got a lot of commendations in it. It's got a lot of letters from family members of murder victims talking about how Detective Schatz was relentless in his pursuit of justice for their loved ones. Folks were grateful that he always seemed to take their losses personally, when other institutional actors seemed indifferent. That's a mark of a good detective. And he seems to have been a good detective. Schatz was willing to work the cases other detectives didn't want, but his clearance numbers were among the best in the department, every year, from the mid-'50s to the mid-'70s.

But the file has also got some complaints about excessive force, and some of the reports that the department produces after internally investigating a police-involved shooting. In every case, Detective Schatz was cleared of any wrongdoing, but there are a bunch of them. He killed a lot of criminal suspects, and he beat up a lot more. I understand you've seen the same documents, so I am not sure what I more I can tell you.

WATKINS: Do you think that's acceptable, all those shootings and beatings?

LYNCH: Well, here's what I can tell you: Memphis is a majority-minority city, and today's Memphis police make community outreach a core value. Our department is headed by an African American police director, and many other top leadership roles are also held by black officials. We're proud, as well, of the diversity we've achieved among our rank and file, and of the trust we've built in Memphis's minority communities. And the work we do to build a police force that represents the community yields exceptional results. The Memphis Police Department clears about three-quarters of our homicides. In demographically and socioeconomically similar cities like Baltimore, New Orleans, Chicago, and Detroit, police clear less than half their murders. Some of them, less than a third.

WATKINS: I'm not sure that answers my question.

LYNCH: The compassion Schatz evidently showed to victims and their families is something we like to see in detectives. And he closed a lot of cases and caught a lot of bad guys. But he was quick to resort to force, and we wouldn't tolerate that from a detective today. And the frequency with which he used lethal methods is honestly shocking.

WATKINS: Do you know any other police officers who have been involved in as many shootings as Buck Schatz?

LYNCH: No. If an officer kills a suspect today, any department is going to take a real close look at the circumstances in which he made that decision. If an officer who has killed a suspect before kills another suspect, every aspect of his conduct in both instances will need to be completely unimpeachable for him to be allowed back onto the street. I can think of a very small number of officers who have fired their service weapons in more than one incident, and none who have done it more than twice. We place a lot of value on our relationship with the community, and we can't maintain that with killer cops running around.

WATKINS: So you're saying that Buck Schatz's conduct is unacceptable.

LYNCH: I'm saying he's from a different time. He joined the force after getting back from World War II, and he was a cop during Korea and Vietnam. He prowled these streets in the middle of a century defined by the worst carnage in human history. Maybe in the '60s it was considered normal for a detective to go out and shoot all the bad guys. I don't know what it was like then, but based on the records, he was viewed as a good cop by the standards of his day.

That isn't how we do things anymore. Modern officers have less lethal ways to deal with violent suspects, things like pepper spray and Tasers and beanbag guns. Schatz only had a nightstick and a sidearm. Today, we have newer, more sophisticated training and tactics, far better communications technology, and a lot more officers. That means it's a lot easier to call for backup, and help will arrive a lot faster. A suspect being pursued by one detective is more likely to flee or resist than a suspect who is surrounded by a dozen cops. So we have fewer incidents in which use of force is likely to be necessary. Officers today also have training on how to defuse volatile situations that Detective Schatz's generation didn't get. And we have officers and paramedics who are specially trained to deal with addicts and the mentally ill.

WATKINS: What do you think about beating confessions out of suspects in detention?

LYNCH: I can't imagine that's ever been an acceptable police practice.

WATKINS: All right, Mr. Lynch. Thanks for your time.

16

The doctor's office didn't look like a doctor's office. Pincus and another headshrinker shared a suite in a regular building off of Poplar Avenue, and his neighbors were lawyers and accountants. It made sense; if people had to come see him every week, they wouldn't want to have to visit a hospital or one of the medical parks and see all the real sick folks in the parking lot.

A little bell rang when Rose opened the door, which let him know we were there. He had a waiting room—windowless, with a couple of cheap-looking sofas and a coffee table with some magazines on it. There was no receptionist. The sofas were low to the ground, and I knew I would have a hard time getting up once I sat down on one, but I didn't know how long Pincus would keep me waiting. Even with the walker to lean on, I wouldn't be able to stand for very long. Damned if you do, and damned if you don't. I lowered myself onto the rough woven upholstery.

Pincus left us in there just long enough that I couldn't have stood, but not quite long enough to make the effort required to sit down and then get back up feel worthwhile. I disliked him immediately, but when he offered his arm to help me pull myself off the couch, I took it.

"Dr. Mohammed has told me a lot about you, Mr. Schatz, and I must say that it's an honor to meet a man with your distinguished record of service."

I recalled something Tequila had said, which seemed appropriate for this situation: "Eat a dick."

"Buck!" said Rose.

"Why don't you step inside, and we can discuss where this hostility is coming from," Pincus said, and he opened his door.

"How about let's not and say we did," I suggested. But Rose walked into the office, and I pushed my walker behind her.

The doctor's inner sanctum was a lot nicer than the waiting room. The office took up a lot of space, for starters; thirty feet by eighteen, I figured. Bigger than the room we lived in at Valhalla. In one corner he had a heavy wooden desk, like the kind a ship's captain might sit behind while he consulted his charts. The walls were lined with bookshelves full of serious-looking medical and psychological texts that Pincus had probably never read. The middle of the room was mostly occupied by a leather sofa and a somewhat imposing-looking armchair. Between the chair and the sofa was a glass-topped coffee table, upon which rested a leather-bound notebook, a Montblanc pen, and a box of tissues. No ashtrays in sight.

"The Kleenex are a nice touch," I said.

"Things can get pretty real in here sometimes, so those are here in case my patients need them," said the doctor.

"You mean because all of this is a big jerk-off?" I asked.

Pincus stared at me, his face expressionless. This guy was about as sharp as a baseball bat.

"You're not as funny as you think you are, Buck," Rose said.

"Yes, I am," I told her.

The doctor smiled at me. He was in his mid-forties and clean-shaven, with thinning hair, wearing a collared shirt with no jacket and a pair of khaki pants. He looked like a church pastor or a child molester, if there's even a difference between those things. "Before we begin, can I offer you a glass of water or anything?" Ever congenial, this guy.

I reached into my pocket and pulled out my cigarettes. "You'd better get me a glass or an ashtray unless you want a mess on your rug," I said.

I expected him to tell me I couldn't smoke in his office, but he flipped a switch on the wall to turn on his ceiling fan, and then he went and found an ashtray in his desk drawer.

While he was doing that, I sat in the armchair.

"Oh, that's my seat," Pincus said.

"Don't worry," I said. "I'm not going to take it with me when I leave."

Pincus shifted uncomfortably from foot to foot. "This is a safe and friendly space, but it has to be bounded by certain rules, and one of the rules is that the chair is mine. I need you to sit on the sofa."

I scratched my chin. "Listen, Dr. Pincushion, I appreciate

where you're coming from, but I am an older gentleman, and it takes a fair bit of effort for me to get up. Perhaps you noticed my mobility assistance device." I gestured toward the walker. "If it's all the same, I'd prefer to just sit here."

"It's not all the same, and you may not sit there," he said. "As soon as you move, we can begin."

I turned to Rose. "Is this guy serious?"

She sat on the sofa. "Why don't you join me over here?"

"Fine," I said, but I made a show of stretching out the process of hauling myself out of the cushy recesses of the armchair. As soon as I was clear of it, Pincus slid into the seat and folded his hands in his lap, to watch as I pushed the walker over to the couch. I grumbled, cursed, and complained the whole way.

When I finally situated myself, he picked up his notebook and unscrewed the cap of his fancy pen. It was a ballpoint, not the fountain. Who buys a Montblanc ballpoint? What a phony.

"You knew when you sat down that this was my chair, didn't you, Mr. Schatz?" he asked.

"I didn't think that much about it, to be honest," I said.

"I don't think you're being very honest at all," Pincus said. "I'm sure, even if you have never been to a psychologist's office, that you have seen one on television. Most people know that a psychologist sits in his chair and the patient sits or lies on the couch. Even if you were unfamiliar with that convention, you could see, based on where my notebook and my pen were situated, that I intended to sit here. I believe you recognized that this was my position, and you immediately moved to occupy it. Why do you think you did that?"

Rose shifted her weight next to me and began pawing around in her handbag, in search of nothing in particular.

"The chair looked more comfortable than the couch," I said. "Like your guy Freud said, sometimes a cigar is just a cigar."

"Well, maybe. But I think you were challenging me, and I don't believe you ever would have trusted or respected me enough to get anywhere in therapy if I hadn't stood up to you in your little dominance ritual."

"And you think I respect you now?" I asked.

"I don't know, Mr. Schatz. But I think, in the future, you will stay out of my chair," Pincus told me.

I laughed at him. He was not smiling.

"Dr. Mohammed referred you to me because he thinks you've had a rough last couple of years. He told me that you were shot and have had a difficult and incomplete recovery. He told me that, as a result of your injuries, you had to move out of your home and into a more accessible facility, and you had to give up driving."

I was holding the pack of Lucky Strikes in my hand. Pincus reached into his pocket, produced a plastic Bic lighter, and offered it to me. I took it from him, lit the cigarette, and tossed the lighter onto the table.

"I'm doing all right," I said.

He leaned forward to get the lighter and slid it back into his pants. "You're all right, relative to what?"

"Relative to the guy who shot me, for starters," I said. "I got that son of a bitch back, and then some."

He wrote something in his notebook with his expensive ballpoint. "And that's a triumph for you? To outlive your enemies even as the quality of your life declines?"

"I have outlived a lot of people."

"Yes, Dr. Mohammed told me about your son, Brian."

"Dr. Mohammed has a pretty big goddamn mouth, doesn't he?" I said. I remembered that I also had a notebook, which Rose kept for me in the front pocket of her purse. I grabbed it and mimicked Pincus's thoughtful scribbling. My notebook was a cheap reporter's pad with a cardboard cover, and my pen was a disposable that I had bought in a package of six for three dollars, but it was the same as the doctor's Montblanc because one ballpoint pen is as good as another.

"My impression of Dr. Mohammed is that he cares a great deal about his patients," Pincus said. "Let me tell you a little bit about myself and about why your neurologist thought it might be useful for you to come here. I specialize in helping people who have endured trauma. I've spent a lot of time working with veterans, soldiers who have been injured in combat—men who have seen their compatriots injured or killed, and who may be struggling to deal with things they have done."

"Well, I ain't got shell shock, Dr. Pink-Ass," I told him.

"I also help survivors of violent crimes, policemen who have been involved in shoot-outs or other use-of-force incidents, and patients who are coping with grief and loss. In other words, all the bad stuff rattling around in your head is precisely my area of expertise."

"The bad stuff in my head is Alzheimer's-type dementia," I said.

"Dr. Mohammed says you've been responding well to Aricept, and your condition has been stable, except for your complete inability to remember anything about certain subjects. That's not a usual pattern for dementia progression, Mr. Schatz. That's why Dr. Mohammed thinks that your situation falls within my area of expertise, rather than his."

"He ain't the first to wish I was somebody else's problem," I said.

"The mind is a versatile and complex organ. It protects itself. It blocks things it isn't prepared to confront. Your inability to remember your wife's illness is your mind's way of trying to guard against further trauma, just like your refusal to talk about your son's death."

"I have Alzheimer's," I said.

He ignored me, and continued: "But even though the mind instinctively tries to protect itself by locking these things away, the only path to healing is through confronting these traumas. You will have to face these things that you cannot remember and will not talk about. They will not go away just because you shut them out. Your wife has cancer whether you remember she does or not. Your son died whether you are willing to talk about it or not."

"I know," I said. "I may be old, and I may be demented, but I am not stupid."

He scribbled something in his notebook, took a moment to read over it, and then looked up at me. "Alzheimer's is a progressive, degenerative condition. But to the extent that certain aspects of your memory disorder are psychological, that is something that is treatable and potentially reversible. I wouldn't ask you to confront these traumas if I didn't honestly believe there was a benefit to it. If you can summon the courage to face these demons in this safe space, with me, I think you could be living a fuller, better life."

"Fuller?" I asked. "Better? I am ninety years old. I live in an assisted-living facility. My life is not getting better or fuller. I just sit in that place, and I wait."

Pincus leaned forward. "For what? What are you waiting for?"

"Oh," I said. "I don't know."

"It's this," Rose said, grasping at my wrist. "We're waiting for this. Everyone there is waiting for something to happen, and the only thing that is going to happen is the last thing that happens. And it's happening to me now."

"Yes," said Pincus. "Let's talk about Rose's condition."

"My wife is fine. I'm fine. Everything's fine," I said.

"I'm not, though," Rose said. "And you're not. And everything isn't. All these years, you've been fearless. Until recently. You can barely walk, but all you want to do is run away. We have to talk about this."

"Not here. Not in front of Dr. Penis," I said.

"Then where? When?"

"Somewhere else. Some other time."

"Buck, I don't know where else to take you, and I don't know how much time we have left."

"Tonight. We will talk about it tonight. Just not here. Not with him."

Pincus snapped his notebook shut. "That's fine. I think this has been a productive first session."

"I've had more productive sessions in the bathroom," I said. "Longer ones, too. We've been here what? Fifteen minutes?"

"If you'd like to talk more, you're welcome to stay another half hour. I just thought I'd let you go since you don't seem to enjoy this."

"Why not? You get paid either way, don't you? I just want to know how much this is costing me."

"It doesn't cost you anything. Medicare covers this. Every week, if you'd like to return."

"Fitting that this racket you've got is subsidized by government programs," I said.

"Programs we get a great deal of use out of," Rose reminded me.

"I think it's important that the two of you try to have an honest conversation about the struggles you're dealing with," Pincus said. "If we've facilitated that here today, then we've made real progress. I want you to try to focus on confronting your problems instead of minimizing them or fleeing from them, and then we will see next week whether you start to notice improvements in memory."

"What a treat," I said. "If I make myself miserable, I might get better at remembering how bad things are."

TRANSCRIPT: AMERICAN JUSTICE

CARLOS WATKINS (NARRATION): The entire Western world has abolished the practice of capital punishment with the exception of the United States. As a nation that executes its convicts, we are in the company of Pakistan, Saudi Arabia, China, and Iran.

In the last thirty years, 159 convicted and condemned men have been exonerated by the discovery of new DNA or other forensic evidence. And those are just the ones who were able to prove themselves innocent. We will never know how many falsely accused people have died at the hands of the state, convicted on the testimony of lying witnesses or on the strength of dubious proof.

So why are we still doing it? Why are we still killing people and calling it American Justice?

I asked Ed Heffernan, the Vanderbilt professor who is representing Chester in his appeals, and he suggested I should talk to one of his colleagues.

PROFESSOR RUPERT FIELDS: There are three rationales underlying all penalties handed down by the criminal justice system. The first is containment: the public interest in neutralizing individuals with known propensities for criminal activity and mitigating the danger they may pose to the innocent. The second is deterrence: the idea that a rational actor considering committing a crime might decide that the risk of suffering a severe punishment outweighs the benefit he will accrue from committing the act and that he may, therefore, abstain.

CARLOS WATKINS: And the third rationale?

FIELDS: Retribution. I think that one's pretty self-explanatory.

WATKINS (NARRATION): This is Professor Rupert Fields, an expert on the subjects of criminal justice and comparative law. He is a graduate of Yale Law School, a former clerk for Supreme Court Justice Antonin Scalia, and he now teaches at the University of Virginia. He has written friend-of-the-court briefs supporting the government in several death penalty cases. If anyone can explain to me how state-sanctioned murder can be justified, it's this guy.

FIELDS: Now, when we're talking about the death penalty, we can take containment off the table. Capital punishment doesn't do a much better job of protecting the public from the offender than life in prison.

Deterrence is a more interesting question, because it's impossible to prove. In theory, there may very well be a person out there who didn't commit a murder because he feared the death penalty. But you can never know how many murders were deterred, and that number might be zero. A lot of the really heinous crimes—those serial killings you love to cover on your true-crime broadcasts—are committed by people with personality disorders that alter the way they perceive risk. And when jurisdictions abolish or suspend capital punishment, we do not see a resulting rise in murders. Over the past couple of decades, the number of executions has declined, and the murder rate has declined as well. If you believe capital punishment deters murder, these phenomena are difficult to explain.

And you have to weigh the theoretical deaths prevented by deterrence against the measurable number of deaths that result from capital punishment. You could argue that killers have so debased and devalued themselves that even an unproven, theoretical innocent life is worth a significant number of actual lives of convicted murderers, but there is a nonzero possibility that our procedural safeguards could fail and that we might wrongfully convict and execute an innocent person, so there is a risk to a theoretical innocent life on both sides of that equation.

WATKINS: But despite all that, you still support the death penalty?

FIELDS: I believe in retribution. I believe extreme violence deserves to be punished in kind. I believe some people are so vile that the world is made worse off by their continued existence, even if they are confined. As Justice Potter Stewart wrote in *Gregg v. Georgia*, which reinstated the death penalty in 1976, "certain crimes are themselves so grievous an affront to humanity that the only adequate response may be the penalty of death."

WATKINS: Explain that to me.

FIELDS: Sometimes you will hear about some particularly heinous crime—an act of terrorism, or a killing motivated by racial animus, or a murder in which someone tortured and raped a child—and you'll think, "I don't support the death penalty, but maybe this guy deserves it."

WATKINS: I have never thought anything like that.

FIELDS: Well, maybe you haven't, but a lot of people have. Most people probably have. Sentiment is divided on the death penalty in this country. Something like 55 percent of Americans favor capital punishment, and 45 percent oppose it. But you've got to get unanimity in a jury room to sentence somebody to death. If people voted on juries the way they respond to opinion polls, we'd never execute anybody.

When you show people what some of these killers have done to their victims, when you show them photographs of the mangled bodies and you hear the coroner describe the extent of the violence these defendants have inflicted, those things will sway a lot of people who would tell you that they oppose the death penalty. When prosecutors present testimony from the family members of the victim, you'll see these compassionate folks crying in the jury box. And, at the end of all that, a lot of good, progressive jurors find that they are prepared to make an exception to their general opposition to the death penalty. The calculus just changes when it's a personal issue rather than a policy issue.

WATKINS: It becomes a personal issue for me when I meet people who are caught up in the machinery of the prison-industrial complex. It's personal to me when I meet folks from marginalized backgrounds who have survived abusive families, worthless, broken schools, and the depredations of thuggish, brutal police, only to find that their opportunities are limited by dense networks of privilege that funnel university admissions and top jobs to a favored elite. It's personal to me when I meet good people who have been rendered unemployable by nonsense criminal convictions, people whose very existence is criminalized by a racist, sexist, homophobic, and transphobic justice system that offers no leniency or second chances to poor people and people of color.

When you say these people deserve to be punished by these systems, it's like saying a steer deserves the abattoir, as if he's had a choice in anything that has ever happened to him.

FIELDS: Well, it's easy to take that view when you frame the narratives of these cases in a way that makes the condemned individual the protagonist of the story, with the state as an oppressive force mobilized to destroy him. Often, these stories are told years—maybe decades—after the crime has occurred, and the victim is a dim memory. The killer looks small and pathetic in his baggy prison jumpsuit, shivering like a scared dog. He is easy to frame as a sympathetic figure.

I've read articles about death penalty cases—articles thousands of words long—which never mention the victims' names and never describe the circumstances of their deaths. But people start to view these situations differently when you tell them a tragic horror story in which the victim is the protagonist and the killer is a monster lying in wait for them. That's not a story you read in most media accounts surrounding executions, but it is the story jurors hear.

WATKINS (NARRATION): I understand what Professor Fields is saying, but in the American criminal justice system, there are horror stories all around, and folks like those nice progressive jurors who are voting to kill people are more sympathetic to some of those stories than they are to others. I was pretty upset after this conversation, so I went back to Ed and played the audio you just heard for him. He told me some things that made me feel better.

ED HEFFERNAN: It may be true that judges and juries are willing to set aside their general opposition to the needless taking of human life after hearing inflammatory details from the prosecution in a murder trial or a sentencing hearing. But it's less true than it used to be. The number of death sentences has fallen to near zero in most states, even where the death penalty hasn't been banned by legislation or placed on moratorium by executive decree. Prosecutors rarely even ask for capital punishment anymore. And a big part of the reason for that is that nobody wants to actually carry out the death sentences after we condemn people.

Defense lawyers file endless appeals for decades and file for delays and continuances that drag out the proceedings. And prosecutors and judges and policymakers and voters all allow it, because, while people like the catharsis that comes with sentencing someone to death, they are deeply ambivalent about executing people. The state of California has nearly 750 condemned people on death row and has carried out only 13 executions since 1977, and zero since 2006. In the meantime, nearly ten times as many people have died of other causes while awaiting execution—some of them have died of old age, although, after years or decades of solitary confinement, a lot of people commit suicide.

And while governors still face political blowback for granting clemency to individual killers, because doing so seems like endorsement of the crimes they committed or an indifference to the victims, there is actually less backlash to simply suspending capital punishment entirely. That is how we got rid of the death penalty in Illinois and New York.

The Supreme Court has already found that it is cruel and unusual—and therefore unconstitutional—to execute offenders who committed their crimes when they were minors, and for similar reasons, that it is unconstitutional to execute offenders with mental disabilities. We are chipping away at it, and sometime pretty soon, the only states that will be executing people will be Texas and maybe Florida and Alabama, and then, in the face of widespread rejection of capital punishment, the Court will find that evolving moral standards can no longer countenance the death penalty. It's not a matter of "if," it's a matter of "when." The end of this story is already written.

WATKINS: Then why are you still fighting?

HEFFERNAN: I'm fighting to save Chester March and people like him, whose fates are still hanging in the balance under this zombie policy. And I will keep fighting until we put an end to the death penalty, and until we get rid of solitary confinement and the other barbarities of our deeply broken criminal justice system.

17

I was sitting in my easy chair, one of the few things I brought over from the old house. We'd had an estate sale when we moved in here, and got rid of most of what we owned: our wedding china, all Rose's kitchen things, and the furniture we inherited from Mother. All told, the accumulated possessions of our long lives didn't amount to much; the lot of it was worth less than what it cost to live in a tiny room at Valhalla for two months.

Rose was sitting across from me on the bed, looking at me like she expected me to say something.

I used to keep the chair in front of the television, but with my hearing fading and my memory going, I rarely turned that on anymore. Instead, we'd had the staff move the chair next to the window, so I could blow my cigarette smoke outside, and that was what I was doing. I had my ashtray sitting on the end table next to me, and there were four spent butts in it already, so I knew we had been here for a while.

I stubbed the fifth one out and reached for the next. This comforted me: the automatic motion of tapping the pack against the palm of my hand, plucking a cigarette between my fingers, flicking the same gold lighter I'd had for decades, inhaling. I could have been doing this in 1950 or 1970, and it would have felt the same and smelled the same and tasted the same. Everything else was falling apart or changing in incomprehensible ways. The only thing that could withstand the onslaught of time was smoke.

"How much do you remember?" she asked me.

"I always feel like I am just waking up from a bad dream," I said. "I've got a sense of dread; I know something is wrong. But I can just let it fade into the background of all the things that are wrong. This place is wrong. Our lives here are wrong. It's all wrong."

She rested her arms on her knees, and her whole body seemed to sag and deflate. "But not wrong like this is wrong."

I rocked back and forth in my seat. "I know that. I know that."

"If you know, then why do you pretend not to sometimes?"

"I'm not pretending. It's just confusing. There are so many doctors and so much to keep track of."

"And it's easier to forget."

"I don't know that it's easier. I'm not deciding to forget anything. It's just what happens."

"You know, Buck, every time you would get a medal for bravery, I'd go to the ceremony, and I'd listen to them tell a story about your heroism. About how you'd chased some murderer down an alley or kicked in a door, faced down some degenerate who came at you with a knife or a gun, and got the better of him. And I always thought, 'What happens to us if it goes the other way? What happens if one of these murderers gets the drop on you? What happens if you're not as fast as the other guy?' And I was afraid to say anything about it to you, because I was afraid saying it would make it happen. Like talking about it would put a jinx on us. I think you know how that is."

I nodded. "I don't like talking about things."

"I know you don't. And that's also why I never brought it up. But I used to think it was unfair that you were the one making the decision to run down that alley or kick in that door."

"That was the job," I said.

"A job you chose. A job you fought so hard for, that nobody even wanted you to have. And it was never my place to tell you not to pursue that dream, never my place to tell you not to be the hero who gets the medal. It was always your decision to run into danger, and I always had to accept that I would be the one to live with the consequences."

I stubbed out my Lucky Strike. "You would have got my pension if something happened to me. I had life insurance. Everything would have been taken care of."

"I know it," she said. "And I always supported your choices. You wanted to protect people. I admired that about you. And I admired the fact that when you had to decide whether to run into danger or let the bad guy get away, you never hesitated."

"I did it for you and for Brian. To keep you and people like you safe. If I didn't get those scumbags, who knows what they would have done, or who they would have done it to," I said.

She wiped at her eyes with the back of her hand. "But you're hesitating now."

"I'm not. It's just hard. I can't remember."

"You were never afraid when you ran down those alleys or kicked in those doors. But you're afraid now. You weren't afraid to die, but you're terrified to be left alone."

"That was never how I thought of it," I said. "I never felt like I was making a choice. Somebody had to go after those guys. Somebody had to stop them. It was my job, and it was more than that. It was a purpose. It was a calling."

She shook her head. "It was a decision, though. There were plenty of detectives who didn't go after those guys the way you did. Plenty of detectives who didn't put themselves in harm's way like you did. I never said anything, because it was your decision whether to chase after the bad guys. And it was a decision that you were always prepared to make. But you're not prepared to make this decision. You're so unprepared to make it that your mind is turning itself inside out to avoid it. And I don't blame you. If you had called me before you went chasing off after some armed psycho and asked me for permission, I don't know what I would have told you. I would never have asked you not to do the thing you were best at. But if I'd told you to go, and something had happened, it would have felt like it was my fault. It was a kindness for you to make that decision on your own. If something had happened, I might have blamed you, but I wouldn't have had to blame myself. And it's selfish of me to ask you to help me make this decision, because you are the one who will have to live with the guilt if it goes badly. It's selfish of me to be angry at you for not being able to make the decision I don't know how to make either. It's selfish of me to be annoyed with you while I am watching you tear yourself apart."

"I want to help," I said. "I really do. I'm so sorry."

"I know what you want. You want me to fight, like you always fought. Fighting has always been the right thing for you to do. But you don't want to tell me to do it, because you're scared that if you do, something will go wrong. Just like I didn't want to talk to you about how scared I was for you."

"I don't know what to say," I said. "Nothing makes this all right. I don't know how to fix it."

She smiled. "You don't have to say anything. Of course, I already know what you think. I've known you long enough that you don't have to tell me. You were always strong on your own. And I have to decide on my own now, about whether to try to treat this cancer. And I'm not going to do it."

The unlit cigarette I had been holding between my fingers dropped to the floor. "What?"

"I'm not going to do chemotherapy. I am not going to put myself through that. I am not going to put you through that. All those hospital trips. All the weakness and sickness and vomiting and the bleeding. I am going to enjoy the time I have left, I am going to take care of you as long as I can, and when it's time, it will be time."

"Is this because of me?" I asked. "That's not what I wanted."

"I know it's not. It's what I want. And I know you will be angry about it, and that's what I want, too. I'd rather leave you feeling angry than guilty. I'd hate for you to spend the time you have left carrying guilt. It will probably be a year or so before I get really sick, and until then, you can just forget this is happening. You probably will, whether you want to or not."

I started to bend down to retrieve the cigarette on the floor, but I felt a little lightheaded. The last thing I needed was to tumble over and cap this night off with a trip to the emergency room. I left the fallen soldier and pulled a fresh one out of the pack instead. "You know, it's not true that I was never afraid when I chased after those scumbags. I was always afraid. I never had any illusions that the things I saw happen to so many people couldn't happen to me. I was scared, and I did it anyway, because it was something that needed doing. What's different now is that I'm helpless. Useless."

Rose stood up, and wrapped her arms around my shoulders. "Don't say that, Buck," she said, pressing her face against my neck. "Don't say that, even if it might be true. You're all I've got."

TRANSCRIPT: AMERICAN JUSTICE

CARLOS WATKINS (NARRATION): As you may recall, I have been trying to get Baruch Schatz to sit down and talk to me on the record about how he extracted the confession that doomed Chester March. He has been evasive. I've gotten him on the phone a couple of times, but he gets cagey when I ask about this case, and he will not agree to sit down and talk to me face-to-face.

Buck Schatz is a lot of things, but he isn't a coward. Even if he knows he did something wrong, he is the type who would want to make excuses or rationalizations rather than hide from a reporter.

And if I am being honest, I expected he'd talk to me when I pitched the Chester March case to NPR. I can tell a version of this story without his piece of it, but it will be incomplete. And listeners have been e-mailing me, asking me what he has to say for himself, and I'm embarrassed to tell them that I don't know. I promise you, I'm not hiding him. I'm not saving him to build suspense. I am trying to get him to talk. That's a big part of what I am doing in Memphis right now. You want to hear from him, and I want to hear from him, and everyone who knows him has told me he certainly has something to say about this. He's got something to say about everything.

So why isn't he talking to me? Well, that piece of the puzzle is Buck's grandson, William Tecumseh Schatz. William recently graduated from law school and will be working at a white-shoe law firm after he takes the bar exam next month. Buck told me William doesn't want him to sit for an interview with me. It sounds like old Buck has lawyered up.

So, if William is going to be the old man's lawyer, then he's got to speak for the old man. I called him up and told him as much, and he has agreed to meet me and go on the record. He doesn't know firsthand what went down in 1976; he wasn't even born yet. But I can look him in the eye and ask him why he's so dead set against his grandpa talking to me. It's better than nothing. I'm still trying to get Buck to sit for an interview. I'm not giving up. But, for the moment, we can have this.

I scheduled the meeting at the lobby bar at the Peabody. It probably would have been better to do the interview in my room, where there would be less background noise, but the mics I have are pretty good at filtering that out, and the room is a little disappointing; it's just, like, a regular hotel room. The lobby, though, is such a great backdrop. It's a two-story space with marble floors and huge columns, and the bar is wood-paneled with a barkeep in a vest and a bow tie. It's like old South meets Coruscant, and it's weird as hell, and I love it.

I was expecting Buck's grandson to look like Buck in those old photos—a thousand-yard stare beneath heavy brows and a permanent sneer, like he was just daring you to try something. The kind of man who can be imposing without being big, because he makes you feel so small. In retrospect, I don't know why I expected that of William. His grandfather came up during the Great Depression and got his education at Normandy and in a German prison camp. William went to NYU.

What William actually looks like is: a white man. I wish I could do better for you, but that's what he looks like. Have you ever been at the airport, waiting to board an airplane, and you saw a white man in a light blue button-down, non-iron dress shirt, probably from Brooks Brothers, and a pair of khaki pants? Because I see a white man like that, and usually more than one, every time I fly. And they all look the same, and they all look exactly like William Schatz. He was even carrying the same black canvas expandable Tumi briefcase that white men in blue Brooks Brothers shirts and khaki pants always carry.

If you squint at his face, maybe you can see a little bit of Buck around the eyebrows. But he doesn't have the stare or the sneer. He doesn't have the air about him that lets you know he's been hungry—really hungry—or that he knows how to hurt you—really hurt you. His face is rounder. He's soft.

William sits down in the leather chair across from me; he crosses his left ankle over his right knee. On his lap, he rests the black canvas Tumi briefcase that is exactly like the black canvas Tumi briefcase that every other white man in a blue Brooks Brothers shirt and khaki pants has. He is wearing lace-up wingtip shoes. This is unsurprising. The shoes are the one thing that varies among your standard-issue airport white men. The ones who wear lace-ups are lawyers; the ones who wear loafers, usually without socks, work in finance; and the ones who wear sneakers work in tech.

CARLOS WATKINS: You're William Schatz, Buck's grandson?

WILLIAM SCHATZ: Yes.

WATKINS: Buck told me on the phone that you like for people to call you Four Loko.

W. SCHATZ: Where did he—how does he even know what that is? No. That is not correct.

WATKINS: What do you want me to call you?

W. SCHATZ: My friends call me Bill.

WATKINS: So you want me to call you Bill?

W. SCHATZ: Call me William.

WATKINS: . . . Okay, William. I've been trying to get your grandfather to speak to me about the investigation and trial of Chester March, and he won't do it. He says you don't want him to talk to me.

W. SCHATZ: That's correct. I've listened to the first couple of episodes of *American Justice*, and it's pretty clear that you're telling this story in a way that downplays the severity of Mr. March's crimes and that you are trying to accuse my grandfather of professional wrongdoing. I'm not going to allow my grandfather to participate in your show. Baruch Schatz is ninety years old. He suffers from Alzheimer's, and he is very frail. I am trying to protect him. I hope you will understand my concerns, and I hope you will stop calling him.

WATKINS: Your grandfather was involved in a gunfight about a year and a half ago. He killed a young black boy.

W. SCHATZ: My grandfather was forced to defend himself when a car he was riding in was attacked by drug dealers and rammed off the road. The armed man my grandfather shot was responsible for the murder of a Memphis police officer. That story was covered extensively by local media at the time, and neither he nor I have anything to add to the ample information that is publicly available regarding that incident.

WATKINS: I'm just saying your grandfather doesn't seem like a weak, confused old man who needs your protection from me. And even if he is, that doesn't mean he should be spared scrutiny when his actions from 1976 continue to have serious consequences. A man your grandfather arrested was convicted of murder on the basis of evidence your grandfather gathered and a confession your grandfather extracted. Every question I want to ask your grandfather deserves to be answered before Chester March is put to death.

W. SCHATZ: Every question that needs to be asked has been asked during Mr. March's trial and during his decades of subsequent appeals. My grandfather's record of professional conduct is exemplary, and he has been retired from the police department for decades. He doesn't need to sit here and participate in your distortion of the facts or the smearing of his name.

WATKINS: I'm not trying to do anything except tell the truth. I'm not looking to distort anything. I'm not planning to engage in any deceptive editing of any audio involving you or your grandfather. I have been interviewing Chester about these events, and your grandfather is the only other participant in this story who remembers what happened. I want to hear what he has to say. If he has a conflicting account, I am happy to air both sides.

W. SCHATZ: If you were really interested in the issues your show claims to cover, you would be talking about how Chester March exploited the privileges associated with his race and his class to escape charges in 1955 after my grandfather arrested him for killing his wife, Margery, and an African American sex worker named Cecilia Tompkins. A racist prosecutor refused to put Chester on trial because the case my grandfather built was centered around the testimony of another African American sex worker, a woman named Bernadette Ward, who identified Mr. March in a lineup as the man who had abducted Tompkins, and described Mr. March's car.

WATKINS: So, you talked with your grandfather about this case, and you don't want him to tell me what he told you about it?

W. SCHATZ: My reasons for preventing him from talking to you have nothing to do with what he told me and everything to do with what I have heard on *American Justice*. I think you are a credulous, ideologically motivated dupe, and I think you are being manipulated by a psychopath. I have listened to you air Mr. March's lies without presenting facts that rebut them.

WATKINS: Baruch is welcome to come rebut anything he wants.

W. SCHATZ: My elderly and infirm grandfather doesn't need to provide you with facts that are available from numerous other sources. The facts are recounted in the appellate record that I know you have seen because I heard you discuss it on the air. Mr. March is guilty, and the evidence supporting his conviction is overwhelming. You have portrayed this evidence as being much more ambiguous than the record justifies. You have uncritically aired Mr. March's risible claims of innocence. I don't want my grandfather to talk to you, because I don't think you are a serious journalist or a good-faith interlocutor.

WATKINS: Edward Heffernan is one of the most respected law

professors in the country, and he's representing Chester and trying to save his life.

W. SCHATZ: Professor Heffernan opposes the death penalty categorically. His current appeals are based on theories that are unrelated to the settled question of Mr. March's guilt and have nothing to do with Baruch Schatz. You've gotten way out ahead of any position he would take with your irresponsible suggestions that Mr. March might be innocent. If you ask Professor Heffernan whether he believes Chester March is a murderer, he will avoid the question and pivot back to his generalized objections to capital punishment.

WATKINS (NARRATION): At this point, William Schatz unzips the standard-issue black canvas Tumi briefcase and produces several Redweld accordion folders from inside of it.

W. SCHATZ: Do you know what Chester March was up to between his wife's disappearance in 1955 and his eventual arrest for murder in 1976?

WATKINS: He was living in California.

W. SCHATZ: And do you know what he was doing there?

WATKINS: How is that relevant?

W. SCHATZ: Mr. March inherited his father's cotton concern in 1961. At the time, March was living in the San Francisco Bay Area. March did not return to the South when his father fell ill. He arranged for the liquidation of the business, and while the agents he hired dumped the company's assets at fire-sale prices, March collected seven hundred thousand dollars after taxes and fees. That's the equivalent of about five million dollars today. Have you asked Mr. March what happened to his money?

WATKINS: Nothing about that is referenced in the case or any of the appeals.

W. SCHATZ: I know it isn't. My grandfather and the Tennessee prosecutors had Chester's confessions for three local murders. There was limited coordination or cooperation between police agencies at the time. In 1976, the Memphis police simply didn't have any way to find out what Mr. March had been up to in California. But that information is now available through various legal and public records databases. I'm not even sure if my grandfather knows about this.

Chester March married a woman named Catherine Wood in 1963. She disappeared under mysterious circumstances in 1967. Local authorities investigated Mr. March in relation to the disappearance but never indicted him. However, in the year after Catherine March's disappearance, Mr. March retained expensive criminal defense attorneys and made several sizable donations to local political leaders. I have those records here, if you'd like to see them. Catherine March's parents, Eugene and Agatha Wood, sued Mr. March in 1968 for the wrongful death of their daughter. Chester March settled for an undisclosed sum in 1971 after their lawsuit survived a motion for summary judgment.

Legal expenses and the settlement consumed the bulk of Mr. March's fortune, and he returned to Memphis to try to borrow money from some of his cousins who were still engaged in the cotton business. He was destitute when my grandfather arrested him for the murder of Evelyn Duhrer in 1976, which is why he was represented by court-appointed counsel at his murder trial.

WATKINS: What does this have to do with any of the subject matter of *American Justice*?

W. SCHATZ: Why have you been trying to convince your listeners that this man might be innocent? Chester March is a serial killer. Women go missing whenever he is around. And you are giving him

a national platform to tell lies about his victims and about the coura-
geous detectives who caught him. My grandfather stopped Chester in
1976 and would have put him away twenty years earlier if it hadn't
been for the bigotry of the police brass and the local prosecutors.
How can you look at this story and think Buck Schatz is the bad guy?

WATKINS: The good guys don't beat up on shackled prisoners.
Good guys don't torture confessions out of suspects.

W. SCHATZ: I just don't think your little crusade is really about
Chester March or Baruch Schatz. I think it is about Marius Watkins.

WATKINS: What do you know about Marius Watkins?

W. SCHATZ: I know he's your father, and I know he's been a guest
of the government at the Dannemora prison for the last twenty years
and will probably remain there for the rest of his life. Like I told you, a
lot of information is available in legal and public records databases.

WATKINS: Well, shit, man, I guess you got me. You figured out that
I am the son of an impoverished single mother and an incarcerated
father. How can any of my listeners ever trust me, knowing that I grew
up in a housing project and attended a crumbling Brooklyn public
school, and then went to Dartmouth and got my master's degree in
journalism from Columbia?

W. SCHATZ: I question your objectivity with regard to allegations
of police misconduct, in light of your father's claims that cops planted
the evidence that led to his murder conviction. I think your journalism
is agenda-driven, and I think you're hostile to police and sympathetic
to violent criminals.

WATKINS (NARRATION): When I looked at William before, I didn't
see Buck in him, but I can spot the resemblance now. He's looking at
me, but he's looking through me. His eyes are set, and his lip is curled
downward, just like Buck's. I'm a puzzle he's solved, a problem he

has dismantled and defused. He has figured out my deal, and now I am no longer a threat. To him, I am nothing.

I haven't spoken much about my life or my past on the air, because I have never considered it relevant to the stories I am telling here, but I don't have any secrets. I'm not trying to hide anything.

My father, Marius Watkins, is serving a life sentence at the Clinton Correctional Facility in Dannemora, New York. He was convicted of killing a man and a woman during a street robbery in 1992. A witness identified my father fleeing the scene shortly after hearing the gunshots. Police searched his residence and recovered a handgun. Ballistics experts testified at trial that the gun was the one used in the murders, and a forensics expert testified that my father's fingerprints were recovered from the gun. Marius has maintained for two decades that he is innocent and that the NYPD planted the weapon. In appeals, he has unsuccessfully petitioned to have new DNA testing performed on the gun, which he says he never touched or saw before police raided his apartment.

I am close with my father, and since I was a child, I have visited him regularly at the prison. I believe Marius Watkins is innocent, I believe he will be exonerated one day, and I don't deny that his circumstances are a reason for my professional interest in the workings of the criminal justice system. If you feel I have misled you in any way by not disclosing this earlier, then I apologize sincerely.

That said, I—along with Marisol Rodriguez, my coproducer on *American Justice*, and the team of researchers and fact-checkers who support us—stand behind everything we've reported. We do not believe that having an incarcerated family member disqualifies a journalist from covering the criminal justice system. We believe the son of a convicted felon is as qualified to tell the story of Chester March as the grandson of a Memphis cop.

W. SCHATZ: You are welcome to keep those documents, in case there's any information in them that is useful to you.

WATKINS: I don't want to look at any of your documents. When can I talk to Buck?

W. SCHATZ: You're never going to talk to him. I will never let that happen.

18

According to the clock on the nightstand, it was 2:24 A.M. The numbers glowed green, three inches tall. The clock was hideous and I hated it, but although it was grotesque, it was also necessary. We needed a large display so we could see what time it was without putting on our glasses. I stared at the green numbers, fuzzy around the edges, hanging in the darkness. 2:25.

Rose snored softly next to me. It would be eighteen months, maybe two years before the cancer did its job on her. That's a long time at our age. Long enough that she could die of something else first. Long enough that she might still outlive me. But she probably wouldn't. I was a survivor. Always had been, since long before I knew what that meant or what it would cost me.

They say that, when you lock a guy up for a crime, if he's guilty, he'll sleep soundly. Once the trap has snapped closed on him, he knows he's caught, so the worst is behind him. It's almost a relief. It's the innocent who fear what comes next, who are anxious about their trials and fret about how to clear their names. That's not true, of course. I've seen plenty of guilty men who were all kinds of nervous, and the worst criminals always believe themselves to be innocent. As they see things, intervening circumstances relieve them of culpability. It's all somebody else's fault. Whatever they've done is trivial next to what's been done to them.

But there must have been a kernel of truth to that old superstition, because, with her decision made and her course set, Rose seemed unburdened. She was done fighting. Done negotiating. Done searching for a way out. And now, she could sleep soundly. I couldn't remember the last time I had seen her look so peaceful, though, admittedly, there were a lot of things I couldn't remember. I was the one lying awake, anxious and afraid.

Rose said she used to worry about me chasing after scumbags and killers. But, if anything, I should have taken more risks. Started more gunfights. Maybe smoked more. It takes a lot of nails to pin a beast like me into a coffin, but I could have found my number. An extra half a pack a day, maybe, and I could have been dead thirty years ago.

They should put warning labels on vegetables. The surgeon general should tell people not to get too much exercise. Somebody needs to get the word out: If you aren't careful, you might live too long.

After I got back from the war—after I had mostly recovered from my injuries—I went out on the municipal golf course at Overton Park. I had my clubs, the same clubs I'd had before I went to Europe. And I pulled the driver out of the bag, and it looked like it always had, and it felt like it always had, and it was a pretty day in April, and everything seemed all right. And for a second, it seemed like I could pick up where I'd left off before the world exploded. And then I teed up, and I squared my hips, and by the time I got to the top of my backswing, I knew it wasn't the same after all, and it never would be. I could feel the pins in my shoulder. I could feel that the rotation of my body was off, in a way I couldn't ever fix.

That wasn't the last time I played golf. I figured out a stiff way to swing the club that could get the ball down the fairway. I told myself I'd compensate for what I'd lost on the drive by working on my short game. Brilliant idea, there. I must have been the first one who ever came up with it. And I told myself that what I'd lost was balanced out by the wisdom I'd gained.

But the truth was, I knew when I took that swing that the best round of golf I'd ever play was behind me. That was the first time I really understood what it means to move through this life, to suffer wear and tear that you can't fix.

The peak comes real early, and when you're there, you never realize it. By the time you figure out that you're on the way down, your best day is already so far behind you that you can't even figure out which one it was in retrospect, and then for the rest of your life, you'll just get weaker and uglier.

At some point, you stop marking time around celebrations and holidays, and start using funerals as your signposts. Remember so-and-so? How long has he been gone? It's been longer than you realize. You mark time by what you've lost and who you've left behind. And you diminish more each day, until you can barely remember your unbowed, unscarred, perfect self, until you don't even recognize what you see in the mirror.

At some point, what are you sticking around for? Why did I want to keep going without Brian? What is there to keep me going without Rose? Maybe there will be something good on TV? There's never anything good on TV.

There's food. You can enjoy a great meal. But even that starts to get away from you. I've forgotten so many things, but here's something I remember: Little children's entire mouths are lined with taste buds. Taste is important to babies; they can taste before they can see, and it's how they first come to know their mothers. Later on, the exquisite sensitivity of a child's sense of taste can warn them if something they're trying to eat is poison, before they've learned what's safe and what isn't. That's why babies are always putting things in their mouths; they can get a lot of information that way. But all those taste buds fall out with the baby teeth.

That means that even if you go to the world's finest restaurants, even if you order the six-hundred-dollar tasting menus at the extravagant New York joints my grandson visits with his lawyer friends, nothing you ever eat will taste as good as a nickel ice cream tastes to a four-year-old. And by the time you turn ten, you will have forgotten what it tasted like. You keep losing taste buds your whole life. Your mouth becomes a dead gray expanse. When I was seventy, I doused everything I ate in hot sauce, and by the time I turned eighty, I'd stopped bothering. Do you want to know why the food in retirement homes is so bad? It's because nobody cares anymore.

I know what my funeral would have been like if, as Rose feared, one of the murderers I went after had got the better of me. There would have been pallbearers in dress uniforms. A eulogy from the police chief, maybe the mayor. A twenty-one-gun salute.

Hundreds would have attended. The entire police force. Folks I helped. People from the synagogue. People who knew my mother. People who knew my son.

My colleagues never fully embraced me on account of my race and my faith, but they'd have shown respect, and they'd have given me a raucous Irish wake. If you die in the line, you get an Irish wake at a downtown bar, even if you're not Irish— even though most Memphis cops aren't Irish. It would have been something to see, all those shitkickers and good ol' boys, toasting my memory into the wee hours of the morning and retelling the stories of the meanest Jew who ever walked these streets.

They're dead now. All those cops. My mother and everyone who knew her. My son.

And as I've diminished these last forty years, so has the mark I've made on the world. I once believed a man's deeds and the things he built became his legacy, but it turns out that those things aren't terribly durable. I've outlived all of mine. The people I saved didn't stay saved. Something got them, eventually: disease or car accidents or old age or whatever. And the killers I stopped were replaced by new ones. And the city I protected remains near the top of every list of the most dangerous places in America, and people tell me now that the way I fought crime was barbaric and racist. When I finally go, if I'm remembered at all, it won't be well.

Who will show up to bury me? Tequila and Fran, I guess.

He'll probably give a speech that makes the whole thing about himself. Perhaps a couple of folks from the Jewish Community Center, but not many. Maybe some of the aides from Valhalla will show up, but probably not. If this place gave the staff leave to attend residents' funerals, there would never be anyone at work, and it's a lot to ask for folks to show up on their time off. There are some local veterans who attend other veterans' funerals. I don't know them, and they don't know me. They fought in other wars. But they'll be there nonetheless. And the department will send somebody. But just as a formality. Then they'll go get lunch.

I like to tell people that I've buried all my enemies. I don't like to talk about how I've buried all my friends. And I don't even know how to think about burying Rose. Seventy years I've been with her, and I don't know how to be without her. Is it something I'll get used to? I don't think so. I haven't gotten used to my son being gone. I haven't gotten used to riding in the backseat of my own car. I haven't gotten used to living in this place instead of my house. I haven't gotten used to the walker. I don't quite understand how all this could possibly have happened. Just when I reached the point where I thought I had everything fixed, it all started falling irreversibly to pieces. Entropy gets you in the end.

But somehow, despite all evidence to the contrary, I can sometimes forget enough to still believe I am the man I was. In my mind, in those moments, I'm still Buck Schatz.

PART 4

1976: BUCK SCHATZ

19

It was clear from the smell that something was very wrong on Alton Avenue. After four days tolerating the stink coming out of Evelyn Duhrer's house, John Clifton had called the police.

The responding officers agreed the house stank and knocked on the door. Nobody answered. They used the two-way in their patrol car to radio the precinct for further instructions, and the precinct captain decided the situation merited the attention of a homicide detective. He called me.

"Lots of houses stink," I said. "Somebody's septic tank is probably leaking. Why are you bothering me with this?"

"It's not a poop smell," the captain told me. "It's more of a chemical smell."

"What kind of a chemical smell?" I asked.

I waited while he conferred with the officers on the radio.

"Like when you pick your kid up from school the day they dissect the fetal pig," he told me.

"That's not a good smell," I said. "Tell the officers not to leave. Have them wait outside, and if anybody tries to go into the house, have the officers stop them, frisk them, and question them. I will be down there in a couple of hours, with a warrant. Tell your boys not to take their eyes off that house until I arrive."

Most officers know what a rotting body smells like; it's a meaty, earthy smell, with a sort of sweet undertone to it, and sometimes a shit smell as well, on account of the guts rupturing during decomposition. That smell signifies an unattended death, but not necessarily a suspicious one. It happens whenever somebody who lives alone dies of a heart attack or a stroke or a household accident, or a suicide, unless somebody finds them quickly.

That smell also signifies that the decedent is well past the point of requiring medical assistance, so we could handle an unattended death carefully, with the knowledge that there was no emergency. When we found a house like that, the department would send out a detective to supervise the collection of the body and to make sure the scene was preserved until the coroner determined that the cause of death was not criminal. You didn't want to have your uniformed officers going through the house, touching things with their bare hands and leaving dirty footprints on the carpets, only to discover a few hours later that your accidental death was less accidental than it initially appeared.

But days-old bodies discovered in houses where there were no obvious signs of breaking and entering almost never turned out to be murders, so attending and preserving these scenes was a boring and undesirable detail. By the 1970s, I didn't have to do garbage tasks like that anymore.

I'd never have been treated as having seniority if the police brass had stayed Klanned up like it was in the '50s, but the most wonderful thing happened over the course of the '60s: All those bigoted schmucks retired or died.

Old Inspector Byrne took his pension in 1961, and he fell out of a bass boat and drowned in a still pond two years later. One might wonder why a man who couldn't swim would go fishing alone in a small boat without wearing a life preserver, and one might also wonder why a man as large and fluffy as Byrne hadn't been able to float in calm water until somebody could rescue him. But apparently he wasn't as buoyant as he appeared, which led to speculation among his kompatriots as to whether he might have had some colored ancestry. Personally, I speculated as to whether there might be more to Byrne's death than was readily apparent at first glance, but he died outside the city limits, which meant it wasn't my problem, and I didn't like him enough to make it my problem, so if the former chief of detectives fell victim to foul play, the crime went unnoticed and unsolved.

Henry McCloskey had a successful and much-admired career in the district attorney's office until 1962, when an anticorruption task force found evidence that he had taken a cash bribe in order to drop charges arising out of an incident in which a prominent and successful local drunk ran a red light and T-boned a Chevrolet, killing two people. Henry was suspended without pay pending the results of the investigation, and he decided to use his time off to undertake a little home improvement project, which involved putting a shotgun in his mouth and redecorating his garage.

And the head of the anticorruption task force just might have been a certain Jew detective! We had a good time at that crime scene. The cause of death was pretty clearly nonsuspicious, so I brought over some beers for my team, and we watched the crew from the coroner's office clean up the mess. The recoil from the shotgun blast knocked all of McCloskey's rotten, shitty teeth out, and one of the coroner's technicians had to crawl around on the floor with a pair of tweezers, looking for them. He told me that the teeth smelled a lot worse than the brains.

I took Brian to McCloskey's funeral. He was ten years old. We sat in the back of the chapel at the funeral home, behind a capacity crowd of weeping, grieving anti-Semites, and I said to my boy, "Look around, at what your daddy did." I had never been so proud.

"Who are those guys?" he asked, pointing toward a cluster of good ol' boys who were glowering in our direction.

"Klan, I reckon," I told him. "But I know just what to do about them."

And we skipped the eulogy and went out to the parking lot, where Brian helped me examine all the cars and write all the license plate numbers into my notebook. We rejoined the funeral in time to watch McCloskey go into the ground, and later on I pulled the DMV records for all of the attendees and made a special project of Henry's Klan buddies, looking into their affairs and seeing if they had skeletons in their closets. I put two of them in prison for wife-beating, which a white man could usually get away with in those days, unless he drew the ire of a mean-spirited kike with a badge and some time to kill. I referred a third to federal agents who ultimately charged him with financial fraud and tax evasion.

A fourth Klansman, a stout middle-aged shitkicker by the name of Gerald Hart, got mighty peeved at me when I was executing a search warrant on his house, on account of my own ethnic persuasion and the fact that I was assisted in tossing his domicile by several colored officers hand-selected for this particular task. Hart had a bulbous nose as cracked and florid as the back of his neck, and his whole face flushed to match it as I directed the boys to start cutting up his furniture with big hunting knives to see if anything was concealed inside. The warrant was for illegal weapons, so we weren't particularly surprised when Hart stormed into a back room and came out of it brandishing a snub-nosed revolver. I had the distinct pleasure of putting four rounds into his chest in a nice tight grouping. It turned out he was a Grand Dragon in the Knights of the Ku Klux Klan. To think, I killed me a Dragon! How many people can say that? And it wasn't just a regular Dragon! I killed a Grand Dragon!

Indeed, the '60s were a decade of progress, with folks like me on the way up and folks like my erstwhile persecutors on the way out. And so, in the later years of my career, despite being descended from a duplicitous race, I was afforded most of the respect owed to a white man by my peers in the department, who had come to admire my careful eye, my preternatural intuition, and my verve for busting skulls. That meant I didn't have to be the one sent to deal with houses that smelled like they might have dead bodies in them.

But this biology class smell didn't signify an ordinary unattended death. Accidental deaths and heart attacks and suicides didn't smell like that. The normal process of decomposition happens when bacteria get into the tissue of a body that is no longer protected by a functioning immune system. The germs that live in the gut and aid digestion while the host is alive multiply out of control and begin liquefying the organs, and the sweet, fermented smell of death comes from those little guys doing their work.

The smell the officers described, however, was the smell of flesh disintegrating in some solution corrosive enough to kill off the bacteria. Unless somebody tripped and fell into a vat of acid, that's something you only smelled when someone was trying to clean up a very bad mess. I explained this in my affidavit to the magistrate, informed Captain Heller that I was planning to search the Alton Avenue residence, and messengered the documents over for my warrant.

An hour later, I was supervising an officer as he broke the locks off the front door with a prybar. Once we got inside, the stink was damn near overpowering. Even with my nose and mouth covered with a handkerchief, the noxious air made my eyes water.

In the kitchen, we found a woman's body in a large plastic tub, not quite covered with a cloudy chemical solution. Her skin was in the process of liquefying and melting off the body, revealing fibrous stretches of exposed muscle tissue and blobby yellow mounds of subcutaneous fat.

I stepped outside the house to await the coroner and took a look around. This South Memphis neighborhood had been mostly white and middle class after the war, but it had begun to turn when the schools were integrated and the whites started fleeing to the outer-ring suburbs. Evelyn Duhrer had been one of the few remaining white holdouts. Maybe sticking around hadn't been such a good idea. This wasn't one of the more dangerous places in the city, but it certainly wasn't as nice as it used to be. Then again, neither was I.

I looked up and down the street. Most of the houses had well-tended lawns and flower beds, but a few were overgrown. John Clifton, the neighbor who had reported the smell, was standing at the edge of his yard next door. I waved him over.

"What did you find in there?" he asked. He was a black man, maybe six feet tall, with a short Afro-style haircut and a mustache. He looked a little bit like my son's favorite foulmouthed comedian.

"What do you think I found in there?" I replied.

He scratched his chin. "Well, we hadn't seen Mrs. Duhrer in a while, and then the house started stinking. Over the next few days, the smell kept on getting worse. I don't suppose the news is good."

"I suppose whether you consider the news is good depends on how much you liked Mrs. Duhrer," I told him. "We found her in a big bucket of acid, about halfway melted."

Clifton clapped his left hand over his mouth and put his right on his knee as he doubled over. I thought his reaction seemed overly dramatic, but when he looked up, he had tears in his eyes. "I consider that bad news indeed, Detective," he said. "Mrs. Duhrer was a very kind woman."

"You know anyone who'd wish her ill?" I asked.

Clifton blinked dumbly. "You mean, you think she was murdered?" he asked.

I considered whether I was far enough away from the house for it to be safe to ignite a flame. I thought it probably was, but I stepped around to the other side of Clifton, to make sure he'd go up with me if I was wrong. Then I reached into my pocket for my cigarettes, but came out with a big double-pack of Juicy Fruit.

I'd quit cold turkey eighteen months previous, after forty years of steady smoking. Brian had been on me about the Luckys ever since he'd started hearing lectures about the dangers of tar and nicotine in his health class at school. When he'd graduated from Knoxville, I asked him what he wanted for a gift. I was ready to buy him a car. He told me all he wanted was for me to give up cigarettes. I told him to go jump in a lake.

But the more I'd thought about it, the more it made sense. I'd always dismissed the dangers of smoking because, between the war and police work, I had always figured something else would do me in before the cigarettes burned my lungs up. But I'd been taking things a little easier on the job as I neared retirement age, and soon I'd be taking my pension. Smoking was just about the most dangerous thing I was still doing. It made sense to give it up, so I could get the most out of my golden years.

But the smokes were like a phantom limb. I was always itching for them, patting my pockets for the lighter I'd stopped carrying. I felt awkward when I wanted to offer someone a cigarette and I didn't have one. Sometimes, in conversations, I found myself unsure of what to do with my hands. And when I reflexively reached for my cigarettes and found chewing gum instead, there was always a momentary shock of confusion and disappointment.

The air stank, and I wanted to smoke. I thought about trying to bum one off of Clifton, but instead I opted to stuff two sticks of gum into my mouth.

Then, I said, "I don't reckon she dunked herself into that bucket of chemicals."

"I see," said Clifton. This wasn't actually an unusual response. Most people didn't know what to say when I told them there had been a murder. "I can't imagine why anyone would want to harm her. She was a very kind woman."

"Do you know if she had anything of value in the house that somebody might want to steal?" I asked.

Clifton shook his head. "She could not have had much. She told us she was left in a tough spot after her husband passed. That's why she took in the tenant."

"The tenant?" I asked. "Somebody else is living in there?"

"Yes, a man rents rooms on the second floor. Mrs. Duhrer figured she might as well rent out the second story since she doesn't go upstairs very well anymore. Or didn't, I guess."

"When was the last time you saw the tenant?"

"Day before yesterday, maybe?"

"He was in there after you noticed the smell?"

"I think so. But it wasn't as bad as it is now."

That didn't matter. The smell wouldn't have been there at all while the victim was still alive. "You know this fellow's name?" I asked.

"Yessir," he said. "It's March. Chester March."

20

In twenty years with the detectives' bureau, I had busted hundreds of killers and thieves and forgotten most of their names. But I remembered Chester March. I remembered the way he'd acted like he was better than me, and I remembered the way McCloskey had let him skate, because, as far as the brass was concerned, March actually was better than me.

And I remember that I caught him, that I had a solid eyewitness who had picked him from a lineup with certainty and accurately described his car. And that he'd gotten off anyway, because my work wasn't trusted. And now here was Chester, twenty years later, still killing women.

"Describe Chester March to me," I said to Clifton.

"He's a white man, in his fifties. Close-cropped hair. Receding hairline. Funny sort of nose, a little bit bent, like he broke it real bad and then somebody tried to fix it." That sounded like my old friend.

"How long has he been staying here?"

"Maybe three months? I think he mentioned once that he'd come back from California."

"You're sure you saw him go into the house the day after you first smelled chemicals coming from in there?" It would have taken at least a few days of the body marinating in that sludge before enough of it would be floating around in the air for people to smell it from outside. That meant Chester was in the house for days while the dead woman was dissolving in the kitchen.

"Yessir," Clifton said.

"And when was the last time you saw Mrs. Duhrer?" I asked.

"Two, maybe three days before I last saw Mr. March."

I wanted to have a talk with Chester, but if he was already on the run, it was going to be hard to find him. If he had any sense, he had already blown town, and if he had, he was out of my reach. All I'd be able to do was get a warrant sworn for his arrest and send it to the Tennessee Highway Patrol and maybe notify authorities in Jackson, Little Rock, St. Louis, and Nashville, in case he popped up in one of those places. But I was going to do my best to throw out the nets, on the slim chance he might still be in Memphis.

I pointed at the dull-gray import parked in the victim's carport. "Is that Mrs. Duhrer's car?"

"Yes, it is."

"When was the last time you were aware of this car being moved?"

He shrugged. "I wasn't really paying attention, but probably the last day I saw Mrs. Duhrer."

"Does Mr. March have a car?"

"Yeah. He drives an old Chevy."

"How old?"

Another shrug. "I don't know a lot about cars. Maybe ten years?"

"Two doors or four?"

"Two." That would make it a third- or fourth-generation Impala. Fast car, if he'd taken good care of it. He'd seemed careless, last I'd seen him, but that was a long time ago.

"Hardtop or convertible?"

"Hardtop."

"What color was it?"

"Metallic blue."

I could put an all-points bulletin out on the car. That was a long shot. The four door was more popular than the coupe, and the car's age and color might stand out. But most likely, if I put an APB on a blue Chevy Impala, the officers would just laugh at me and ignore it. There were an awful lot of blue Chevys on the road, and nobody had time to stop them all.

"Did you happen to see the license plate?" I asked. I offered him my pack of gum. He took a piece, but gave me an odd look. Giving people gum felt weird. I missed my cigarettes.

"There's no way I'd remember the number," Clifton told me.

"That's all right," I said. "Do you happen to recall if the car had Tennessee plates?" If I knew the car was registered in Tennessee, I could pull all the records for cars matching its description, and that could get me the number or, if the car was

registered to a known associate, a lead on who might be shelter-
ing him.

"I'm sorry," Clifton said. "I didn't pay attention to that."

So the car was probably a dead end.

"Did March have any friends? Did you ever notice anyone
coming to visit him?"

Clifton shook his head. "Nobody ever came to see him here,
but he said he had some rich relatives. He seemed bitter that they
weren't doing more for him."

I nodded. "If he were in trouble, do you have any idea where
he'd go, or who he might turn to for help?"

Clifton showed me his empty palms. "I'm sorry. I really didn't
know him very well."

That seemed reasonable. I thanked Clifton, gave him my card
in case he remembered anything else, and returned to the house.
While I'd been talking to Clifton, Dr. Engels, the medical examiner, had arrived with an ambulance to take away the body. I
found him inside the house standing over the tub, looking at the
corpse. He turned toward me as I approached, and I saw that he
was wearing goggles and a surgical mask. I wondered how safe it
was to breathe the air in the house if the coroner was taking such
precautions. I figured it was probably okay, as long as I didn't stay
inside for too long. Engels was a wimp.

"This is a troublesome situation," he said. "I don't know how
to get her out of there. This corpse has roughly the consistency
of a Jell-O mold. Even the bones have softened. I am afraid if
we attempt to lift her out of the solution, the cadaver will burst.
What I would like to do is puncture the bottom of the tub, drain
off the liquid, and then cut the side off the vessel so we can slide

her onto a gurney. But we can't dispose of this fluid here. It needs to be strained, and any solids that are suspended in it need to be examined during autopsy," he said.

"Sounds like a fun evening you've got planned," I said. I offered Engels my pack of gum. He held up his hands, which were sheathed in thick, elbow-length rubber gloves. The gloves were covered in corrosive Evelyn Duhrer soup. He sighed in a way that let me know he thought I was the dumbest idiot who ever lived. I wanted very badly to blow a cloud of smoke in his face, but I didn't have any goddamn cigarettes.

"Maybe we should get a lid for the tub, and transport the entire thing, with the corpse inside it, and then figure out how to drain the fluid and remove the body once we get her to the morgue. But God help us if we spill any of that liquid during transport. If any of that comes in contact with somebody's bare skin, the chemical burns will be horrific. And if the body is damaged, it will be more difficult to identify wounds inflicted by the killer. This is troubling."

That possibility troubled me as well. In cases where coroners had failed to distinguish between fatal injuries and postmortem damage to a body, criminal defense lawyers sometimes pursued a strategy of admitting that their client had tried to dispose of the body, but denied that a murder had occurred, claiming that the defendant panicked and tried to get rid of the evidence after the victim suffered a natural or accidental death. And juries had sometimes believed them.

"I'm sure you'll figure it out," I said. "Do you know what kind of chemicals he put her in?"

"It's sulfuric acid," Engels told me. He waved a paper pH testing strip in front of my face, in case I needed further proof. The end of it was charred, and it smelled terrible. I pushed his arm away.

"I'll take your word for it," I said. I'd have to check the file, but I was pretty sure that I'd found sulfuric acid in Chester's garage twenty years earlier.

"It's the same stuff they use to unclog drains," he said.

"Drain opener will dissolve a human body?" I asked.

Engels waved a soiled glove in front of my face. "Drain opener isn't quite this concentrated. But yes. Drains get clogged with organic materials. Hair, soap, food waste. Drain cleaner dissolves organic materials. People are also made of organic materials. Acid will dissolve people. But you need at least forty gallons to liquefy a body. There's only maybe twelve to fifteen gallons in here. This killer is clearly an imbecile. If he'd done this right, he would have dissolved the body completely in about seventy-two hours. Since he didn't, I have to devise a way to transport these delicate remains and perform what will be an unpleasant autopsy."

"When I catch him, I'll ask him to consult with you on body-disposal techniques before he kills again," I promised. "What can you tell me about the body?"

Engels bent over the tub. "Preliminary examination suggests the victim was killed by beating and strangulation. I'll figure out which of these wounds killed her and which are postmortem burns when I perform the full autopsy."

"I'll let you work, then," I said. I figured I'd breathed enough fumes for the moment. I took a short detour outside to gulp some fresh air—or fresher air at least. The stink hung over the yard and was noticeable all the way down the block. When I thought

I could stand to go back in there, I returned to search the house. I checked all the floors and walls for blood, but didn't find any. Under normal circumstances, I might be able to identify an area where bloodstains had been cleaned by the smell of bleach or ammonia, but even if March had performed a cleanup here, it was impossible to smell anything but the dissolving body.

However, I noticed an oddity in the great room: Next to the fireplace, there was a shovel and a pair of tongs, but no poker. There was an empty peg to hang an extra implement on the rack for the fireplace set, which meant something was missing. Happy for an excuse to leave the house, I went outside and searched the yard. I found a spot in the flower bed where the soil appeared to have recently been turned. I photographed it and then dug it up and found the poker, visibly stained with blood. I took more pictures to document the location of this discovery and then had this likely murder weapon bagged for further forensic testing. This substantially assuaged my fear that March might try to deny he had committed murder and claim that his decision to place a woman's body in a tub of acid was the result of some misunderstanding.

The rest of my search of the house was less productive. Chester had removed every sign of his habitation before he fled. And I still had no idea how to find him.

TRANSCRIPT: AMERICAN JUSTICE

CHESTER MARCH: I want to be clear, I didn't kill that woman. I had, admittedly, been involved in a dispute with her over rent. I was past due to pay her, and I was living in her house. I needed my cousins to give me some money so I could cover my debt, but they were recalcitrant. She floated me for a couple of weeks, but then she started to get frustrated.

When I was out of the house, she decided to rifle my things looking for money or valuables, so she climbed the stairs to try to search my room. Unfortunately, the reason she was renting out the second floor of her house in the first place was that she wasn't getting around so well. She must have fallen on the way back down. And that's how I found her when I returned to the house. Stone cold, crumpled on the floor at the bottom of the staircase.

Surely you can understand my panic at finding her this way. Given my history with the local authorities, I was terrified to report the accident and so I decided to try to get rid of the body. I can admit that what I did was wrong. Desecration of a corpse is a crime. But it is not a crime that carries the death penalty, and it is not a crime I should have spent thirty-five years in solitary over.

CARLOS WATKINS (NARRATION): I want to believe Chester when he tells me he's innocent. I want to believe that the charming old man who tells me funny stories about things that happen in prison is really a victim of systemic abuses. But is he lying to me? And am I broadcasting his lies on the radio? After my encounter with William Schatz aired, a lot of you e-mailed to reiterate your support for this program and to tell me you thought that the way he treated me was racist and way out of line. But was he right about Chester? Am I being manipulated by a psychopath?

I decided to talk to Professor Heffernan about my concerns.

CARLOS WATKINS: Have you been listening to *American Justice*?

ED HEFFERNAN: Yes, I heard all about your euphoric visit to Interstate Bar-B-Que in Memphis.

WATKINS: (LAUGHTER) I'm sorry about that, Professor.

HEFFERNAN: I forgive you, Carlos. That experience is part of my larger point, you see, that these unethical systems are so deeply embedded in our society that they're almost unavoidable. You're right that it's hard not to eat barbecue in Memphis! Living by ethical principles is difficult, and systemic factors will constantly undermine your attempts to do so. But when you get back to Nashville, I can recommend some excellent vegan restaurants.

WATKINS: I wanted to ask what you thought of my encounter with William Schatz.

HEFFERNAN: That must have been a very difficult experience for you.

WATKINS: But was he right? Is Chester lying to me?

HEFFERNAN: There is an organization called the Innocence Project—actually an affiliated group of organizations called the Innocence Network—that works to exonerate the wrongfully convicted using new or overlooked forensic evidence. I admire their work and support their goal, but my project is a different one. We discussed this distinction when you first asked if you could cover my appeals on behalf of Chester March, and I believe you understand it, because I have heard you talk about it on *American Justice*.

WATKINS: Right. This isn't about what Chester did. It's about what has been done to him.

HEFFERNAN: It's about what has been done to him and about the horrible thing that will be done to him if our appeals are unsuccessful. Chester is about to be murdered by the state of Tennessee. He is terrified, and he is desperate. Will a person in his predicament lie? Will they equivocate? Will they manipulate? Of course they will.

I have no doubt that my clients often lie to me. They have been mistreated and abused their whole lives, and they don't know how to trust or how to be trustworthy. The criminal defense lawyers who are trying to help them look and talk just like the prosecutors who are trying to put them away. They don't feel safe. They aren't safe. And so they try to defend themselves as best they can. And sometimes their defensiveness can seem incriminating or confusing or counterproductive because they don't know how to act in these contexts. But they can't help themselves, any more than you could help yourself at the barbecue restaurant, because they are operating within systems.

The only lawyers who get to represent exclusively innocent clients are Ally McBeal and Daredevil. Those of us who practice in the real world know that being a criminal defense lawyer means standing on the side of people who may have done bad things. And people who may have done bad things need and deserve to be protected from the excesses of powerful and often brutal systems.

It's my view that the process that convicted Chester March was irreparably flawed and insufficient to resolve the question of his guilt or innocence. So when you air his claims and his narrative, that's just his side of the story, and obviously those facts are disputed by Detective Schatz, and by Schatz's grandson and by the state. And, at this late date, it is difficult or impossible to figure out which set of facts is true. But considering that Chester March was denied a fair trial, I don't think airing his narrative is the wrong thing to do, even if his version of the facts is unconfirmed.

But I do not need to know whether Chester March is innocent to know that he should not be killed by lethal injection. An eighty-year-old man shouldn't be injected with drugs when we don't understand how those drugs will interact with his physiology. Nobody should be given a lethal injection when we don't know whether death from potassium poisoning is torturous. That's what I'm fighting for.

WATKINS (NARRATION): I agree with everything Heffernan said, but here's what I find disquieting: William Schatz said that if I asked Heffernan whether he thought Chester was innocent, Heffernan would avoid giving me a straight answer by pivoting from the question of Chester's guilt back to generalized objections to capital punishment.

And that's exactly what he did.

21

checked local DMV records for a car fitting the description of the Chevrolet Impala that Clifton had described. There was no such car registered in Chester's name in the state of Tennessee. I phoned in a request for records from San Francisco, to see if he had registered one in California. That was a pointless formality; it would take days at least, and probably weeks, for someone to get back to me with the license number, and by then, it would be too late to use any information they provided. If I didn't catch him soon, he would leave town. And they'd only be able to give me a license number if Chester had registered the car in his own name in California. It was possible he'd bought the car from somebody and it still had that person's plates on it.

I could contact every person in Memphis who had registered a car matching the description Clifton had given me and find out if any of them might have sold a car to Chester, but, once again, doing that would take a lot of precious time, and the effort would only bear fruit if Chester had bought the car from someone local.

Getting the license number would mean that the all-points bulletin would be more likely to flush him out, but every way I knew to try to find it was uncertain to do anything except occupy my time. I decided to hope somebody would spot the car without the plate number while I pursued other options. I had dispatch radio the APB out for a '60s-vintage metallic blue two-door Chevy Impala, possibly with California plates. I didn't have much faith that I'd catch him this way. There were too many blue Chevys for officers to pay attention to.

The best lead I had was Chester's relatives. Clifton said Chester mentioned visiting family. Chester had two first cousins, brothers named Forrest and Lee. Maybe they'd know how to find him. They operated a business concern in downtown Memphis called March Mercantile Partners. I called down there, and a secretary told me that Forrest March was available to speak with me.

March Mercantile had a medium-size suite on a high floor of a downtown skyscraper, with views overlooking the river. Forrest March's secretary met me at the elevator. She was a pretty white girl in her mid-twenties. She told me her name, and I immediately forgot it.

I took a look around the place. It seemed prosperous. I counted eight office doors around the perimeter of a central bullpen where a dozen secretaries and clerks were occupied doing what were, as far as I could tell, legitimate business activities.

The secretary escorted me toward Forrest's corner office and asked me if I needed coffee. I declined. She knocked on his door, and told him that a policeman had arrived. Without waiting for him to invite me in, I pushed past her.

His space was large, and everything in it looked expensive. Two of the walls were floor-to-ceiling picture windows, a third was lined with bookshelves containing a full set of World Book encyclopedias that had never had their spines cracked but seemed to have been frequently dusted. The fourth wall contained a fireplace, which was a gratuitous thing to have in a centrally heated office. It was clearly a gas-burning fireplace with fake logs, since there was no chimney, but its mere presence communicated that this was a man who had accumulated so much wealth that he had run out of non-absurd things to spend it on.

Forrest March was not a man to bother with pleasantries or formalities. He looked me over as if he was appraising me, and then he asked, "How much?"

"I beg your pardon?" I replied. If Forrest March thought he could buy me, he'd better have been prepared to pay a hell of a lot more than it cost to put a fireplace in a thirtieth-floor office.

He lit a cigar. I wanted one, too, but he didn't offer to share. I stuffed two sticks of Juicy Fruit into my cheek, instead. "You're here about my cousin Chester, right?" he said. "Well, what's the damage? What will it take to make this go away?"

"Sir, are you trying to bribe me?" I asked.

His eyes narrowed. "Are you not a deputy from the sheriff's office?"

"I am a detective from the Memphis Police Department."

"And you're looking to collect on a debt my cousin owes, or a judgment or something. I'll square it for him, if it's a reasonable amount. How much do you need?"

I chewed my gum, and I took the measure of Forrest March. He was a few years younger than me, maybe late forties, with his hair combed back from his receding hairline and held in place with something that made it look wet. He was heavyset and jowly, but in a way that seemed formidable rather than sloppy. He wore a three-piece suit, expensively tailored. He had his jacket and his vest on, even though he was sitting at his desk, and I did not get the impression that he'd donned the garments for my benefit; rather, he struck me as the sort who would wear his jacket all day.

I remembered Chester's imperious, emotionless gaze. Forrest wasn't as cool; he was sizing me up. Even though he was clearly making every effort to exude power, there was a nervousness to him. Chester had presented himself as a Southern dandy, and Forrest was presenting himself as a successful businessman, but in both cases, the appearance was affected. Forrest and Chester March were nothing but white Delta trash who had got their hands on some money and were putting on airs. The only difference was that Forrest was afraid of being exposed, and Chester wasn't, because Chester was a psychopath.

I decided to treat Forrest like the important man he wanted to be—at least at first. If I needed to scare him, I could let my mask drop and show him that I could see what he really was. And if push came to shove, I would show him what I really was.

"I think you may have misunderstood me, sir," I said. "I'm not here after money. I need to speak to Chester. Can you tell me where to find him?"

Forrest tapped his cigar against the side of a large stone ashtray on his desk. His hand shook a little. He was nervous. "I'm sorry. He came in here a couple of weeks ago, telling me he needed money to pay his rent. I thought maybe you were here about that."

"I'm not," I said. "Not exactly. It's just important that I find Chester and talk to him, so I can straighten things out."

"It was clear he was in trouble, but I didn't know what kind of trouble he was in. He's had a history with alcohol. Maybe with drugs. We thought it was gambling, or maybe a woman. I'm a charitable Christian, but giving a man the means to further indulge his vices is like giving him rope to hang himself with, so we turned him away. He inherited a lot of money from his father, and Lee and I have no idea what happened to that."

Either Forrest didn't know where Chester was, or he didn't want to tell me. Maybe he knew exactly who I was and what I'd done to his cousin. Maybe he didn't know anything at all. I needed to figure him out before I decided if I needed to squeeze him. I slid into one of the heavy leather chairs opposite his desk. The chairs were big, and the desk was big, and the office was big. But this guy wasn't big enough to be safe from me. "Why don't you tell me what you know about Chester, and what he's been up to," I suggested.

Forrest shrugged. "Not much to tell, really. We hadn't seen him in years before he showed up a couple of months ago. His father was our father's brother, but those two didn't really get along. The family business in my grandfather's day was growing cotton on our farmland and selling it to textile producers up North. My father and my uncle inherited the company, but they could never agree on how to run it. My uncle thought our fortune was tied to the land. We'd made our living from the Mississippi soil for generations, and he felt there was value in preserving that legacy. My old man didn't want to be a farmer. To him, cotton was a commodity, and the money was to be made in shipping and selling the product, which we could import from India and China. Even after you factor in the cost of moving it across the ocean, their cotton is cheaper than ours, and the quality is indistinguishable. We haven't been able to match their labor costs for the last hundred years, if you take my meaning."

"Yeah, I follow you," I said. "You used to be allowed to own black people, and now you can't anymore, and that's been a challenge for your business."

He frowned. Apparently, he disapproved of my phrasing. "Not a challenge. A change. And an opportunity. Domestic cotton costs more than Chinese or Indian cotton, so there's no reason to be in the business of producing domestic cotton, and no need for capital investment in land or machinery or an agricultural workforce. My uncle never saw things that way, though. He had a romantic attachment to the land, so he and my father eventually split the business. My uncle took the farmland, and my dad took over shipping and sales. They both prospered, I suppose, but they were glad to be rid of each other. Lee and I were boys when that happened, and we rarely saw that side of the family after the schism."

"And what about Chester?" I asked.

"Well, that's the point," Forrest said. "He was on that side of the family, and we rarely saw him. He married a woman around 1950. Strong-willed, that one. She abandoned my cousin and ran off with another man. I think Chester took to drinking after she left. He was in a car accident, and he got hurt pretty bad. Lee and

I would have gone to see him in the hospital, but our uncle had taken charge of the situation, and he made it clear that Chester didn't want visitors. We didn't think this was terribly unusual. Like I said, we hadn't been close since we were kids. I didn't even go to Chester's wedding."

"Were you in Korea?" I asked.

"No," he said. "You could get a deferment if you were a newlywed, so I got hitched to stay out of the draft."

"I see."

"Anyway, after Chester's accident, his father sent him to someplace in the desert to recuperate and to dry out, and he stayed out West after that. When my uncle died, Chester sold off the agricultural properties, which Lee and I thought was a smart move. No future in farming cotton in Mississippi. I don't know what he did with the proceeds of that sale or why he is broke now. Like I said, I am not close with my cousin. And the reason I'm telling you all this is to make it clear that the business Chester inherited hadn't been connected to March Mercantile for decades, since my father and my uncle split up their concern. This belongs to me and to my brother. Chester doesn't own any of it, and neither Lee nor I nor this business entity in which Lee and I are partners bears responsibility for any of his liabilities. We can involve lawyers if we have to, but I hope you'll take my word that there's no money for you here, excepting any sums I may willingly give over in the spirit of Christian generosity."

I reached into my mouth with my thumb and forefinger, and pulled out my big, sticky wad of chewing gum. Then, while maintaining eye contact with Forrest March, I leaned forward so that the red leather upholstery of my chair squeaked beneath me, and I stuck the gum to the underside of his antique desk. "Mr. March, I am a police detective," I said. "I am not looking for money. I am not collecting a debt. I need to find Chester and talk to him. All I need from you is any information you have pertaining to his whereabouts." I leaned back in the chair, unwrapped two fresh sticks of Juicy Fruit, and began chewing them loudly, with my mouth open. I rolled the foil wrappers into little balls, and I threw them on the floor.

"We didn't give him the money he asked for," Forrest said. "I don't know where he is."

"How about Lee? Can I talk to him?"

Forrest shook his head. "He's not in the office. I haven't seen him today. And if that concludes our business, I think you had better go."

I was not ready to leave, however. Forrest and Lee were my only leads on Chester, and I was convinced Forrest knew something. I decided to tell him some things and see how he'd respond. "Chester's wife didn't run off twenty years ago. She vanished. She left her car, her luggage, and all her clothes and jewelry. Her family never heard from her again. Did you know that?"

His jaw dropped open, and he set the lit cigar directly on his desk blotter. "All we knew about that was what my uncle told the family. That she had left, and that he had been in an accident, and that he was going someplace to dry out."

"He didn't get in a drunk-driving accident," I said. "He wrecked his car trying to flee arrest for murder. I was the one chasing him. Your uncle bribed a prosecutor to get the charges dropped. Then your uncle sent Chester to California to prevent these scandals from embarrassing your family. I am here now because we found a woman's corpse dissolving in a tub of acid. Chester was renting a room in her house and is currently a suspect in her murder. And we don't know where he is. But I will find him, and I intend to send him to the electric chair. And, if you are covering for him, you're an accessory after the fact. It will be my sincere pleasure to see you go to prison, Mr. March."

The blotter paper was starting to smolder. I really wanted to see how Forrest would react when his desk caught on fire, but it seemed like he might be about to tell me something, and I didn't want to give him a break that would allow him to think better of it, so I grabbed the cigar and deposited it in the ashtray, and then I pounded my fist a couple of times on the spot where it had been resting, to smother any embers.

Chester looked at the burned spot on the blotter, and then he looked up at me. "I had no idea about any of this," he said. "I am not protecting Chester. He has been here several times in the last six weeks, asking for money. My secretary may be able to give you the exact dates of his visits. I offered to get him help and encouraged him to go to my church, but I wouldn't give him any cash. As far as I know, Lee hasn't given him anything either. If he comes here again, we will call you at once."

"I think he is on the run now," I said. "I think he murdered the landlady because she was trying to evict him and he wanted to stay in her house. But he had nowhere to dispose of her body, and the smell of it drove him out. He has to know she's been found by now. He has to know that we're after him. I need to know where he'd hide out. Who might help him if he were in legal trouble? Does your family own a cabin or a lake house someplace where he might go?"

"Oh my God," Forrest said. He leapt up out of his chair, and I reflexively put a hand on my gun. I thought maybe he was about to make a break for it or something, but instead, he just started screaming, "Christine! Christine!"

The secretary who had greeted me at the door rushed into the office, eyes wide with real terror. "What do you need, Mr. March?"

"Send Amelia in here right away, and try to get Lee on the line," Forrest demanded.

"Of course," Christine said, and she raced back out of the office.

Forrest leaned forward and put his hands flat on his charred blotter. He was breathing fast and ragged. I decided not to say anything.

A second girl, younger, prettier, and whiter than the first one, scurried into Forrest's office.

"When was the last time you saw Lee?" Forrest demanded.

"Yesterday," Amelia said. I gathered she was Lee's secretary.

"Did he have any plans last night? Is he entertaining any clients?" Forrest asked.

"I don't know. He didn't mention anything."

"Did he tell you he wasn't going to be in today?"

"He didn't say anything."

Christine appeared in the doorway. "There's no answer at Lee's house."

"Detective Schatz," Forrest said, "Lee split up with his wife last year, and he lives alone. If Chester was desperate and in need of money and he was willing to use force to get it, he would go after Lee."

"All right," I said. "Let's go find your brother."

22

Forrest was able to reach his wife by phone, as well as Lee's ex-wife. Neither of them had seen anything unusual, but we didn't know what Chester might do next, so I called for units to watch both of their houses and to pull Forrest's daughter out of school and take her home. No sense taking chances with a psycho on the loose. Forrest and I would go check on Lee.

Forrest's hands were visibly shaking as we rode the elevator down to the parking garage, so I offered him a lift to his brother's house.

"Is this a police car?" he asked when he climbed into my vehicle.

"It is when I'm driving it," I said.

The car I drove during the final years of my career as a Memphis detective was a 1970 Dodge Challenger. I had been in the habit of replacing my car every three years or so since I'd come back from the war; I figured life was too short to spend driving a shitty car. But I'd hung on to the Challenger because, in the 1970s, cars stopped getting better. Everything stopped getting better.

Beginning with the 1964 Ford Mustang, American automakers had been competing to make the most powerful two-door sports cars. The Challenger line was designed to match up against the Mustang, the Chevy Camaro, the Pontiac Firebird, and the Mercury Cougar, and in 1970, it kicked the shit out of all of them. Mine was the Road/Track model with the 440 Six Pack engine and a four-speed manual transmission with a pistol-grip shifter. It displaced 7.2 liters and was rated at 390 horsepower. The speedometer went to 150, but if you had a clear stretch of road and a reasonable tolerance for danger, the beast under the hood could bury the needle without much effort.

But the 1970 Dodge Challenger was also the last of a dying breed. Detroit started sacrificing performance for fuel efficiency as early as 1971, and when the price of oil quadrupled during the 1973 gas crisis, automakers quit building powerful gas-guzzlers like the Challenger, which only got about ten miles to the gallon on the street, and replaced them with fuel-sipping compact cars. New emissions standards and environmental regulations guaranteed that, even when gas prices returned to sane levels, the days of the great American muscle car were over.

It did not seem like a good time to explain this to Forrest March, however, who was in a state of near panic over his brother.

"It's nice," he said. "Real nice."

I put a flashing bubble light on the dash and got us to Lee's residence in the Central Gardens neighborhood as quickly as I could, though the Challenger's giant engine was of no particular benefit in midday traffic on city streets.

Forrest jumped out of the car and ran up the porch steps as soon as I pulled into the driveway, but when he reached the door, he hesitated.

"If he's in there—if something has happened—I don't want to be the one to find him," he said, when I walked up behind him.

"I understand," I said. "I'll try to make sure you don't have to see anything you don't want to see." I was feeling a lot more sympathetic toward this guy now that he was potentially a victim, and now that he was being helpful.

I rang the doorbell several times, and then I knocked loudly, even though I could hear the bell inside the house. There was no response.

"I have a key," Forrest said, and he unlocked the front door.

I drew my .357 from the holster in my armpit. "I'm police," I shouted into the darkened interior of the house. "Mr. March, your brother is here, and he has opened the door for me. I am coming in."

"What should I do?" Forrest asked.

"Step back, off the porch," I told him. "I'll let you know when I'm sure it's clear."

I flipped on the light next to the door and spent the next five minutes checking every room in the house and opening every closet in case there was a body or an assailant hidden in one of them. The house was empty.

The last place I looked was the attached garage. There was a late-model Cadillac Eldorado—a go-kart engine wrapped in luxury trim—parked inside. I stepped out onto the porch, where Forrest was pacing back and forth.

"There's no body," I said. "And no signs of a struggle."

"That's good news, right?" Forrest asked.

"Good news would be if he was here and he was fine. He is not here, and we still don't know where he is. Is the Cadillac in the garage your brother's car?"

"Yes," Forrest said.

"Does he have another one?"

"No."

"Well, it's here, and he's not. That gives me cause for concern."

"Oh God."

"But, like I said, there's no blood, there's no signs of forced entry. It looks like Chester took Lee someplace, but he took him alive. Chester is after money, as best we figure, so he won't kill Lee until he gets it. He hasn't got it already has he? There isn't a safe full of cash or valuables in this house, is there?"

"Not a safe. My brother has a Rolex and some other jewelry, and he kept a few hundred dollars in cash. Maybe a thousand. Nothing significant."

A thousand dollars and a handful of gold didn't sound insignificant to me, but it also didn't sound like enough to maintain the lifestyle to which Chester March was accustomed. He was looking for a bigger score. "Then we know where he's going."

"Where's he going?"

How could a man so rich be so dumb? "Wherever the money is," I told him. He nodded, but didn't say anything. I intuited that he was just pretending to know what was going on. "Where is your brother's money, Mr. March?"

"Oh. We do our banking at First Tennessee," he said. "The downtown branch."

Okay. This was information I could work with. I didn't know where Chester was, but I had an idea where he was going to be. I sent Forrest into the house to phone his banker and to find out if any withdrawals had already been made on Lee's accounts. I returned to my car and used my portable radio to call for units to stake out every First Tennessee bank in the city and to keep an eye out for Chester, Lee, or the metallic blue Impala.

I returned to the house to find Forrest on the phone. I took the receiver from him.

"This is Detective Lieutenant Buck Schatz. To whom am I speaking?"

"My name is Victor Burton. I am head teller on duty at First Tennessee," said the voice on the line.

"One of your clients, Lee March, is missing, and I have reason to believe he may have been abducted by someone who is trying to extort money from him. Can you tell if someone has made a withdrawal or cashed a check on one of Mr. March's accounts since yesterday afternoon?"

I waited while Burton consulted his ledgers, or whatever he used to keep track of account balances.

"Nobody has," Burton told me. "At least not for any significant amount."

"How sure are you of that?" I asked.

"We keep records of any transactions conducted from this location. If someone attempted to make a sizable withdrawal or cash a large check at one of our other branches, the teller there would call here first to verify that the account has the funds on deposit, and to notify us of the transaction. A teller might cash a small check and put the paperwork through a day or so later, but we would know about any transaction larger than around two hundred fifty dollars."

"Somebody may try to withdraw money from Lee March's personal accounts, or from the March Mercantile business account, or else cash a large check drawing down one of those accounts. This person might come into the branch with Lee March, or he might come in alone, pretending to be Lee March, in order to make this transaction. I need you to make sure that nobody can clean out those accounts, and I need to find that man. If he gets the money, he will kill Lee March and leave town. If he comes in, have your people try to delay him as long as possible and call the police. There will be officers nearby, prepared to assist. And warn the folks at your other branches. I will be there shortly."

I hung up the phone and headed back out the front door and down the walkway, toward my car. Forrest paused to lock up the house, and then he followed me.

"What are we going to do now?" he asked.

"We are going to wait here until units arrive to watch this house, and then I am going to take you back to your office. We'll have somebody there as well, in case Chester turns up again. At close of business, an officer will escort you home, and if Chester is still at large, we'll leave units outside your house overnight."

I slid into the driver's seat, and Forrest walked around to the passenger side. And then the radio crackled to life: "Officers in pursuit of a metallic blue Chevrolet Impala. California plates. Heading toward I-55 southbound."

"Get out of the car," I told Forrest.

"But—my brother," he said.

"I'll do what I can to get him back. But you aren't coming with me," I said. "It's not safe, and the extra weight slows the car down. Go back to your office, and I'll radio the officers there as soon as I have news."

He hesitated briefly, and then he stood up and closed the car door. I backed out of the driveway and headed for the on-ramp to I-240. I was ten minutes away from the pursuing officers, which meant the Challenger could catch up to them in six. Traffic was light, which was lucky. I upshifted, and the 440 engine bellowed. I was going to get this son of a bitch.

TRANSCRIPT: AMERICAN JUSTICE

CHESTER MARCH: The history of my family is a little bit complicated. If you talk to the prosecutors, they'll tell you that I kidnapped and tried to extort my cousin, but they won't tell you about what my uncle and my cousins did to my father and to me.

CARLOS WATKINS: Okay, I'm here to listen.

MARCH: My grandfather built a business on growing cotton and selling it to textile manufacturers. But, after the war, growing cotton in Mississippi wasn't as lucrative anymore, and selling imported cotton had become a booming trade. After my grandfather died, my uncle tricked my father into an unconscionable division of the family firm, which stuck my dad with the debt-saddled, underperforming agricultural properties, while my uncle's side of the business became a thriving shipping concern.

WATKINS: My understanding is that, when your father died, you liquidated his cotton-farming business for hundreds of thousands of dollars.

MARCH: A fraction of what my inheritance should have been. What you have to understand is that, in 1976, my cousins were very rich and I was destitute because my uncle conned my father out of my birthright. All I was trying to do was rebalance those scales. It was about justice. Do you understand that?

WATKINS: I think so.

MARCH: My cousin Forrest certainly did not. When I went in and explained to him that some of his money was actually my money, he asked me if I had a gambling problem, and if I needed to go to church with him. You wouldn't think someone could be so avaricious and so sanctimonious at the same time, but my cousins were sincerely bad people. When I went to my other cousin, Lee, I had to be a bit more persuasive.

WATKINS: You abducted him at gunpoint.

MARCH: Look, the key thing to understand is that they robbed me first. I didn't choose to be in a situation where I had to approach them, hat in hand, and beg for my supper. And I didn't choose to be in a situation where I had to force the issue. I'm the victim here. I had no choice but to stick a gun in Lee's face, because of what he and his brother and their father did to me. Maybe if my uncle hadn't betrayed him, my father would have lived longer. Maybe a lot of things would have been different. You think about that a lot, when you spend a few decades in a place like this. All the people who failed you or screwed you to cause you to end up here.

WATKINS: Let's talk about what happened when Buck Schatz entered the situation.

MARCH: I had Lee's identification and his bank ledgers. He had a checking account with a quarter million dollars in it. A checking account. In 1976. That doesn't even include his houses or his retirement account or his brokerage account or his stake in March Mercantile. He could have just given me that money, and he still would have been rich, and everything would have been fine.

But he wasn't willing to be reasonable, so, if I was going to get what I was owed, I was going to have to take it. I figured that he and I looked enough alike that I could pass his identification at an out-of-the-way bank branch and clean out the account from there. So, I wrote a check for the whole amount on deposit, I made him sign it, and I tried to cash it.

The tellers were suspicious of me immediately. One of them sidled away from his window and went into the back office, and I could tell he was going for a phone. The manager was giving me some rigmarole about how they didn't have that much cash on hand, and that I was going to have to wait for them to bring some more over from another location. I could tell that they were stalling me, and I suspected that Lee had already been missed. So I ran out the door. And, sure enough, I saw flashing lights in the rearview before I even got to the on-ramp for the interstate. If I'd stayed ninety seconds longer, they'd have cornered me in the bank. But I'd caught on to their ploy, I had a lead on them, and I was heading south on I-55 in a fast car. I was fifteen minutes from crossing the bridge into Mississippi, and the police cars were falling farther behind me. I knew the local cops wouldn't chase me across the state line, so I thought I was going to make it.

And then I heard this noise, a rumble at first, and then as it got closer, it became a roar, overwhelming the sound of the sirens. It was so loud I thought they must be chasing me with a helicopter, but then I checked the rearview, and I saw an unmarked Dodge with a flashing blue light on its dash. I was probably doing ninety, and he was closing distance on me like I was standing still. I don't know if someone your age has ever even seen a car like this. It was a sports car, but huge—something like fifteen feet long—to accommodate an enormous engine. It was hideous and impractical and dirty and noisy, and a car like that appeals to a particular kind of man.

And even though I couldn't see past the glare on the windshield, I knew who was behind the wheel.

When he pulled alongside me, his window was already rolled down, because he already knew what he was going to do. He gestured at me to let me know he wanted me to pull over, but I was so close to the bridge over the river. I floored the pedal; opened my old Impala all the way up. And I lurched out ahead of him. I was going so fast that I was wrestling the steering wheel just to keep the car going straight. It felt like any crack or bump in the road would set me spinning or flip my Chevy.

But the Dodge was so much more car than I was driving, and he pulled even with me again. And then he looked right at me, and he waved. He took his hand off the steering wheel doing a hundred and thirty miles per hour so he could wave at me, so he could let me know that all my efforts were futile, that Mississippi might as well be the moon as far as my hopes of ever getting there were concerned, and that I was living my last free moments. And then he had a gun in his hand, and he opened fire on me.

Have you ever been shot, Carlos?

WATKINS: No, Chester, I haven't. Why would you ask me that?

MARCH: I don't mean no offense by it. You'll have to excuse my manners. They've suffered a bit, on account of my situation here. Of course that's a strange thing to ask in polite society. I just forget that sometimes, because most of the folks I run into have caught one at one point or another, whether they're white or black or purple polka-dotted or whatever. Even the guards here are rough-living types, or they wouldn't be working in this godforsaken hellhole. And there have been wars going. A lot of people have been shot.

WATKINS: I went to Dartmouth, and I work for NPR. So, no, I have never been shot.

MARCH: All right then, let me tell you what it's like. You'd think it would hurt, but it doesn't. Not exactly—at least not at first. Your nerves don't know how to register that kind of trauma. You know how it hurts worse to stub your toe than it does if you cut yourself real bad with a sharp knife?

WATKINS: Yeah, that's more within my range of experience.

MARCH: Well, getting shot feels like getting punched by some-body wearing a boxing glove; you don't realize, right away, what has happened or how bad the damage is. Especially since adrena-line dulls the pain response. When you injure yourself a little bit, your body gives you a shock so you'll stop doing whatever dumb thing you're doing, but if you're hurt real bad, your body doesn't want to do anything that will keep you from trying to fight back or run away. It works that way because of evolution, or something.

I didn't even really think I'd been hit at first. Schatz fired three times, and I knew one had busted the windshield and one had hit the door. And I felt a pressure in the middle of my left biceps, but it didn't really hurt, so I didn't realize I had been shot until I noticed that my arm didn't work. I couldn't keep the car straight at that speed with just one hand, and I lost control of it.

WATKINS: He could have killed you.

MARCH: He was trying to kill me, or, leastaways, he didn't care whether I lived or died as long as I didn't get away. I wanted to sue him or open a personnel complaint or something over him shooting at me like that, but every lawyer I talked to said he was within his rights.

I lost control of the car, but I had the presence of mind to turn the wheel into the spin and pop the handbrake, or I probably would have died. The median was sort of a grassy ditch, and the car skidded in the dirt and then rolled over once. The windows shattered, and I was showered with broken glass, and the dash caved in some, so the steering wheel hit me pretty hard. I crawled out of the wreck just in time to see Schatz running at me. The way he moved was still sort of clumpy, but he was somehow pretty quick on his feet. He mule kicked me right in the stomach, and that took the wind out of me and knocked me flat on the ground.

WATKINS: What happened to your cousin Lee?

MARCH: He was in the trunk. I think he was pretty lucky. The front end of the car took most of the damage. He got banged around a little bit in there. Broke his arm and cracked a few ribs. But he recovered.

I'm not saying what I did to my cousin was right. If he were still around, I'd apologize. But my actions have to be looked at in context, you know? In the context of family history. In the context of my unfair situation. And, anyway, if I'd been convicted of kidnapping or robbery or corpse desecration or any of the stuff I did—the stuff I was forced to do by my circumstances—I would have been released long ago. I would not have been convicted of murder without the confession, and I would not have confessed if I hadn't been tortured. The reason I am still in prison, still in solitary, and facing execution is what Buck Schatz did to me in that interrogation room.

23

hester sat in a steel chair, in front of a steel table, in a window-less interrogation room. In the middle of the table, there was a large crystal ashtray with five or six spent butts in it. That wasn't supposed to be in here, but the last detective who had used the room must have left it. I wanted a cigarette so badly that the smell of the ashtray made me want to climb the goddamn walls.

Chester was shivering, even though the room wasn't cold. He was pretty messed up. I'd let the paramedics look him over and bandage the gunshot wound to his arm, but he needed a doctor to tape his cracked ribs and sew up the bullet hole. I wanted to question him first, though, while the events were still fresh and his emotions were still running high. I figured he probably wouldn't die as a result of a couple hours' delay in getting medical treatment, and if he did, well, that would be a real shame, and we'd all feel really bad about it.

Department policy by the mid-'70s was to have two detectives in the room whenever a suspect was being questioned. That way, the detectives could corroborate each other if the suspect tried to deny giving his statement at trial, or if he tried to claim he'd been mistreated. The second detective in the room with me and Chester was a guy named Morris Bentley. Bentley was in many ways my opposite: a tall, blond-haired patrician WASP with a gentle disposition.

Bentley wasn't somebody I'd want stepping on my toes during an investigation, but I had taken to calling on him when it was time to question a suspect, because we played off each other well in an interrogation room. I sometimes struggled to build rapport with criminals, particularly the ones I had beat up or shot while I was trying to arrest them. When he was in the room, I could snarl and bellow and stomp around, and the suspect would come to rely on Bentley to keep my rage in check, and Bentley could exploit that trust to extract a statement. Bentley, meanwhile, wasn't great at physical intimidation. He didn't like to get his hands dirty, and the suspects sensed that and perceived it as weakness. If Bentley had a suspect who needed to be slammed against the wall a few times, I could do that for him.

One example of how this worked: I'd wanted to keep Chester's arms shackled behind his back, which would have been extremely painful during his interrogation, but Bentley had prevailed on me to shackle them in front of him, so he could sign his *Miranda* waiver. I had to admit, that made sense.

But Bentley could be threatening as well. His face was the face of the system, and he could take on a cold, regal demeanor that reminded suspects that they were at the mercy of people who looked like him and would decide their fates without much empathy or compassion. The threat he posed was less immediate, but perhaps more chilling. Being in a room with him reminded suspects that they could be thrown away and forgotten.

The way we divided up the responsibilities was: He was the good cop when we were interrogating white suspects, who viewed him as a comforting authority figure who could keep the hotheaded, ethnic attack dog on its leash. I was the good cop when we were interrogating black suspects, who perceived me as a bleeding-heart Jew who might protect them from Bentley's dispassionate judgment. With Chester March, I was obviously the bad cop, and Bentley was a perfect good cop.

"You have the right to remain silent," Bentley told Chester. "Anything you say will be used against you. You have a right to an attorney. If you cannot afford an attorney, one will be provided for you. Do you understand your rights?"

"Yes," said Chester.

"If you would like to speak to an attorney, you can just let us know, and this conversation will end. But as soon as you do that, Detective Schatz is going to go write up the paperwork to charge you with capital murder."

"And you're welcome to go ahead and ask for your lawyer," I said. "We have you dead to rights. We found the bloody fireplace poker you beat Evelyn Duhrer to death with buried in the backyard. We recovered your fingerprints from the murder weapon. The neighbor, John Clifton, saw you entering the house several days after he could smell the stink of the dissolving body from the street. He has identified you from a photo lineup, and he accurately described your car. Your cousin Lee is also ready to talk about how you kidnapped him and tried to take his money. I am

ready to ship you off to death row, and I don't need to hear another goddamn word from you."

The Supreme Court had ruled that we had to inform a suspect
of his constitutional rights before interrogating him, but outside
of the court-mandated warning, we were not obligated to tell him
the truth about anything. In fact, we had not recovered any fingerprints from the fireplace poker. John Clifton, who was not a keen
observer, had failed to pick Chester's face out of a photo lineup of
white men, despite Chester's distinctive broken nose. And I had
not yet interviewed Lee; he was expected to recover, but he was
under sedation at the hospital. Lee was an actual person, unlike
Chester, who was a ball of shit with eyes and false teeth. So Lee's
medical needs took priority over my investigation.

That meant we actually did need Chester's statement. If he lawyered up without talking, the district attorney would look at our
evidence and offer him a plea deal for murder two, which carried
fifteen years to life with parole eligibility after ten. That wasn't good
enough. For what he'd done, Chester needed to ride the lightning.

"Detective Schatz," Chester said, "have you been waiting here
for me since last we met?"

He smiled at me. His teeth were flawless, undamaged in the
accident. The porcelain implants were harder than bone. I figured I could probably find something that would break them if I
really tried, though. Maybe a wrench.

"I should have shot you twenty years ago," I said.

"Well, you shot me today."

"I should have shot you in the head. Your daddy's gone, and
your money's gone, and the only family you have left are your
cousins, and I don't reckon they're too fond of you at the moment.

There's nobody left in the world who likes you, Chester. Anything could happen to you, and nobody would care."

Bentley put a firm hand on my shoulder. "Take a step back, Detective Schatz. That's not an appropriate way to talk to a suspect."

Chester smirked at me, and despite his busted face and the adverse dermatological effects of twenty years of being a vile, murderous scumbag, I saw him as he had been when I first encountered him sitting on his porch sipping his rum drink in his white summer suit. He thought he was going to do it again. He thought he was going to kill a woman in my town and get away with it. I gripped the edge of the table with white knuckles to keep myself from reaching for my nightstick.

"Can I get some coffee or something?" Chester asked Bentley.

"Of course," Bentley said. "Buck, why don't you fetch Mr. March some coffee."

"You've got to be kidding me," I said.

"Mr. March has asked for some coffee. We would like to engage him in civil discourse. There's no reason we can't be civil, is there, Buck?"

"This is ridiculous," I said, as I stomped out of the room.

This exchange was rehearsed; every interrogation of this type had to involve a moment where Bentley could demonstrate authority over me to the suspect, so the suspect would seek to ingratiate himself to Bentley in order to get protection from me. The truth was, I was senior to Bentley, and I was at a stage of my career where nobody really told me what to do anymore. But even though I knew this was all just routine interrogation schtick, it enraged me to be dressed down in front of Chester. I felt like I was back in that cramped office in 1955, smelling Henry McCloskey's shit breath and thinking I was about to be fired or worse by a couple of Klanned-up hillbillies who were universally considered to be my social betters.

I walked down the hall to the coffee pot, poured two cups of black coffee, and returned to the interrogation room. I slammed one of the cups in front of Chester, spilling a little bit, and gave the other to Bentley. I didn't want coffee. I wanted a cigarette, and the smell of the butts in the ashtray was driving me nuts. I crammed two sticks of Juicy Fruit into my mouth and started grinding them between my teeth.

"I think, if you can make a show of contrition—a demonstration of humanity, really—I can persuade the district attorney not to seek the death penalty. What we really need to know is where Margery March's body is," Bentley said.

Chester flashed his fake teeth. "How should I know that?" he asked.

Bentley leaned forward and spoke softly. "You're already facing capital murder for killing Evelyn Duhrer. You are drowning. I am trying to throw you a life preserver. I just need you to prove to me that you're not totally irredeemable."

I started laughing. "Fat chance of that."

"Shut up, Buck," Bentley said. He turned back to Chester. "Her family has been grieving for twenty years. All they want is to be able to inter their daughter's remains in the family plot in Nashville. If you can help them do that, if you can make that showing of genuine remorse, maybe I can go to the prosecutor and get you a lighter charge."

There was a long pause, while the killer seemed to consider his deeds and the opportunity he had to show remorse or contrition.

And then Chester started laughing. "This has been really great, watching you guys put on this little show," he said. "I certainly believe that the two of you don't like each other. I don't blame you. You guys are a couple of assholes. I don't like you, either."

"Goddamnit," I said, and I grabbed the heavy crystal ashtray off the table and threw it at Chester. Because of his gunshot wound and the fact that his hands were shackled, he couldn't raise his arms fast enough to protect his head. The corner of the ashtray hit him right in the middle of the forehead. I had expected it to shatter against his skull, but it didn't even break when it hit the floor. Chester fell face forward, banged his head a second time against the side of the steel table, and then slid over the side of his chair.

"Jesus, Buck," Bentley said. "What the hell was that?"

"I don't know," I told him. "A pratfall maybe? Is that the right word for it? It feels right. I think that was a pratfall."

"Is he dead? Did you just kill him?"

I bent over and looked under the table at Chester. "Naw, he's breathing. I think he's probably fine."

"This man needs medical attention," Bentley said.

I grabbed Chester under the arms and hauled him up into his chair. "No. He needs to confess. The best thing for him is to unburden his soul. This man does not leave this room until he gives us a statement."

Bentley yanked his tie loose and unbuttoned his collar. "My God, Buck. I've never seen a man take a blow to the head and then just shut off like that."

Chester's face was twitching a little bit.

"I think he's coming around," I said. I smacked Chester lightly on the cheek. "Wake up, Shitbird."

Chester's eyelids fluttered. "What happened? Where—Where am I?"

"What did you do with your wife, Margery, Chester?" I asked.

He looked at me, without recognition, and he said, "Out on Dad's property. There's a stand of trees along the edge of the cotton fields. I buried her there."

"Wait a second," Bentley said.

"Are you going to make this a problem?" I asked.

"No, we just need to get the waiver. Chester March, you have the right to remain silent. Anything you say will be used against you. You have the right to an attorney. If you cannot afford an attorney, one will be provided for you. Do you understand your rights?"

"I guess so," Chester said. The pupil of his left eye was huge and dilated. The pupil of his right was a pinprick. His upper lip twitched.

Bentley had the Miranda waiver form. He slid it across the table to Chester. "You just need to sign this," he said.

Chester reached for the pen and seemed surprised to find his wrists shackled. "What is this? What's going on?" he said.

I uncuffed his wrists and put the pen in his hand. He signed the form in a tremulous, spidery script.

"Now, let's start from the beginning. Why did you kill Cecilia Tompkins, the black prostitute?"

TRANSCRIPT: AMERICAN JUSTICE

CARLOS WATKINS (NARRATION): If you're going to appreciate just how profoundly Detective Schatz is alleged to have violated Chester's rights, first you need to understand what those rights are, so I asked Ed Heffernan to help explain.

PROFESSOR EDWARD HEFFERNAN: So, you want to know about the rights of the accused? I bet you and your listeners know what they are already. You know what they say, every time they arrest somebody on *Law and Order*?

WATKINS: You've got a right to remain silent. Anything you say can be used against you.

HEFFERNAN: That's it. Do you know the rest of it?

WATKINS: You've got a right to an attorney. Um . . . If you cannot afford an attorney, one will be provided for you?

HEFFERNAN: Yep. The Fifth Amendment to the Constitution guarantees a right against self-incrimination. It's there to prevent people from being forced to confess to crimes and then having those coerced confessions used as evidence at trial. And the Sixth Amendment guarantees a right to counsel, to keep the accused from getting railroaded. The right against self-incrimination isn't much good if police can rake people over the coals until they get a statement out of them, so any time an arrestee asks for a lawyer, police have to stop questioning him until he's had a chance to consult counsel. In 1966, the Supreme Court held in *Miranda v. Arizona* that accused individuals must be informed of their rights before they can be questioned. That case is why the police have to give you that warning. Not that it does a whole lot of good.

WATKINS: What do you mean?

HEFFERNAN: Everybody's heard the Miranda warning a million times on television. So the police recite it, and people just think it's a formality, like the fine print you click through when you update your iPhone software. When the police give you the warning, they ask if you understand it. Everybody says they understand it. But if people really understood what it means that everything they say is going to be used against them, a lot fewer of them would talk.

When they sit you down to interrogate you, they give you a form that explains your rights in greater detail. The form says you can stop questioning any time you want a lawyer. And then they ask you to sign the form to waive those rights.

WATKINS: Why do people waive their constitutional rights?

HEFFERNAN: Because once the police give you the Court-mandated warning, they're allowed to lie to you, to manipulate you. You're in trouble, and they're your only friend. They just want to get it right or hear your side of it. They're trying to help you, but you have to talk to help yourself. They're the ones protecting you by standing between you and the DA or the hanging judge or the inmates who will rape you in prison, or the other cops. They'll tell you your friends are ratting on you and your only chance to avoid taking the fall is to rat on them first. But what you don't realize is they're asking for things, but never offering anything. Because cops can't grant you immunity in exchange for your testimony. Cops can't offer you a plea agreement. All those things are at the discretion of a prosecutor. They'll tell you that if you exercise your rights and get yourself a lawyer, then they can't help you. But they can't help you anyway, and they don't want to. All they want is a confession.

WATKINS: So when should you talk to a cop?

HEFFERNAN: Never. Well, I mean, you can feel free to talk to them if you're a victim. I wouldn't want to discourage victims from reporting crimes, especially violent ones. But if you've done something, or you think they think you've done something, shut up. If they give you that *Miranda* warning, shut up. Shut up, and lawyer up.

WATKINS: And how was Chester March deprived of his rights?

HEFFERNAN: It's undisputed that Chester March was suffering from a serious head injury at the time he confessed to the murders. Chester has alleged that the injury was inflicted by Detective Schatz, during the interrogation. Schatz and other police witnesses dispute that claim, but they admit that Chester had been involved in a high-speed car accident while evading arrest, and that he was interrogated before his injuries had been treated by a doctor.

WATKINS: And judges have upheld the use of the statement against Chester?

HEFFERNAN: The state contends that Chester was not in apparent distress at the time of the interrogation, and that he had received first aid from paramedics prior to being interrogated, which was sufficient for the interrogation to pass muster under the Eighth Amendment.

During that interrogation, Chester told the police that he had buried his wife, Margery, in a wooded spot on an agricultural property in Mississippi that his father had owned. Based on what Chester told them, police excavated the site and uncovered human remains. It's really hard to get a judge to throw out a murder confession that leads police to a body. Judges will twist the facts to the limits of reasonableness and sometimes beyond to avoid finding that a constitutional violation requires them to exclude evidence collected from a victim's body.

The Tennessee Supreme Court ruled that since the detectives didn't know that Chester was suffering from a brain injury, they were not obligated to seek immediate medical care for him, and they did not behave improperly in questioning him or taking his statement. They analogized the case to cases in which suspects who were intoxicated or under the influence of drugs at the time of their arrest made damaging admissions to officers and those admissions were admitted as evidence against them.

WATKINS: What do you think about that?

HEFFERNAN: I think interrogating a prisoner who has suffered a serious head injury is not analogous to questioning a prisoner who is under the influence of substances he has voluntarily consumed. I think it is cruel and unusual to delay medical treatment to an injured prisoner while he is subjected to questioning from police. And, in light of Buck Schatz's lengthy record of violent behavior, I think the courts didn't give enough consideration to Chester's allegation that he suffered the head injury during the interrogation, rather than in the car crash.

But, unfortunately, none of these issues are currently live. We're now just days from the scheduled execution, and what we are now arguing before the court is the constitutionality of the lethal injection protocol the state plans to use on Chester.

WATKINS: How do you feel about your chances?

HEFFERNAN: Optimistic. Other than maybe Buck Schatz, I don't think anyone wants this to happen. In the latest round of oral arguments, the judges had some sharp questions for the state about their knowledge of the effects these drugs would have on someone of Chester's advanced age, and I don't think they got very persuasive answers to those questions. I think we'll get a stay of execution.

WATKINS: I hope so.

PART 5

2011: AMERICAN JUSTICE

24

t's good to see you, Mr. Schatz," Dr. Pincus said as he opened
the door to his office.

"Wish I could say the same," I told him as I pushed my
walker past him and made my way to the couch. I didn't bother
trying for the chair anymore. I was seeing Pincus twice a week,
and this was my seventh session. I didn't exactly like coming here,
but it wasn't like I had anywhere else to go. I figured Pincus was
slightly better company than Gus Turnip and the Lunch Bunch.

"How have things been with Rose?" Pincus asked as he fetched
the ashtray from his desk drawer and turned on the ceiling fan.

"Normal," I said. I tapped my pack of Lucky Strikes against
my palm and one popped out of the pack. I stuck it between my
lips and flicked my lighter. "I don't think we've really talked about
it since we had, you know, the conversation. But William has been
coming by every day for half an hour or so. He's taking the bar

exam soon, and he's been spending most of his time studying, but he's making a point of seeing us. He's not really doing anything but studying, and we aren't up to much either, so we never really have anything to talk about, but he keeps showing up. I know the only reason he's still in town is because of Rose's illness. He obviously knows about her decision, but I don't remember telling him about it, so either she told him when I wasn't around, or I was there and I just don't remember it. It's nice of him to think about us, but it feels ominous, like he knows we don't have much time left."

He set the ashtray on the coffee table and slid into his chair. He tapped his ridiculous Montblanc ballpoint against his pretentious leather-bound notebook. "Has your memory improved since you started confronting this problem?"

"I'm not sure," I said. "It comes and goes. I still forget it's all happening sometimes, but when something reminds me of it, it rings a bell. It's not like I am hearing about the whole thing for the first time anymore. Maybe talking to you doesn't do anything. Maybe it just sank in, through repetition."

"Maybe," Pincus said. "But you told me the first time we met that things don't get better, that everything is on a downhill slide, and that what is lost is irretrievable. Do you still believe that, Buck?"

"My wife is dying, and my son is dead. My outlook has not changed much."

Pincus wrote something in his notebook. I sat and watched him and puffed on my cigarette. When he finished, he looked up and said, "This is the second time you've come here without Rose. I asked you why she wasn't here last week, and you said she was busy. I didn't believe you."

"I asked her not to come," I said.

"She wasn't very happy about that, was she?"

"I think she's glad I'm still doing this. But I don't think she was pleased to be left out of it."

"Why don't you want her here?"

"I don't agree with the decision she's made. I am angry, and I'm sad, and I don't want to talk about it."

"You don't want to burden her with your feelings about what's happening."

I nodded. "Yeah, something like that."

"You think you're being stoic by dealing with your feelings this way, but have you considered the fact that while you're dealing with it on your own, she is having to deal with it on her own? You're not taking a burden off her shoulders. You're compounding her sorrow by being aloof and unavailable during these difficult times."

I stubbed out the cigarette I was smoking. "When you put it that way, you don't make me sound like such a good guy."

"Then maybe you should reconsider how you respond to these difficult situations. Do you think you withdrew from Rose after Brian died?"

"I don't like to talk about that." I lit another cigarette.

"I think that's my answer, then," Pincus replied. "Do you think that made things easier for her?"

"I guess it just made things easier for me. I just don't know how I could stand to have handled it any differently. I could hold it together as long as I didn't talk about it. I don't see how anyone would be better off if I'd allowed myself to fall apart."

"If you just let these things fester, you will never get past them."

"I won't get past them anyway. How am I supposed to get past losing Brian? How will I get past losing Rose? Where am I even trying to go that I need to move past these losses? You are wrong. Things are irreparably worse than they were before, and they're going to continue to get worse. I will suffer every day of the few remaining years I have left, and I will die miserable. I just don't see any point in whining about it all the time."

Pincus scribbled in the notebook. When he was satisfied with whatever he had written, he leveled his eyes at me. "Do you want Rose to die miserable, Buck?" he asked.

"You know I don't."

"Well, what are you going to do about that?"

I stubbed out my second cigarette and immediately lit a third. "I don't know. What do you suggest?"

Pincus clipped his stupid pen to the front of his stupid notebook and set it on his stupid coffee table. "Being aloof and closed off may be the easiest way for you to bear your pain, but it doesn't seem to make things easier for Rose. Your goal needs to be to get to a point where you can talk to Rose about these things. And I think, the sooner we can get you there, the better it will be for everyone."

"Maybe after Tequila leaves town," I said. "He's taking us up to Nashville tomorrow, and then he'll be flying back to New York." I lit another cigarette. "When he's not around to distract us, we'll have to deal with this."

"You're going to Nashville for the execution?"

"Yes. Unless the Supreme Court or the governor intervenes, we're going to go watch Chester March die."

"You know, I've been listening to Carlos Watkins's radio show," Pincus said.

I snorted. "Isn't that delightful to hear. Do you think I need to talk to him as well?"

"I'm not sure. There's been a lot of discussion on the Internet. Some people think that Carlos has been way too trusting of Chester, but a lot of people think his conviction should be overturned because of your conduct."

"If it was their daughters or sisters he killed, I bet they'd think differently."

"I can understand that, but Professor Heffernan is also very persuasive. It's not about what Chester did or what he deserves. It's about what kind of country we want to live in."

I stubbed out my Lucky Strike, and that meant it was time to go. I could tolerate three cigarettes of Dr. Pincus, but any more pushed my limits. "I want to live in a country where innocent women don't get murdered. And I'm happy to kill a few scumbags like Chester March if that's what it takes to get us there. I think our time is up."

"All right, Buck. Think about opening up a bit more with Rose this week. I think you'll have fewer regrets that way."

"When she's gone, you mean?"

"Well, yes."

"When she's gone, I'll have nothing left but regrets. Enjoy the rest of your week, Dr. Pincus."

TRANSCRIPT: AMERICAN JUSTICE

CARLOS WATKINS (NARRATION): The Tennessee Supreme Court has ruled against Professor Heffernan, finding that the lethal injection protocol does not need to be modified to account for the age, weight, or health status of the condemned individual, because the drug doses administered are sufficient to sedate and then kill a human being of any age and any weight.

They also rejected the contention that lethal injection is cruel and unusual. Time grows short, and hope dwindles for Chester March. Professor Heffernan has filed an appeal to the U.S. Supreme Court, and there is a petition begging Tennessee governor Bill Haslam to intervene on Chester's behalf, but the Supreme Court rarely stays executions, and governors almost never grant clemency. At Riverbend, corrections officials have begun preparing for an execution. And Ed Heffernan has been preparing as well, in his own way.

ED HEFFERNAN: I didn't think it would come to this. I really didn't. It's been several years since we last put someone to death in Tennessee. Every time we kill somebody, I tell myself that this will be the last time. And I believe it, too. It's incredible to me that we keep putting ourselves through this process.

You know, the prison hires grief and trauma counselors to be on-site to talk to the staff that participate in the execution? The journalists who witness these always come away horrified. I read the same article in *The Tennessean* after every execution; in the abstract, people don't think much about it one way or another, but if you make them watch, they're shocked that this kind of thing still happens in America. You know how Professor Fields told you that jurors' views toward capital punishment change when you show them crime-scene and autopsy photos and make them listen to victim impact testimony? Well, I'd hypothesize that those views would shift the other way if more people had to watch executions. There's a reason states kill inmates in the middle of the night and carefully control the list of approved witnesses.

We have a lucky class of students at the capital defense clinic this year. Most lawyers don't get the unique experience of having their first client get tortured to death because they lost an appeal. So, I'm sure this will be an edifying professional development opportunity for them.

As for me? Well, you'd think I'd be used to this, after so many years of capital appeals. But I'm not. I mean, I don't think I will break down and weep in front of the students this time, but I'm honestly shocked that this is happening. I thought we had the better argument. I thought the justices finally heard us, about the barbarity of using drugs in unmeasured, untested dosages and the suffering inflicted during death by lethal injection. I thought the tide of public opinion was turning in our favor.

And this shouldn't matter, but I like Chester March on a personal level. He's charming, he's cultured, he's personable. Even though the Supreme Court has held that it's unconstitutional to execute the cognitively disabled, it's up to the states to determine what constitutes a disability, and most states have set that bar at profoundly low levels—IQs in the sixties—and continue to execute relatively low-functioning individuals. And that's its own separate horror; individuals with often no more than a sixth- or seventh-grade education, many of whom suffered horrific childhood abuse, being killed by a system they can barely comprehend as punishment for acting on impulses they can't control.

But Chester is one of very few college graduates who has been convicted of a capital crime. In some ways, if you believe he is guilty, that makes him less sympathetic; unlike some of these other offenders, he should have known better. But in certain ways—and maybe this reflects biases on my part—he's also easier to relate to. I care deeply about all my capital clients, but this execution is going to haunt me.

WATKINS (NARRATION): Corrections officials have already taken Chester from the secure wing of the prison where he has spent the last thirty-five years and put him in a special cell adjacent to the execution chamber. Ed hasn't left the prison since they moved Chester down; he is showering in the guards' locker room and napping in his car when Chester is asleep. Otherwise, he is by his client's side.

A Riverbend spokesman told me that the Department of Correction has obtained the drugs for the lethal injection and that they are on-site. The protocol calls for a cocktail of three drugs. The first is sodium thiopental, a sedative that will render Chester unconscious. Then comes vecuronium bromide, a powerful muscle relaxant that is commonly used in surgical anesthesia. This drug will paralyze Chester's skeletal muscles so he won't twitch or convulse. It will also shut down his respiratory function; when this drug is used in therapeutic settings, the patient under its effects will typically be kept on a ventilator. Finally a lethal dose of potassium chloride is administered, which will cause massive cardiac arrest.

The process will take ten to fifteen minutes, and if the sodium thiopental isn't effective in rendering him totally insensible, Chester will endure the experience of being slowly suffocated as his pulmonary system struggles and ultimately fails to operate under the effects of the vecuronium while, at the same time, his heart is being melted by corrosive potassium.

I caught up to Tennessee deputy attorney general Peter Clayton outside the prison, where he'd been speaking to corrections officials about the preparations for the execution. Clayton argued on behalf of the state against Heffernan in the final round of appeals, and he, along with Buck Schatz, will be the law enforcement representatives who will witness Chester's execution.

I'd sought him out for comment previously, but he had declined to speak to me while Chester's appeals were still pending in state court. He agreed to talk to me now only if I promised not to share the audio until after the U.S. Supreme Court had ruled on Heffernan's petition. He didn't think they were likely to grant a stay.

PETER CLAYTON: I've been listening to your show. I always follow the media coverage of the cases I work on, but I've never experienced anything like this. Oral arguments at the Supreme Court are public proceedings, but there usually aren't many people in the galleries, and *American Justice* had them packed for Chester March. I'm a trial lawyer, so I am used to arguing in front of a crowd, but I think Ed had a little bit of stage fright.

CARLOS WATKINS: They were pretty supportive of him.

CLAYTON: Yeah. And a tough room for me. I suppose I have you to thank for bringing them out. This has been—I'll call it interesting. I did not expect these routine appeals in a case from the '70s to cause this kind of a circus.

WATKINS: Happy to be of service.

CLAYTON: Ed has fans now. He has, like, groupies. That is so weird. You turned Ed Heffernan into a rock star. There are women on the Internet writing erotic fan fiction about how they want to strip Ed out of his Costco sweater and his stain-resistant Dockers and do shocking things to him. The world is a strange place. I wonder what Judith thinks about all this. That's his wife. I don't know if you've met her.

WATKINS: Do you know Ed well?

CLAYTON: I was his student. I took two of his seminars at Vanderbilt, going on twelve years ago. The guy's brilliant. I'm only talking to you because he asked me to.

WATKINS: And you just beat him. How does that feel?

CLAYTON: I wouldn't say I beat him. I'd say the court wasn't willing to hand down a ruling at this time that would have brought about the policy shift Ed was advocating. If he'd won, it would have probably ended capital punishment in this state. Technically, execution by electric chair is still legal in Tennessee, but I don't think we'd go back to electrocuting people if the Supreme Court overturned lethal injection.

WATKINS: Do you think that would be a bad outcome?

CLAYTON: I wouldn't be here arguing for Chester March's execution if I disagreed with it. Prosecutors have a lot of discretion in our criminal justice system, and I believe we have a duty to use that discretion to avoid wielding state power to immoral ends. That's why I've fiercely advocated inside the AG's office against seeking prison terms for low-level marijuana offenders.

WATKINS: If you know Ed, I'm sure you're familiar with his arguments against capital punishment.

CLAYTON: I am. And I disagree with him. I think we've got maybe thirty-five inmates from West Tennessee on death row and fewer than sixty statewide for offenses dating back forty years. We've had six executions since 1976. We had a hundred and twelve homicides in Memphis alone in 2010, and that was a record low. We haven't had fewer in a year since 1971. The police popped champagne to celebrate having only a hundred and twelve homicides.

Nationwide, there are maybe two dozen executions a year, and around fifteen thousand murders. We sentence more people to death than we actually execute, but capital cases are still a tiny fraction of the total set of murders. We reserve this sanction for the worst of the worst. Child murderers and sex killers. People who commit bias-related murders. Serial killers like Chester March, who killed three women that we know of. Terrorists like Timothy McVeigh, the Oklahoma City bomber. I'm aware of the suffering that the lethal injection supposedly causes, and I don't think it's disproportionate to the suffering these people have inflicted. In general, I'm a lot more concerned with the people who die by murder than the people who die by execution. Ed and I just disagree on how we balance our compassion for these perpetrators with our outrage on behalf of these victims.

CARLOS WATKINS (NARRATION): We tried to find a family member of a victim to talk to us about the death penalty, but nobody we contacted would go on the record. All death row inmates are somewhat famous, and all famous killers have fans, and the families of the victims are understandably frightened of those fans and tend to avoid speaking publicly.

Family members often give what's called victim impact testimony in the sentencing phase of a capital case, where they talk about the pain and loss that the crime has inflicted on their families. Criminal defense lawyers view this kind of testimony as unfairly prejudicial against their clients, and the constitutionality of this kind of evidence was actually challenged and upheld by the U.S. Supreme Court in an appeal brought by Pervis Payne, an inmate here at Riverbend, who was sentenced to death for the double murder of Charisse Christopher and her two-year-old daughter, Lacie, in 1987, after a jury heard testimony from Charisse's mother about the crime's impact on three-year-old Nicholas, who was stabbed during the attack but survived. Payne insists he is wrongly accused and is currently seeking new DNA testing on evidence taken from the scene.

But while many victims' family members offer testimony in support of prosecutors' attempts to secure a death sentence, over the course of decades of appeals, they often change their minds, in some cases publicly forgiving the killers and calling on governors to grant clemency.

Family members who arrive to view executions at Riverbend are brought in through a side entrance, to avoid contact with the protesters who gather at the prison gates, and corrections officials keep the media away from them. They rarely speak on the record, so we don't know how most of them feel about what they see here. A reporter from *The Tennessean* told me she has sometimes seen victims' family members crying as they leave the prison.

Since nobody would talk to me about the experience of witnessing a loved one's killer being executed, we can only speculate as to whether this experience brings comfort or catharsis, or whether it just dredges up old pain. But we know it can't undo the loss they've suffered. Misery begets more misery.

25

So, there are two things on our Nashville itinerary," Tequila said. "First, we're going to see this asshole get a lethal injection, and then we're gonna get hot chicken. Or do you think we should get the hot chicken before we see the execution? Do you think we're going to be hungry after we watch this guy die?"

"What is a hot chicken?" Rose asked.

"It's a Nashville delicacy," Tequila said. "It's fried chicken sauced with a cayenne pepper paste so spicy that they warn you not to touch your eyes after you touch the chicken. They serve it on white bread with pickle chips."

Rose grimaced. "That sounds horrible. Why does that even exist?"

"Supposedly, a gentleman named Thornton Prince III was running around on his lady friend, and for revenge, she doused his chicken in pepper. But it turns out that Thornton Prince liked pepper, and he thought it was delicious, so he opened Prince's Hot Chicken Shack, which has been in business since 1945."

"That sounds unpleasant," Rose said.

"It sounds like something I'll actually be able to taste," I reminded her. "Let's go for the chicken afterwards, so you won't have a stomach full of hot sauce if the execution makes you feel sick."

"We can go whenever we want," Tequila said. "Hot chicken is as delicious as a late-night snack as it is for breakfast."

"Ugh," Rose said.

The road trip wasn't too bad. The car Tequila was driving us in was my 2006 Buick Lucerne CXS, which had the special distinction of being the last car I would ever own. The 2006 Lucerne's front fender was adorned with porthole details that echoed the famous "ventiports" Buicks had sported in the 1950s. Back in those days, Buick competed with Ford and Chevy at the top of the market, and a bells-and-whistles model like Chester's Roadmaster Skylark, with its scowling grille and its four portholes on the front fender, was just about the nicest ride a rich man could buy with his money.

In the twenty-first century, the once-revered Buick line was now a range of sedate midrange sedans targeted at drivers who were old enough to remember when those portholes signified something more exciting. The wood details on the Lucerne's dash were actually plastic. But the car had standard heated and cooled seats, which I enjoyed more than I cared to admit.

My CXS model also came with the same 4.6-liter Northstar V8 that GM put in the upper-end Cadillacs, and according to the pamphlet the guy at the dealership showed me, it could do zero to sixty in just under seven seconds. It wasn't as muscular as my 1970 Challenger, but it was a lot quieter and the gas mileage was better. I'd never had much occasion to stretch the Buick's legs, anyway. When I bought it, I was a little peeved that the only option was an automatic transmission, but that turned out to be for the best, because the aides at Valhalla didn't know how to drive stick, and I don't think Tequila did, either.

The drive to Nashville was short enough that the Buick made it on one tank of gas, and my car didn't have a Bluetooth, so Tequila couldn't hook his Internet phone up to my stereo and play his godawful music. Rose sat in the front with him; he was leaving town after this trip and probably wouldn't be back until Thanksgiving. And maybe that was going to be her last Thanksgiving. Ordinarily, I probably would have tasked Tequila with taking me on this jaunt, and Rose would have stayed behind; we were just going to see the execution, get Tequila's chicken, maybe sleep a few hours at a motel, and then drive back. I don't think Rose had any powerful desire to witness this event. But William wanted to spend time with her before he left, and I felt wrong leaving her behind, so we'd brought her with us. Even now, she was making sacrifices for us. For me, really.

Maybe I should have skipped the execution, in light of other things that were going on. But these connections to the past felt so important, now more than ever, and I had promised to watch Chester die.

It was unusual to be permitted to bring two guests to an execution; this kind of invitation doesn't typically even come with a plus-one. Since I had mobility issues and needed assistance, I probably could have got Tequila in, but Peter Clayton, the man from the attorney general's office, really came through for me in getting the prison to let Rose to join us as well. I think Clayton fixed it with the corrections people for Tequila and Rose to witness the execution as a way of razzing Watkins. A bunch of *American Justice* listeners had booed him during his oral arguments before the Tennessee Supreme Court, and he hadn't seemed pleased about that.

Clayton said it hadn't been too hard to arrange two guests for me because there were no families of victims coming to see Chester off. Margery's parents passed years ago. Evelyn Duhrer's closest living relative was a niece who lived in Oregon. She had declined to come to Nashville for this. Cecilia Tompkins had no next of kin on record. Chester also didn't have any family, except Forrest's daughter. She had apparently wanted to witness the execution, but the last time Chester saw his cousins had been at his trial, when they testified against him, so he asked that she not be allowed to attend. I'm sure he also would have objected to Rose and Tequila, but I guess nobody told him they were coming.

There was a crowd of demonstrators around the prison's front gate as we pulled up. On our left side were death penalty opponents. One guy had a sign that said ALL KILLING IS WRONG, and a bunch of people were wearing T-shirts that said SAVE CHESTER. On the other side, a smaller crowd of supporters had signs that said things like BURN IN HELL. I also saw a woman with a sign that said FUCK ME ED HEFFERNAN. So there was room here for many agendas.

The parking lot was outside the prison's main gates where the demonstrators were gathered, and normally, to get into the prison, a visitor would have to walk in past that crowd. but following directions Clayton had provided, Tequila drove past the parking lot and pulled up to the main entrance. The crowd encircled the car, and I worried that Carlos Watkins's listeners would recognize me, but the prison guard manning the gatehouse yelled at the protesters to step back, and he waved us past his checkpoint and into the prison complex. Tequila's directions instructed him to pull up next to one of the nondescript buildings that apparently housed the execution chamber, and Clayton, who must have been informed of our arrival by the guard on the gate, came out to greet us. I opened my door but stayed in my seat, waiting as Tequila fetched my walker from the trunk and began unfolding it. Clayton waved at him to stop.

"You can't bring that inside the prison," he said.

"How am I supposed to get around, then?" I asked.

"We'll have to see if the prison has a mobility aid you can use. Your walker is not going to be allowed in the building. It could be broken apart, and the pieces of it could be used as weapons, and it's made from hollow tubes that could be used to smuggle contraband."

"They can't really think Buck is going to smuggle contraband into the prison?" Rose asked.

"The rules of this place aren't exactly built on a foundation of trust," Clayton said with a shrug.

"I'll go see what they have that you can use," Tequila said. "Just wait here for me."

He went into the prison with Clayton. I turned to Rose. "Look at me," I said. "I can't even get out of the car until he gets me something to lean on."

"It's all right, Buck," she told me. "Most people don't even get close to ninety. We've had a lot more good years than we had any right to expect."

"And now we've got nothing but bad ones left, and not very many of those," I said. I turned sideways in the seat and dangled my legs out of the open door. I lit a cigarette.

"Can I have one?" Rose asked.

I handed her the one I was holding and lit another. "Be careful with these," I said. "They will give you cancer."

She laughed, bitterly, and we both blew plumes of smoke into the heavy July air. It was 5 P.M., but it still looked like midafternoon.

"You know, we passed a sign on the way in that said no tobacco products were supposed to be used on the prison grounds."

"What are they going to do?" I asked. "Lock us up?"

She laughed again.

"It's not a bad evening," I said. Nobody wanted to live near a prison, so Riverbend was on Nashville's outskirts, past the airport. It was called Riverbend because it was situated at a bend in the Cumberland River. Beyond the fences we could see the water and, past that, wooded hills.

"You always find the nicest places to take me," Rose said.

I flicked ash onto the pavement. "Thank you for coming on this trip. I know you wouldn't have chosen to spend this day driving up here and doing this. I hope you understand why I need to be here."

"It's because the more you lose, the more you cling to the past," Rose said.

"It used to be that I could deal with things," I said. "If it was something about money or something at work, or if I was going after somebody who scared me, it was always best not to talk about it. If I took care of things myself, I could spare you, and Brian and Mother, from having to worry. Now I can't fix anything, but my instinct is still not to talk about things. I don't want to make this harder for you. I don't want to be a burden. And I don't know what I can do or say that will help."

"You make me laugh," she said. "That was always, by far, your most redeeming characteristic. Even if your idea of dinner and a show is witnessing an execution and then going to a shack to get horrible chicken that is painful to eat. I know you, Buck. I've always known you. I knew what I was getting into when I married you. I don't expect you to fix this. I don't expect you to come up with anything that makes it better. There's no way to do that. I just need you to stop running away from it."

We both threw our cigarette butts on the ground, and Rose stomped on them and kicked them under the car while I stashed my pack and my lighter in the pocket on the back of the seat. I knew those wouldn't make it past the prison's security check. Tequila came out of the building pushing a wheelchair, the flimsy kind with the cloth back.

"They don't have a walker?" I asked.

"Apparently walkers are dangerous weapons," Tequila told me. "You can either sit in this, or you can hold my arm and walk in."

"How far is it?" I asked.

"I'd recommend the chair," he said.

"Goddamnit." I gripped his arm to steady myself as I climbed out of the car, and I slid into the wheelchair. He pushed me around to the curb cut and up the accessibility ramp into the building. Rose and Tequila walked through a metal detector, but I had to climb out of the wheelchair and let a corrections official run a wand over me, on account of the pins in my shoulder and in my hip. Once we were past the security check, Peter Clayton caught up to us and walked us down a fluorescent-lit hallway and through a door into a room about the size of a large closet. The walls were constructed from concrete blocks, painted white, and there was nothing but a couple of folding chairs in it, and a window. The window had blackout blinds on the other side, and they were snapped shut.

"When it's time to rock and roll, these blinds will open, and we'll be able to see into the execution chamber," Clayton said. He pointed to an intercom speaker on the ceiling. "We'll hear if he has any last words he wants to say, and the audio will remain on for the duration of the execution, until he is pronounced dead."

"Is this two-way glass?" Tequila asked.

Clayton shook his head. "Clear glass. He'll be able to see you. Most of the time, the victims' families want their faces to be the last thing these guys see before they go. It's soundproof, though. You can't hear what's going on in the chamber unless the microphone in there is on, and they can't hear what you're saying in here."

"When does the show start?" I asked.

"It's probably going to be a while," Clayton told me. "They have one room for law enforcement witnesses and the victims' families. That's just going to be us tonight. There's a second room for the family of the condemned and his lawyers. That's going to be Ed Heffernan and some of his law students. Finally, there's a third room where Carlos Watkins and the other media witnesses

will observe. Corrections staff move everybody in and out sep-
arately. They don't want the victims' families running into the
killer's, and they don't want the reporters to corner anyone who
doesn't want to talk to them. We don't have any victims' families
here tonight, and Chester doesn't have any family either, but the
Department of Correction likes to stick pretty close to the rule-
book for things like this.

"The last I heard, Mr. March had just been served his last
meal. When he's done with that, he'll have an opportunity to pray
with his pastor, and then they have to get the intravenous line
into him. I will step out to observe them doing that, but you will
have to wait in here. That can sometimes take a while, because
it's hard to find a good vein in some of these guys. Mr. March
doesn't have a history of drug use, which hopefully means that
will go a little quicker. The junkies sometimes have collapsed
veins, and that makes it very difficult to get an IV into them. But
March is elderly, so that could make getting the line in tricky as
well. If all that goes smoothly, the blinds might open in an hour
and a half. If they have trouble with the IV, it could be longer.
I've heard about a case where they spent hours trying to get a line
into a guy—stuck him in his arms and his legs and his groin—
and couldn't get the IV in, and he was bleeding all over the place,
and they had to call off the execution. That wasn't in Tennessee,
though. I think it was in Ohio."

"So what you're saying is we might be here all night?" I asked.

"Yeah, pretty much," Clayton said.

Rose sat down on one of the folding chairs. "I should have
brought a magazine or something."

"If I'd known this would take so long, I definitely would have gone for the hot chicken beforehand," Tequila said. "Then, afterwards, we'd probably have been ready for round two."

I shrugged. "Live and learn."

TRANSCRIPT: AMERICAN JUSTICE

CARLOS WATKINS (NARRATION): The U.S. Supreme Court has denied Chester's appeal. Governor Bill Haslam has rejected Chester's plea for clemency. He released a short statement saying a jury decided Chester's fate, and appellate courts upheld it, and it's not his place to relitigate the matter or question their decision. I think it's exactly the governor's place to do that, since he has the power to grant clemency or to suspend capital punishment entirely in Tennessee. But he's not willing to do it. I called his office and asked to interview him, but he doesn't want to talk to me about this. At Riverbend, plans for the execution move forward.

I still can't go in to see Chester, but he has access to a phone, and he called me with an update.

CHESTER MARCH: They've given me a white prison uniform. I've never seen one of these before. The uniforms are color coded, and white is just for being executed. It's like this is my wedding day, and I'm the bride. On death row, we wore light green. The general population wears beige. So I feel very special right now.

They came in a while back and asked what I wanted to eat. On death row, the prisoners spend a lot of time talking about what they want for their last meal. I think we do that in part because the prison food is so bad, and in part just to pass the time. To tell the truth, even on death row, it didn't really seem like we were actually going to get executed. For the first twenty-some years I was in here, Tennessee didn't have a single execution. The first one was in the year 2000. They did it five more times in the last decade or so, as people's appeals began to run out, but still, it's so hard to wrap my mind around. Even now that it's happening, I can't believe it. Talking about last meals always seemed like kind of a joke.

I always thought I would get something lavish: steak and lobster, tins of caviar, bottles of champagne. But it turns out that the budget for a last meal is only twenty dollars, so it doesn't look like I'm going to get to go out in style.

I think the best bet is to go with fast food, because if you ask for a steak or seafood, it is coming from the prison kitchen. Inmates do the cooking here, guys from the general population, so I don't know them. I always had to eat in my cell. A guard would bring a tray and slide it through a slit in the door. I think if I asked those guys to cook my last meal, they'd probably do their best to make it a good one, but the food would still be coming from the vendor who supplies the prison kitchen. I could ask them for a rib eye or a filet mignon, but I'd probably get the same meat we get when they serve us "steaks" on Christmas. It's a sandwich steak or some shitty cut that they call a steak, but isn't really a steak. Like a Denver steak or an Omaha strip or a Toronto tip or some bullshit like that. It's pretty good by prison standards, but it's not the piece of meat you want for your last meal.

I asked them about lobster, and they said they couldn't do that. Shrimp is as close as I can get. They told me they can do either a shrimp cocktail or fried shrimp. I don't think I want to eat shrimp from the prison food vendor. Though I guess I don't have to worry about getting food poisoning or diarrhea, do I? The real dream—the lottery ticket—is if you can get them to serve you your last meal and then you get a last-minute stay and they cancel your date and send you back to your cell. So maybe I'll avoid the seafood, just in case that happens for me. Isn't that pathetic? That my greatest hope is to get to eat a twenty-dollar dinner and then not have to die right afterwards?

There was a guy, Ronnie Lee Gardner, out in Utah, who got steak and a lobster tail and then they let him watch all the Lord of the Rings movies before they killed him. He also got to be executed by firing squad, which you can't get in Tennessee. If you ever commit capital murder, I recommend doing it in Utah. The Mormons handle their executions real classy. I wonder if they will set up a TV in here and let me watch a movie if I ask. They might. The guards all seem to feel real bad about having to do this. But I don't even know what I'd want to watch. I doubt I could pay attention to it right now.

I am going to ask for a bucket of Kentucky Fried Chicken with all the sides, a carton of Häagen-Dazs, and a Coke. I figure they can't screw that up too bad, though I am sure the biscuits and mashed potatoes will be cold by the time they get them to me. Maybe they can reheat them.

CARLOS WATKINS (NARRATION): I wanted to send Chester a bottle of champagne to drink with his last meal, but the corrections staff said they wouldn't take it back to him. I called Ed to see if he could intervene, and he told me that Chester can't have any alcohol anyway, because it might interact with the sodium thiopental.

Outside the prison, there are about a hundred and fifty protesters. People always show up to demonstrate when there's an execution, but Ed told me that this is an unusually large crowd.

Past the parking lot, a local pastor has set up a revival tent. In the tent, the faithful are praying for Chester, and also for Cecilia Tompkins, Margery March, and Evelyn Duhrer. I went out there and sat for a while. I'm not a religious person, but the atmosphere was loving, and it was a welcome escape from the deeply negative energy of the prison.

About 80 percent of the demonstrators seem to be opposed to the death penalty. The rest are here to jeer and celebrate Chester's death. There's one guy in a cowboy hat who loves executions and shows up to stand outside the prison for every one of them.

He likes to hold up a boom box when the execution begins, and he plays "Hell's Bells" by AC/DC while the condemned prisoner dies. The building where the execution takes place is a couple hundred yards away, so nobody in there will be able to hear him, but I don't think that's the point. Anyway, I'm trying not to pass judgment. I don't know what has happened to this guy in his life to make him want to do this. I tried to ask him, but he stopped talking to me.

I'm starting to see cars being let in through the front gate, and I think these are witnesses arriving for the execution. A Buick pulled through a few minutes ago, and I am about 90 percent sure that William Schatz was driving it, which must mean Buck has arrived. I've called him several times since I spoke to William, and he hasn't been picking up his phone.

I will be one of seven reporters who will witness this execution. Chester doesn't have any family, so he offered to put me on his list of invited witnesses, but the American Justice team decided that, although our coverage of this event has an unambiguous editorial viewpoint, it was still a bridge too far, ethically, to attend the execution as Chester's guest if we had an alternative. This is especially true since my objectivity and credibility have been the topic of a lot of the discussion surrounding this show since my interview with William Schatz aired.

The Department of Correction has a set of guidelines for media invitations, and it seems complicated, but it really isn't. It also seems like a lottery among media outlets, but once again, it mostly isn't. The seven witnesses are picked from six categories. The first spot goes to the Associated Press. The second spot goes to a news agency from the county where the murder occurred. The third goes to a Nashville print publication. This doesn't necessarily have to be *The Tennessean*, but I think it always is. Then there is one spot for another Tennessee print publication, two spots for TV news, and one spot for radio. Journalists typically decide amongst themselves who gets the spots, and it's customary to defer to local media from the city where the murder occurred. It only really becomes a lottery if a bunch of national media outlets want to witness the execution.

That happened in some of the categories this time. The popularity of *American Justice* has generated a lot of interest around this case, so CNN, Fox, NBC, CBS, and ABC all wanted the two spots for TV reporters. The big winners were NBC and the Memphis Fox affiliate, which wouldn't give its spot up for Fox News. Luckily—or perhaps un-luckily if you're looking for work in the field of radio journalism—there wasn't as much competition to be the radio witness, and the outlets who were interested in covering the execution were all NPR affiliates who graciously stepped aside for me.

The main drawback of covering the execution from the media pool is that I won't be with Ed Heffernan, and I won't get to see firsthand how he reacts. There will be three separate rooms where different groups of witnesses observe the execution, and the media is separated from both victims' families and law enforcement witnesses and the condemned's family and his lawyers.

I also won't be allowed to bring any recording devices into the building where the execution will occur, so unfortunately, you will not get to hear Chester's last words or my live response to what I am seeing in the moment. I can have a pencil and a legal pad. I can't even bring my own pencil. They'll issue me one. Maybe somebody could conceal a camera or a recording device or some other kind of contraband in their pen or something. But the prison-issued pencil will be good enough to take notes with, and I'll record my narrative of the event as soon as the execution is over, so it's as fresh in my mind as possible.

This is going to be an emotionally trying experience for me. I've gotten to know Chester over the phone for the last couple of months. I will see him in person for the first time this evening, and then he will die. I know, as much as I don't want to believe it, that he is probably a murderer. Knowing that really doesn't make this easier.

I'm going inside now. I'll have more to tell you after Chester March is dead.

26

Peter Clayton waited with us for an hour, and then a uniformed guard knocked on the door, and Clayton left with him.

It was probably good for William to get some quality time with his grandmother, but we'd all run out of stuff to say to each other on the car ride up. So we mostly sat in silence, waiting for something to happen. It's surprising how boring it can be to sit and wait to watch somebody die. I think I dozed off a bit while I was in there.

After about forty-five minutes, Clayton returned.

"The IV is in," he said. "They should be ready to get started any minute."

I wheeled my chair closer to the window. The blinds opened to reveal Chester March, dressed in a clean white jumpsuit, lying on a gurney. The years had not been kind to him. What little was left of his hair was lank and yellow-white. His face was deeply creased, and his eyes had sunk deep into his skull. The only parts of him that looked the same were his porcelain dental implants. His arms were outstretched, like Jesus on the cross, and restrained. He also had restraints around his chest and his legs. A plastic tube ran from his right arm to a clear IV fluid bag, which hung above the gurney. To his left stood a man in a suit. To his right was another man, this one wearing scrubs and a surgical mask.

"The guy in the jacket is the warden," Clayton told us. "The one in the mask is the executioner. He's not a doctor. There is a doctor here, but he won't participate in the execution. He won't even go in the room where this is happening. He'll come in afterwards, to declare the time of death."

The executioner flipped a switch on the wall, and the intercom hissed a little.

"Do you have anything to say, Mr. March?" the warden asked.

Chester lifted his head up, and looked straight at me. "I'm a Christian," he said. He hissed the *s* sound. "I'm right with God, and whatever I've done, He forgives me. I'm ready to face His judgment. But this? This is wrong. This is evil. This is so much worse than anything I ever did. Some of y'all are all right. I've been praying for you. I forgive you, and I think, if you let Him in your heart, Jesus will forgive you too. But some of you? What you've done, I don't see how you'll ever get square with the Lord. I fear for your souls, and I feel sorry for you."

"Is that all?" the warden asked.

"Yeah," Chester said. "I ain't got all night here. Let's give the people what they want!"

The warden nodded at the executioner, who injected a drug into Chester's IV line.

"That's sodium thiopental, the first of the three-drug cocktail," Clayton said. "It's a sedative. It should knock him out in less than thirty seconds."

Chester laid his head back onto the gurney. The warden stepped forward and examined him. He snapped his fingers in front of Chester's face. He bent over and shouted, "Chester! Chester! Can you hear me?"

"He's making sure March is unconscious," Clayton said. The warden seemed satisfied. He took a step back and gestured toward the executioner, who injected a second, and then a third needle into the IV line. "Now he's administering the lethal drugs. March should stop breathing in a few minutes."

But Chester's breathing did not slow. Instead, over the next couple of minutes, it seemed to become more rapid. His arms tensed, and his fists clenched and unclenched. The skin around the spot where the IV was inserted into his right arm was turning red.

Next to me, Tequila had risen from his chair and stepped forward, so his face was inches from the glass. Behind me, Rose had her hands clenched in front of her, knuckles white, staring wide-eyed at Chester. Blisters were emerging on his hot red forearm, seeping pink fluid. Around the spot where the tube went into his arm, his skin had started to turn gray. His whole body was tense, and the cords of his neck stood out as he pulled against the restraints.

"Something is very wrong," Clayton said. "He should be completely paralyzed. I have to stop this." He rushed out of the room.

Chester lifted his head, and his eyes opened. "The fires of

Hell!" he shouted. "Oh, God, why? It wasn't supposed . . . It wasn't supposed to hurt so bad!"

The skin on Chester's arm tore loose and slid down to his wrist like the sleeve of a stretched-out sweatshirt, revealing the pale white flesh of his forearm. The fluid seeping from the injection site had left a pink puddle on the floor. The warden hit the button on the wall. Chester sat partway up again, as far as his restraints would allow, his eyes bulging and his mouth wide, but the microphones were off and the chamber was otherwise soundproof. I watched him scream silently until the warden hit another button, and the blinds snapped closed.

I looked at Tequila, who still had his hand pressed over his mouth, and then at Rose, who was rocking back and forth in her chair.

"So, who's up for hot chicken?" I asked.

"You know what?" Tequila said. "I could eat."

TRANSCRIPT: AMERICAN JUSTICE

CARLOS WATKINS (NARRATION): By time I get this recorded, edited, and on the air, you'll likely already have heard about what has happened at Riverbend from TV news or social media. The execution of Chester March was horribly botched, with gruesome results.

A few minutes after the procedure began, it became clear that the sedative, sodium thiopental, had not rendered Chester unconscious. He sat up on the gurney and began screaming. At that point, the executioner cut off the microphones and closed the blinds, leaving me and the other media witnesses in stunned silence. Here's Ed Heffernan with a better explanation.

ED HEFFERNAN: As soon as it was apparent that Chester March had not been properly sedated, I left the witness room and ran to the death chamber to demand that the warden stop the execution. By that point, the executioner had already injected Chester with the vecuronium bromide and the potassium chloride. Chester was awake and was clearly in considerable distress, and the warden agreed to stop the execution and called upon the doctor in attendance to attempt to resuscitate Chester.

Unfortunately, it was too late. Chester March entered cardiac arrest after forty minutes of unimaginable agony and died an hour after the first part of the lethal injection was administered. While we won't know for sure until we have a full autopsy, the most likely cause of this tragedy is something doctors call "infiltration." The person who inserted the intravenous line pushed it through the wall of the vein, and as a result, the drugs were injected into the subcutaneous tissues of Chester's arm instead of entering his bloodstream in quantities sufficient to ensure a quick death.

Sodium thiopental does not render a subject unconscious when it is administered subcutaneously instead of entering the bloodstream. However, when allowed to pool in the tissues of the arm, it will cause severe chemical burns. Potassium chloride, similarly, must hit the heart in a large dose to cause cardiac arrest. Vecuronium bromide injected into the flesh of the arm will eventually paralyze you, as it is supposed to. It just takes longer to do the job than it would if it entered the bloodstream.

That means that Chester did not get a proper dose of sedative, and he did not receive the drug that was intended to ensure a quick death, but he did get the drug that paralyzed his lungs and diaphragm, causing him to slowly suffocate while he was conscious and aware, and while this was happening, he was suffering chemical burns the severity of which were analogous to what you would experience if you plunged your arm up to the elbow into the pile of smoldering charcoal briquettes at the bottom of a hot barbecue. In short, Chester March was tortured to death by the state of Tennessee.

This tragedy is the result of several of the problems I warned the Tennessee Supreme Court about. The lethal injection is a complex medical procedure that is administered by executioners who are not medical practitioners. These people have no business inserting intravenous lines or handling such dangerous drugs. Further, Chester was unusually prone to this kind of complication from an IV line because he was eighty years old and had spent thirty-five years in a tiny cell, leading a sedentary lifestyle. He was in poor circulatory health, and as a result, his veins were overly prone to tearing.

Because the state applies its lethal injection protocol uniformly, without regard to the age or health status of any particular inmate, it risks serious complications of this type when it attempts to perform this procedure on inmates who are elderly, infirm, are former intravenous drug users, or are in otherwise poor health. That's every death row inmate. No one can stay healthy in an environment like that.

I am appalled and traumatized by what I have witnessed, and I am ashamed that I wasn't able to protect my client from this nightmarish outcome. But Chester March's death will not be for nothing. I will be petitioning the Tennessee Supreme Court to enjoin all further executions until we can reevaluate the state's lethal injection protocols. And I will be calling on the governor to put capital punishment in Tennessee on moratorium.

On a personal note, I'm just sickened by this whole debacle. This is the first time I've witnessed a botched execution, but working in capital defense, it was as inevitable as it is unnecessary. I'm sorry that you had to see it, and I'm sorry my students had to see it. For that matter, I'm sorry that I had to see it, and I am aggrieved and horrified that Chester had to endure it, but you've done a great service by drawing attention to this case. This kind of thing has happened before, with disturbing frequency, and when it does, it generates very little mass outrage, because people don't care very much about death row inmates. Hopefully it will matter that we've brought this injustice to your audience's attention.

CARLOS WATKINS (NARRATION): I don't know what I expected to happen when I started reporting this story, but it wasn't this. Our production team thought Heffernan had better than even odds of winning at least a stay of execution for Chester and that our coverage would conclude on that victory. I thought that Ed had the situation under control that a man like this—educated, eloquent, and white— could get the attention of the people who controlled these systems and make them listen to reason. I never expected that I would end up witnessing a botched and torturous execution firsthand.

And, unfortunately, I do not share Ed's view that these events or my coverage of them can be a catalyst for real change. Maybe if we had audio or video or photos to show people what death by lethal injection looks like, it might make a difference, but describing it isn't enough. My suspicion is that Chester March was supposed to be put to death, and he's dead, and as far as most people are concerned, the system worked within acceptable parameters.

And maybe there will be a temporary moratorium on executions as a result of this, but Tennessee has a Republican governor and a Republican legislature, and those institutions appoint and confirm Republican judges. I suspect Riverbend will be back to executing people sooner than Ed would like to imagine.

I said I would write down Chester's last words and convey them to you, and I have. Before he got the injection he gave a speech he must have spent quite a while preparing. It was a speech about faith and about forgiveness, about how he forgave the people who were poised to kill him, and about how he hoped to find absolution in the arms of Christ. If that had been the last thing Chester March said, his last words would have been eloquent and dignified. But those were not Chester March's last words.

After the lethal injection had been administered, when Chester was supposed to be unconscious, he sat partway up on the gurney, and he screamed, "Oh God, why? It wasn't supposed to hurt so bad!" So, those were Chester March's last words.

On the way out of the prison, I ran into Buck Schatz. Buck steadfastly refused to meet with me, so throughout my entire coverage of this story, I had never actually seen him, and I was shocked by his appearance. I knew he was ninety, but I hadn't fully appreciated what it meant that he was so old. When I thought of him, I thought of the detective I saw in those old archival photos. The reality is quite different.

His grandson, William, was helping him move from a wheelchair into the backseat of their Buick, and his wife was sitting in the front passenger seat, staring blankly ahead. She seemed stunned by what we had just witnessed, but Buck, who has seen a lot of carnage in his day, was in high spirits. Nevertheless, I was shocked by his frailty. Chester had said he was never exactly a big man, but age has reduced him, and he seemed tiny. His skin was like parchment. He wore thick glasses and a hearing aid, and when he looked at me, it seems like he looked past me. His hands trembled.

He was wearing a baggy sweatshirt with an NYU logo on it that his grandson must have given him, and a pair of chinos that were too big for him, leaving drapes of fabric falling off his skinny legs. But the detail about him I really wouldn't have guessed were his shoes. They were slip-on canvas Keds, the kind of kicks you get at a Payless store in a run-down strip mall for fifteen dollars, and there was a hole in the toe of one of them. I'd have guessed Buck Schatz was the kind of guy who spent two hours a week spit-shining his lace-ups.

CARLOS WATKINS: Are you finally going to talk to me, Detective Schatz?

WILLIAM SCHATZ: Piss off, Watkins.

BARUCH SCHATZ: No, I'll talk to him.

W. SCHATZ: We've discussed this. We decided this was a bad idea.

B. SCHATZ: Feh. At this point, what's the harm?

27

Carlos Watkins looked younger than I expected him to. Listening to his program, I imagined somebody who looked kind of like Bryant Gumbel, but this kid couldn't have been more than a couple of years older than Tequila.

He was wearing a light-yellow oxford shirt tucked into dark-blue straight-leg jeans, with a navy blazer but no tie. And he was wearing red Converse sneakers that looked exactly like the ones I used to wear to play racquetball at the Jewish Community Center fifty years ago.

He had close-cropped hair, what I'd call a medium complexion if I were describing him to a police sketch artist, and his eyes were red-rimmed like he'd just been crying and was on the verge of crying again. Over a scumbag like Chester March. Wasn't that something?

"Okay," I said. "You've been wanting to talk to me. So, let's talk."

"I think this is a bad idea," Tequila said.

"My grandson is worried that you're not going to be . . . What did he call it? A good-faith interlocutor. Are you going to be a good-faith interlocutor, Mr. Watkins?"

"I intend to be," he said. He pulled a little recording device out of his pocket and showed it to me, to make sure I knew I was being taped. I nodded at it, and he pushed the button on the side of it.

"Well, you see there, Limoncello, you've got nothing to worry about," I said to my grandson. "Me and Carlos, here, we're just a couple of good-faith interlocutors, interlocuting in good faith. It's a regular meeting of the minds."

"If this goes off the rails, I am putting a stop to it," Tequila said.

"However could I survive, without you around to protect me?" I asked my grandson. Then I turned to Watkins. "So what do you need to know so bad that you won't stop calling me?"

"Did you beat a confession out of Chester March?" Watkins asked.

"No," I said. This was the truth. I did not strike Chester. He just had a close encounter with an unidentified flying ashtray.

"Did you interrogate Chester after he'd been injured in a car crash, but before he had received medical care."

"Yes," I said. "He was a murder suspect. He crashed his car trying to escape from police pursuers and flee across the state line. He had a hostage he'd kidnapped in the trunk of his car. His injuries didn't appear immediately life-threatening, and we decided to question him before we sent him to the hospital."

"Were you aware, when you interrogated Chester, that he was in a diminished cognitive state as a result of a serious head injury?"

"I asked Chester what he did with his wife, and he told me. We went out and dug where he said he buried her, and we found her remains. Maybe he only told me that because he bumped his head, but I'm not one to look a gift horse in the mouth." I found my cigarettes and lighter in the seat pocket. I lit one. "You want one of these?" I asked.

"We're not supposed to use tobacco products on prison grounds," Watkins said.

"What are they going to do? Lock us up?"

"Well, maybe not you, because you're a ninety-year-old retired cop. But I am a black man, so, very possibly."

"All right," I said. "Point taken." I threw the cigarette on the ground and stepped on it, and stuck the pack back into the seat.

"Can you see the direct line between your decision to interrogate Chester without treating his injuries and what happened here tonight?" Watkins asked.

"I see a direct line between Chester's decision to murder three women and what happened here tonight."

Watkins sat down in the wheelchair. "I don't know why you're being so flip with me, man. Can you at least agree that what we just saw was horrifying?"

"Sure it was horrifying," I said. "But I've seen a hundred years of horrifying things, and a lot of those things happened to people who were a lot nicer than Chester March. The crime scene where I discovered Evelyn Duhrer's body partially dissolved in sulfuric acid was a horrifying thing. The corpse was so fragile that it broke apart in transit to the morgue, which made it difficult to ascertain which injuries had killed her, and I needed a confession to make sure that her murderer got justice. So, when I had to consider whether to interrogate that woman's killer or send him to the hospital and let him have time to recuperate and get his lies straight, it wasn't a hard decision for me. Why are you so much more horrified by the execution of Chester March than you are by the murder of Evelyn Duhrer?"

"Because Evelyn Duhrer's murder wasn't systemic," Watkins said.

"What difference does that make?"

"Dismantling corrupt and oppressive systems is the definition of justice."

"Jesus Christ," Tequila said. "Grandpa, I've heard enough of this. Let's go get chicken."

"Hold on," I said. "Isn't the pursuit and capture of a man who beats a woman to death with a fireplace poker and tries to dissolve her body in a tub of acid also justice?"

"No," Watkins said. "That's the operation of a coercive system. You're exacting retribution on the symptom while you're working in the service of the disease."

"So you want to let men like Chester get away with murdering women?"

"No. In a just world, Chester wouldn't feel a need to murder women."

"Wait a second," I said. "You think Chester had to murder Evelyn Duhrer because he didn't inherit a large enough fortune from his cotton-baron father?"

"No, but I think systemic causes can explain Chester's alleged crimes," Watkins told me. "If you repair or dismantle oppressive systems, you solve your Chester problem. But torturing Chester to death does nothing to fix any systemic problems."

"Let me tell you a story about fixing systems," I said. "My father was a communist. He worked down on the Memphis waterfront. He hauled freight all day, and at night he looked around and imagined how the world could be a better place.

"At that time, the labor union that represented the longshoremen was pretty ineffectual. They'd go to the bosses and ask for more money, and the bosses would threaten to fire them all and bring in black workers who would happily do their jobs for less pay. The bosses never actually did it; whenever they came close, old Mr. Crump would intervene. Crump was the mayor in those days, but he was more than that. He was the boss. He was the bosses' boss. And how he said things were going to be, things were. When it came down to it, the unions and their votes were his, and he wasn't going to let them get pushed out by the blacks. But he made sure they never got the wages they deserved either, by hanging the threat over their heads that black replacements were ready to walk onto the site the moment the white workers became more trouble than they were worth.

"So, my father got the idea that what the union should do was let in the blacks. The fight, in his view, wasn't between the white man and the colored, but between those who lived by the labor of their hands and those that controlled the purse strings—the ones who operate the systems, as you put it. If workers of all races could unite, they could all negotiate for a fair wage together, and the bosses couldn't use them against each other. But it was 1927, and my father was a little bit ahead of his time.

"He went to the union hall, and he told them his big idea, and they threw their beer mugs at him. And a week later, somebody ran his car off the road. His body was ten feet from the wreck. He was drowned in a shallow ditch. The police called it an accident. Just a Jew who couldn't keep his mouth shut, even when his head was underwater.

"My mother never believed Mr. Crump was behind that. It was too brazen to be the work of a man with so much to lose. It was the workers, the ones my dad was trying to elevate. They were so disgusted by the idea that they might be equal to the blacks that they lynched my father for trying to teach them about class solidarity. That's what happens when you try to fix systems. You get distracted by your ideals, and you don't see a couple of mean, dumb, white-trash longshoremen coming up behind you. Systems didn't kill my father. Small, petty violent men did. And men like that are a problem I know how to solve."

"That's the Buck Schatz origin story?" Watkins asked. "That's why you think crime isn't systemic? That story is about nothing but systems. Racism is a system. Capitalism is a system. Man, the Crump machine is the very definition of a corrupt system. It's all systems within systems, turning people against each other for the benefit of the operators. Those longshoremen were so blinded to their own interests by the workings of networks of corrupt systems that they killed your father so Crump didn't even have to deal with him. And then you spent your whole life trying to get your hands on the longshoremen and serving the same interests in the process. Your father understood how the world works better than you do. You've spent ninety years going backwards. All those decades, going after the longshoremen, going after Chester, going after whoever. And what did you accomplish?"

"I got him," I said. "I got him and several hundred others like him. He died tonight for what he did, and he spent thirty-five years in a cage waiting for it. If it hadn't been for me, he might be out there somewhere right now, drinking champagne and plotting another murder."

"He died screaming," Watkins said. "His damn arm melted. It was the worst thing I've ever seen."

"It wasn't the worst thing I've ever seen," I said.

"No, I guess it wouldn't be. Your whole life has been a cavalcade of horrors."

He had me there. That was indisputably true.

"Why did Chester March kill Cecilia Tompkins?" I asked. "What systems explain that?"

"She was a black sex worker. She was the most marginalized possible victim," Watkins said.

"But why was he looking for a victim in the first place?"

"Capitalism."

I shook my head. "Capitalism had nothing to do with it. He didn't make a thin dime off that killing. He had nothing to gain from it, except maybe it got his rocks off. He was just a goddamn psycho, and he'd be a psycho if he was rich or if he was poor. He'd be a psycho in your communist paradise, or in whatever kind of utopia you think you can build. There are always going to be monsters. The systems don't make them. We make the systems to protect the rest of us from them."

"Look, man, you can beat the shit out of Chester and everyone

like him for as long as you want, and you'll never make any head-
way against solving the real problem. All the heads you busted,
all the men you arrested, all the lethal injections—what have they
accomplished? You kill one monster and another takes his place,
and the system persists. How is that justice?"

"I did the best I could," I said. "I saw men like the ones who
killed my father and men like Chester out there, doing the things
they do, and I thought somebody ought to stop them. Somebody
ought to get them. So I went out and I got them. That was justice as I understood it, and I meted out as much of it as I could.
Maybe I was wrong. Maybe I spent my whole career trying to get
my hands around the problem, and I retired without solving it. If
you've got your own idea of justice, who am I to tell you whether
it's right or not? I wouldn't have ever let anyone tell me justice
was anything other than what I felt it was in my guts, and I don't
suppose you should either. All you can do is fight for whatever
you believe in until you're too old to fight anymore, and then you
can take a look around and see if any of it made a damn bit of
difference."

Tequila smacked his hand against the hood of the Buick. "Is
that enough?" he asked Watkins. "Have you got what you need?"

Watkins looked at me, and then he looked at the recorder in
his hand. His jaw clenched and unclenched.

"No," he said. "This wasn't what I came here for. Nothing
about this is right. And maybe it doesn't matter, and maybe nobody
even really cares, but you did it. You tortured that confession out of
Chester. You did it, and I know you did it."

"Yeah? Well, you know what you know, and I know what I
know," I told him.

"Splendid," Tequila said. "We've reached an impasse. A man is dead and none of us are sure whether or not we've accomplished anything."

I nodded. "Sounds about right."

"Then let's get the hell out of here, because I am ready to go eat some chicken," Tequila said. "Put your goddamn seat belt on, Grandpa. We've done about as much damage as we can do in this dump."

I was already sitting on the side of the backseat, with my legs hanging out of the car, so I turned and slid them inside, and Tequila shut the door. He walked around to the other side of the car, climbed into the driver's seat, and turned the key in the ignition. As we backed out of the parking lot, Carlos Watkins stood in the pool of the headlights. Then, Tequila cut the wheel, and Watkins receded into the background.

"I'm going to call Dr. Feingold tomorrow," Rose said.

"What?" I asked.

"I'm going to do the chemotherapy. I'm going to do whatever it takes. I don't want . . . that."

"All right," I said.

So, all in all, it was a pretty good night.

ACKNOWLEDGMENTS

Running Out of Road is a work of fiction, but the Riverbend prison is a real place and real people work for the Tennessee Department of Correction, so it's important to acknowledge that I took some creative liberties with the layout and security procedures of the prison, and the execution protocols described in this book are based on those used in various states but may not all match the procedures used in Tennessee.

I am of the opinion that the needless complexity of execution by lethal injection creates the risk that any execution could be botched, but no execution has been botched in the manner described in this story in the state of Tennessee, with a condemned prisoner suffering chemical burns due to the infiltration of lethal drugs into the flesh around the injection site. What happened to Chester March is based on the 2006 execution of Ángel Nieves Díaz in Florida and the 2014 execution of Clayton Lockett in Oklahoma.

However, after the 2018 execution of Billy Ray Irick, during which witnesses said Irick moaned and pulled against his restraints, three condemned inmates in Tennessee opted to be executed by electrocution rather than lethal injection.

During my research for this book, I relied on the excellent coverage of executions at Riverbend by reporters from *The Tennessean*, including Dave Boucher, Jamie Satterfield, and Adam Tamburin. The guy who shows up with the boom box to blast AC/DC during executions at Riverbend is real, and I know about him because of the coverage in *The Tennessean*.

A 2014 *New Republic* article about the execution of Ángel Díaz by editor Ben Crair was also a valuable resource. If you found the descriptions of the chemical burns and skin slippage that occurred during the execution of Chester March insufficiently detailed, I recommend looking up Crair's article, which contains photos from Díaz's autopsy. If you would not like to see photos of those things, I looked at them so you don't have to.

I'd also like to give a special acknowledgment to the great James Ellroy. I met Ellroy at the Southern Festival of Books in Nashville in 2014, and I asked him if he had any writerly advice to offer. He told me that I should start introducing myself to people as "Donkey Dan" to see if I could get a rumor started. But over the course of 2015 and 2016, I read his L.A. Quartet and the Underworld USA trilogy, and those books are fantastic.

My original plan for this book was that Buck's antagonist in the present-day scenes would be Ed Heffernan, the appellate lawyer. The problem I had was that, since there is no witness testimony in an appellate proceeding, there was no occasion for there ever to be any sort of confrontation between these characters. A dramatic scene in which Heffernan pleads for Chester's life before the Tennessee Supreme Court didn't work, because there was nothing for Buck to do there except watch. In the end, the appellate argument, which I thought was going to be the climax of the book, was something I cut out entirely, and the solution to my boring lawyer problem was Carlos Watkins and *American Justice*. Ellroy's books inspired the idea to frame Watkins's narration as transcripts from his radio broadcast— Ellroy used a similar device to depict J. Edgar Hoover in the Underworld USA trilogy.

So, you should read James Ellroy if you haven't; he's a peerless eminence in crime fiction, and his books are a hell of a lot of fun. And I will pass along and endorse his indispensable advice that you should always boast about the size of your genitals to people you just met, particularly in professional contexts.

I want to thank my agent, Victoria Skurnick, and the team at Levine Greenberg Rostan, particularly rights manager Elizabeth Fisher. I'd also like to thank my editor, Hannah Braaten, and editorial assistant Nettie Finn at Minotaur, as well as my former editor Marcia Markland. Also, many thanks to Yuriko Noguchi, who translates these books into Japanese for Tokyo Sogensha. My understanding is that he makes me look very good.

Thanks as well to my mother, Elaine Friedman, my bubbi Goldie Burson, my brother Jonathan Friedman, my sister-in-law Rachel Friedman, and my nieces Hannah and Lyla.

This series would never have existed without my grandparents, Buddy and Margaret Friedman. Buddy passed away in 2014, and Margaret hung on until 2018. She was born on the Oklahoma frontier in a house without plumbing or electricity, and she lived to be 101 years old. She built the preschool at the Memphis Jew- ish Community Center, and she outlived both of her sons. She witnessed things nobody now alive remembers, and she suffered losses no one should ever have to endure. We're better off for having known her, and we will never again see her equal.